D1478606

# THE

# FIVE-FINGERED

# ELF

## LOUISE GORDAY

Copyright © 2022 by Louise Gorday All rights reserved.

This book or any portion thereof may not be reproduced or used in any manner whatsoever without the express written permission of the author except for the use of brief quotations in a book review. This is a work of fiction. Names, characters, places, and incidents either are the product of the author's imagination or are used fictitiously. Any resemblance to actual persons, living or dead, events, or locales is entirely coincidental.

Book Cover Design by Damonza.com
Formatting by Polgarus Studio

Printed in the United States of America

To Aiden
You can already spin a whopping good tale

# Also by Louise Gorday

# Contents

# Chapter One

# En Garde

Santa's chubby hand shot through the air and snatched the sealed white envelope from the fairy's grasp. "Didn't I say to leave my things alone? I haven't even read that one yet." He slid the missive underneath his tablet and resumed writing.

"Mmm," the fairy said. He fluttered back down to the desk and settled on the edge of a pile of books, where he looked like nothing so much as a small and oddly shaped red feather duster. "I don't believe you have an ounce of fun in you." He stuck out his lower lip and bounced the heels of his black cowboy boots against the book spines. "I think we need what's-his-face back." He leaned over and pulled a quill pen from a pencil cup and began waving it around like a saber.

Santa kept writing. "Solomon, as you very well know, his name was also *Santa*, and right about now I couldn't agree with you more." He dotted an "i" and crossed several "t's" that he had missed, then glanced over the top of his glasses at the little red fairy. "I'm pretty sure I wasn't put here purely for your entertainment, and yes, it would be wonderful if my predecessor could be sitting here once more and I could go back to going what I do best: putting in a full day of whittling and wood sculpting at a workbench. If wishes were fishes," he said, poking Solomon in the belly with the eraser end of his pencil, "we would all be fat as Santa."

"That's my boy," Solomon said, parrying the pencil aside with the stiff quill. He hopped up, placed his feet in an L position, and raised his weapon. *"En garde! Prêts? Allez!"*

Santa cocked an eyebrow and chuckled. "I'm afraid you'll have to try harder than that. I have too much to do and too little time to do it in." He dropped his pencil in the cup with the others and stood up.

Solomon heaved a sigh. "Solomon Grundy," he began, fluttering across the bedroom after Santa. "Born on a Monday. Christened on Tuesday. Married on Wednesday. Took ill on Thursday. Grew worse on Friday. Died on Saturday. Buried on Sunday."

"Seeing as how it's Wednesday, shouldn't you be busy elsewhere?" Santa opened his bedroom door and invited Solomon out with a flourish of his hand.

Solomon shot out the opening in a scarlet blur. Just Santa's luck, he'd be back by late afternoon with a honey on each arm, reeling out some fascinating but ridiculous tale about some hidden corner of the North Pole. Santa vowed to keep the door shut and locked for the rest of the day.

With Solomon off sowing wild oats, Claus settled back at his desk. Issues, issues, and more issues. Six months into the job, and he didn't have a clue what he was doing. From a bottom drawer, he pulled a suede bundle tied with a leather thong and withdrew a pocketknife and a fist-size piece of Iowa Butternut tree. He turned the wood around in his hands several times before putting the blade to it. This he knew how to do, thanks to the best dad an elf ever had. But who could teach him how to be the Claus?

Christmasville's infrastructure was crumbling, and only he could do anything about it. Inherited a mess, he did. But he couldn't fault his predecessor for that. Elves might be a joyful, singing, dancing lot dedicated to bringing Christmas cheer around the world, but they were also a mischievous group who enjoyed partying with abandon. He couldn't count the number of times he had pulled festoons of toilet paper out of the evergreens, rescued a reindeer that naughty workers had stranded on a Quonset hut roof, or ordered new computer keyboards because someone thought it funny to pry off all the punctuation keys. The Clausian role was a busy one, and contending with the high jinks ate up precious time better spent elsewhere. How could he concentrate on protecting and improving elf life under the great biodome when all these piddling things kept sucking up his time?

Santa shaved three slivers of wood off, blew softly on his work, and held it out for inspection. The beginnings of a dragon's head, and it looked good. A familiar calm spread through him. He continued carving.

Christmasville operations needed updating. Quonset Hut Boston Charlie had conveyor belts powered by equipment cobbled together from old Model T Ford parts—yes, the car was versatile, but after a century, surely they could find something more efficient. And did elves using the toilets in Quonset Dickens really need to yell *Flush!* to warn those showering that their water was about to become scalding hot?

And don't get him started on inefficient management practices. He sliced the wood again and grimaced at too deep a cut. With a sigh, he shoved the whole project back into his drawer. Manual posting of personnel shift changes in Christmasville's main square had gotten out of hand, with shoving (and even some fisticuffs that he would prefer to forget) and general destruction of the lovely flower beds that had ringed the area. Why couldn't someone create an IT system and put this stuff online?

Santa looked over at his bookshelf, which was crammed with red and green three-inch binders. He simmered just looking at this manifestation of gross inefficiency. Why did everything *really* need to be done in triplicate—a white working copy, a yellow for Santa's information, and a blue for the archives? He would soon run out of shelf space.

*Well, Claus, it's you or nobody, so elf up.* On his notepad, he made a short list of the people he might need to call on for assistance: mostly the Angelic Corps, and the Weigh Station. If they couldn't help him, where on earth would he find someone to take on such an arduous task?

He picked up the letter that Solomon had been toying with. *Santa Claus, North Pole.* The return address read: Federal Aviation Administration, 800 Independence Ave. SW, Washington, DC 20591. Had he forgotten to drop off some Christmas gifts? He slit the envelope and unfolded the enclosed two-page letter—on administration letterhead with an original signature—and skimmed it. Then he read it a bit more slowly and finally a third time, underlining the salient points. His driver's license had expired and he needed another? No, that wasn't quite right. His *predecessor's* license had expired and needed to be renewed immediately. The second page referenced two webcams and included two traffic camera citations dated December 24, 2021, for driving without a license. He looked in the envelope and found two nighttime photos showing the Christmas sleigh in flight. They were over New York City if he recalled rightly (and exactly as documented in the citation). The letter also stated that any further driving of the sleigh required an FFA license and that an assessed five-hundred-dollar fine must be paid before said license would be issued. Failure to comply within ten days could land him in lockup for up to sixty days. And if, God forbid, he insisted on being naughty a second time, that jail time could be bumped up to twelve months. Who knew that a Claus had to have a license of any kind? He tipped back in his chair and focused on the ceiling—in particular, an industrious spider, spinning its web in a corner. The ticket was just one more thing added to an already full plate. He scribbled on a sticky note for Herbert, his first assistant, to look into the issue.

Today would be one of those days, he decided, and he would just have to shake off such distractions. He retired to his bed for a short, rejuvenating nap.

His eyes had barely closed when the clock began chiming. By the time he dragged himself from his bed, the clock's charming little dancers were almost finished twirling and toe-tapping. He left his office suite in Quonset Hut Alpha and headed for the cafeteria. Although his nap had been cut short, his path had become clear. The helpers and allies he had listed earlier—angels and the Weigh Stationers—were the immortal power players in the universe, and Christmasville would be in good hands if he turned to them. But shouldn't those hands belong to St. Nicholas, the Sinterklaas, the one and only Santa Claus? Half a year into the job, and he was ready to throw in the towel. He shook his head. Bad move, Nicholas.

The sound of screeching brakes brought him up short, inches away from becoming the hood ornament on one of the service vehicles that flitted about day and night under the dome, ferrying people and whatnot.

"Ride, sir?" the driver asked.

Santa smiled politely and shook his head again. "No, sorry. I guess I should pay attention, shouldn't I?"

"It's quite all right," the driver said, and with a loud backfire, he putted off again in a sooty puff of smoke.

"New fleet of vehicles," Santa muttered, vowing right then to begin a separate list of the things that needed to be fixed or replaced.

And in that moment, inspiration hit him. Who better to analyze and solve the Pole's problems than Jetsla, the company owned by one of the greatest creative minds of the day! Oh, dear me, that was it—it didn't get any better than Noël Rusk! Now, there was a genius who could get to the heart of a situation and come up with an innovative solution. No need to call on an immortal. Santa balled up his original list, swished a three-pointer in the trash can, and hurried on his way. He was quite capable of handling the situation. He just had to convince larger-than-life Rusk to pay them a visit and understand it, too. If the billionaire entrepreneur agreed to take his call, Santa knew he could persuade him to take on the arduous task of making Christmasville run more smoothly.

## Chapter Two
# The Christmas Baby

North Pole First Assistant Herbert Tuddy ran his fingers along Santa's shelf of red and green notebooks, found a small space between two volumes, and tried to jam the book in his hand into the open spot. "Bonbons," he mumbled, smacking the edge of the book against the notebook spines several times before giving up. With a quick glance over his shoulder, he turned the book horizontal and shoved it into the empty space above the other books. If someone needed it, they could find it. It was still filed alphabetically. He noticed five little mouse figurines sitting on the top shelf. Where had these come from? They seemed to be metal. The smallest was deceptively heavy. He gave another quick look around, slid the tchotchke into a pocket, and zipped it shut.

He returned to the desk in the command room's center to begin his daily cleaning. He put the shiny paper clips—January through June—in the left-hand desk drawer and shut it. Then he scooped the red ones—July through September—into the middle drawer and closed it hard, too. And the big green ones—October through December, indicating priority reading and immediate action—he dumped in the right drawer. And yep, he slammed that one hardest, jingling every silver bell on his green elf hat.

He peeked through the door into the next room, which doubled as Santa's bedroom during the busiest part of the Christmas season. The Claus was still at his desk, head down, pen in hand as he read and commented on the latest Christmas directive. Was the jolly fat man *deaf?* Herbert initiated a prolonged coughing spell and finished by clearing his throat in a loud, phlegmy way.

Santa Claus looked up from his work. "Having a bad day, Herbert?"

"No sir." Which was true. There was no one bad day. Indeed, they all were awful ever since the previous Santa Claus passed on to his reward, and Ethan was anointed his successor. It should have been Herbert. Hadn't he toiled for years as number two at the Pole, meeting each challenge with a smile and as quick a fix as he could manage?

Santa got up from his desk, scroll in hand, and stuck his head into the control room. "I'm sorry. If you're not feeling well, maybe you should go home, climb into bed and recuperate. I'll get Christie or Patterson to handle this. It's a shame, though," he said, shaking his head as he reread his list of third-quarter production estimates. "You would have enjoyed this one."

Herbert blew his nose, stood up, and gave Claus a crisp salute. "Herbert Spanky Tuddy reporting for duty, sir. I'm feeling much better. I'm sure Christie and Patterson are too busy overseeing the production schedule for tutus and hula hoops. Eyes on the production team, know what I mean?"

Claus lowered his glasses until they rested on the bridge of his nose. "Oh, yes, I understand you completely."

"Good," Herbert said, nodding agreeably. "Then what is it, exactly, that you want me to do?"

"A delegation will be arriving bright and early tomorrow morning. I will be indisposed. I need someone I can trust to show them around."

"Oh, oh! Me! Me!" Herbert bounced up and down with his hand in the air.

"And *that's* the old Herbert! The biodome will open precisely at nine hundred hours. Be prepared to greet them at Quonset Hut Boston Charlie."

"It would be an honor," Herbert said, his hand sweeping the floor in a grandiose bow. "And whom will I be greeting? Do I need to prepare a speech or something?"

Santa shook his head. "Actually, the less said, the better. Just be there on time, take them through our production facilities, offer them lunch—which they will refuse—and then stand on the tarmac smiling and waving good-bye." Santa handed him the communiqué. "I have no doubt you will be magnificent."

"Uh, Santa," Herbert said, catching the Claus before he could sit down again. "Exactly who am I providing a tour for?"

"Jetsla."

Herbert fumbled the communiqué and it wafted under a chair. "We're now delivering *cars* for Christmas?"

Santa chuckled. It was a full-bodied sound, and his middle jiggled just the way one would expect from a flabby elf in a body-hugging T-shirt. "Wouldn't that be a hoot? Ah, me," he said, wiping tears from his eyes. "No, I'd like to get some advice on improving operations. Who better than Noël Rusk?"

"Nooo! The Christmas baby? The best billionaire in the world?"

"Yes, well, er, not him personally touring," Santa said, his eyes now sparkling. "It will be his representatives. But Noël has thrown his full support behind us." He reached out and spun a black knob on a piece of electronic equipment. It came off in his hand. "I think it's time we buffed up the old place, don't you? We shouldn't continue to run on a lick and a stardust promise." He set the knob down on the table beside the equipment. "Best go do a quick study-up on Jetsla: electric cars, space travel—so many great things! Tomorrow will be quite a treat."

Herbert looked around conspiratorially. They were still alone. "You can tell me, and I won't repeat it to another soul. Is it true what they say about him? A Christmas present to a childless couple who in turn dedicated their cherished gift to world peace and charitable good works for all mankind?" He sighed dramatically. "Tell me what you know. Is it true that he was born on Christmas Day and that he's destined to save the world?"

"Oh, Herbert, don't put any stock in those old stories. He's a man just like any other—trousers on one leg at a time."

"Understood," Herbert said, giving him a wink as he inched toward the door. "Well, if you have nothing further for me, I'll be off."

"That's it—"

Herbert scampered out the door without letting him finish. He had caterers to instruct, a grounds crew to wrangle, and a quick but thorough meeting with all the department heads. He stutter-stepped to a halt in the corridor, pivoted 180 degrees, then 180 more, and continued on the same heading. His desk calendar would be most helpful at the moment. This was what, Wednesday? He mentally ran through current production activities: woodworking, metals, plastics, sewing and upholstery . . . Everything was operating at full throttle—a perfect day to shine and impress! In a world of geniuses and well-oiled machines, Noël Rusk and his Jetsla Enterprises ranked right up there. How else could one achieve billionaire status?

Herbert's brow knitted into a frown. Why on earth would such a company show interest in Christmasville and its operations? Energy, aerospace, artificial intelligence—those weren't exactly part of the

North Pole's daily operations. He tut-tutted the idea of their improving anything around here. Nothing ran more efficiently than Santa's workshops.

He turned right at the hall's end and bounded down the stairs to the offices in the bunker, his suede-soled elf shoes hitting the thirteen steps with barely a sound. Things could be more automated, sure, but that simply wasn't how things were done around here. Elves weren't interchangeable, not like grocery cashiers who could be assigned to other duties when self-checkout lanes came into vogue. Elves were dedicated servants from birth; sewing elflings became tailors, whittlers advanced to fine woodworking, and reindeer whisperers embraced animal husbandry. Santa, the elves, and the sleigh were an august institution. The Eternal Order of the Elves, the Seamsters Union, and the Brotherhood of Animal Maintenance, on the other hand—they just *were*. Herbert drew his eyebrows down until the ends met at the top of his nose, and held them there a moment before shaking his head. The status quo just worked so well, he couldn't imagine anything different.

At the bottom of the steps, Herbert took a quick left down another hallway, stopping briefly to pull down a red and blue crepe-paper festoon announcing last week's keg party, and entered the door marked *H. Tuddy*. As was his custom, he stopped just inside the door and admired the smartly furnished office. The cherrywood desk, conference table, and chairs were stunningly carved and inlaid, and a miniature fountain on a side table added just the note of peaceful ambience he sought. He broke into a smile. His office might be hidden away in the basement of the North Pole, but that didn't make him any less a mover and shaker. He was still number two elf, right behind the Claus himself. Yes, sir, H. *Spanky* Tuddy had arrived. He would make Christmasville shine for Jetsla and Noël Rusk, baby. He'd make it shine! And

11

considering what a buffoon the new Claus was shaping up to be, it was only a matter of time until he inherited the big guy's office upstairs.

As much as Herbert loved his little basement command center, he had to acknowledge that not being in closer physical proximity to the Claus—and hence more visible—may have hurt his chances at securing the Santa Claus mantle. He needed to ride the coattails a little longer. He made a mental note to broach the idea of his moving up into the empty office that Ethan had vacated when he moved into the Santa suite. Right after Jetsla's visit would be a good time.

He took the pilfered metallic mouse from his pocket and placed it beside a bluebird feather, a tall and regal Mr. Peanut coin bank, a majestic plastic palomino horse rearing back on its hind legs, a small wooden dog carved by the Claus, and half a dozen other treasured curios that stood neatly aligned on his bookcase. He needed to stop this. It would get him into trouble one day—preferably not until he secured the Claus mantle. What could they possibly do to him then?

# Chapter Three

# Jetsla

Herbert and Hoho, his sometime assistant, stood outside the entrance to Quonset Hut Boston Charlie, sporting fresh haircuts, new green uniforms, and megawatt smiles that threatened to dazzle any eye careless enough to glance their way. Flanking them on either side were the various department heads, who had been given their spit-and-polish marching orders twenty-four hours ago. Everyone had been pumped about the Jetsla visit, and they hopped to action with an esprit typically reserved for the twenty-four-hour runup to Christmas Eve.

Herbert gazed across the biodome that covered Christmasville. He was as thrilled as anyone at the prospect of meeting Noël Rusk's staff, yet he had to wonder why the new Claus had decided to take on a revitalization project so soon after taking office. The gently falling snow, the to and fro of airport baggage handlers, the steady stream of elves flowing between buildings—it was like a ballet. What could Jetsla possibly offer that would improve on this magic? A little more snow? he thought, noting an unusual bare patch of ground here and there. But nature would soon deal with the anomaly—that is, if global warming didn't get here first.

He watched the sky window on the great dome roll back, and a blue Gulfstream jet with an elaborately scrolled "J" on the tail dropped in and touched down on the tarmac. A couple of small skips, and the pilot nailed the landing. Herbert felt his legs turn to jelly, and Hoho began humming "We Three Kings." Just as Herbert had feared, Hoho was an embarrassment. But no, Claus had insisted. What if Herbert needed a runner to go hunt down information for Jetsla? Herbert wanted to say that Hoho was too fat to run and a little too slow to be informative, but he held his pettiness in check. It wasn't smart to tick off a new boss. Smarter to work quietly behind his back.

The jet's Airstair descended, and two elves busied themselves unrolling a green carpet from the bottom of the stairs to the entrance to Boston Charlie. Santa seemed to be sparing no expense. What next? Little cocktail weenies and a champagne toast to a fruitful working relationship?

A plump man in a snappy dark-blue suit disembarked first. Herbert assumed him to be Daniel Sossaman, right-hand man to Noël Rusk. He bore himself regally and looked every bit the king come home after vanquishing foes on foreign soil. Herbert harrumphed to himself. This was a guy who took all the fancy wrapped soaps and such when he checked out from the Hilton.

When Sossaman reached the carpet's end, Herbert extended his hand. "Herbert Tuddy, at your service. It will be my pleasure to escort you around our facility and answer any questions that you may have." He nodded to the four assistants in Sossaman's entourage.

Sossaman consulted his watch. "I have an hour before my itinerary requires me to be somewhere else," he said. "Shall we get right to it?"

Herbert bobbed his head. "If you'll follow me, we'll begin with the main toy manufacturing facility." Once inside, he picked up a construction helmet as they passed by a table full of them. "Please wear it. We don't want anyone needlessly putting themselves in harm's way."

\*\*\*

As Herbert led Sossaman and his entourage into the workings of Christmasville operations, a second Gulfstream—larger and bearing no markings on the tail other than its identifying "N" number—touched down and rolled toward Quonset Hut Alpha. Santa welcomed the solitary passenger—a tall, thin man with light-brown hair cropped close—and they disappeared into the hut together.

Inside the command center, Santa ushered his guest past the enormous gray metal desk stacked edge to edge with computers and beeping, blinking electronic equipment, to a couple of rocking chairs sitting on a braided rug before a roaring fire in a broad stone fireplace. "Your thoughts?" Santa asked the moment the doors closed. "I hate to be rude," he continued, "and my seeming lack of hospitality is regrettable, but I fear there is no time to waste. If we are to continue spreading Christmas cheer throughout the world, we must bring Christmasville's operations into the twenty-first century."

Noël Rusk waved aside the Claus's discomfort and said, "I don't believe in wasting time either." He pointed at the coffee service on a side table beside the fireplace. "If you would be so kind . . ." Then he sat down in an armchair and unbuttoned his rumpled plaid jacket, which looked as if he had slept in it. Since he had just had a fairly long flight, maybe that shouldn't be a mark against him, but the worn spots on his shoe soles spoke volumes about where this man's priorities lay.

Santa sat down in the chair opposite him. "Noël, I am desperate," he said. "Our assembly lines are jerry-rigged from hundred-year-old car parts, the purity of our drinking water is one step above a science experiment, and we had two elves in sickbay last week with second-degree burns because you can't flush a commode and run cold water in a shower at the same time. We're killing half a rain forest with our reliance on paper reporting, and tin cans connected by a string would be better than our current system." He handed the billionaire his to-do list. "It's all right here, except for what we'll soon face from global warming. I don't know how effective Christmas magic will be when Christmasville is marooned on an ice floe in the middle of the Arctic Ocean. I'm open to whatever you can envision, Noël."

"We *are* wasting each other's time if you think one person can correct the adverse effects of climate change. It's a global problem."

"Yes," Santa said, swirling his teaspoon around in his cup. "But if you're willing to tackle some of our infrastructure problems, why not address the effects of climate, too? A wickedly smart entrepreneur such as yourself, with your means"—here he gave Rusk a quick glance—"can help set us right again."

Noël set his cup aside on an end table and stared into the dancing, crackling fire. He rocked a moment in his chair, then gave Santa a smug look. "Much as I'd like to throw a lot of money at the problem and fix it, that method rarely accomplishes anything. People lose focus. When too much money is involved, there's usually too little accountability."

"Oh, I'm not asking you to open your wallet, Noël. I can assure you, we here at Christmasville are not driven by money. And we insist on total transparency in all our operations."

Noël cocked an eyebrow. "All?"

"Well, within reason, of course. We do have proprietary considerations just as I'm sure you do. Unlike you, we don't resort to patents and other legal instruments to protect our secrets. Christmasville is a city-state, only slightly larger than Vatican City—"

"And it is that very independence that will save you." Noël began strolling the room. "Imagine a working environment free from governmental constraints, leaving one free to concentrate on humanity's woes without getting caught up in endless red tape and second-guessing," he said, his hands moving as if to add meaning to ideas that the words alone could not encompass. "That's what I'm looking for, Nicholas, and you are in the unique position of being able to provide it."

Santa frowned. "You want to establish a base of operations at the inhospitable North Pole?"

"Would you call this inhospitable?" Noël asked, gesturing to their surroundings. "A gentle snow on the tarmac? Bright green grass surrounding the houses behind this building? I would suppose, any microclimate you want," he said, smiling.

"Christmas magic," Santa said, nodding.

"If you want me to help you with your difficulties, what I ask in return is space in your biodome that I can use exclusively for Jetsla operations—the very first of which would be to analyze your problems and draw up a blueprint to solve them. That can include milestones, costs to implement—whatever you want."

"And the other operations? I should at least know—"

Noël stopped at the big picture window that looked out on a snowy field of white-kissed evergreens and five reindeer grazing in the distance. "Proprietary, but rest assured that preserving the magical beauty and purpose of this place would be a priority."

"This may be a temporary partnership," Santa said. "If the ice continues to melt at the present rate, even I can't guarantee that Christmas magic will be enough to maintain the increase in population that you're talking about."

"And that means you can trust me, then, doesn't it, Nicholas? Because otherwise, why would I pump effort and money into a project that is doomed from the start? Don't you see? What benefits Christmasville also benefits Jetsla. I will give you our best."

Sitting and rocking in front of the roaring fireplace, Santa felt a chill run up his spine. Was he really willing to give away part of Christmasville to save it? And give it to this man, who could be impulsive and, at times, too bold for his own good. And would he stay the course, or would his mercurial disposition soon find a shinier object to tinker with? Santa listened to the crackling fire and imagined Christmas traditions going up in flames and raining down in dirty black ash. His eyes flicked to the billionaire, who was staring at him intently.

"I need more details and I need it in writing."

"No problem," Noël said. "We can do that. I'll fill you in on Jetsla's grand vision for combating climate change, and then we can discuss improving the operations that you're concerned about."

"So your base here would be dedicated to stemming climate change? I know that's a focus for Jetsla."

Noël wagged his head back and forth. "Some. We do maximize opportunities where they present themselves. Listen, Nicholas, with a name like Noël, I think you can trust me. I hold the North Pole in high esteem—an appreciation my parents nurtured in me from an early age. I would never sacrifice what you have here for the sake of profit or notoriety."

"I see," Santa said, though actually, he didn't. While Noël didn't seem disingenuous, he seemed to be choosing his words very carefully, and they seemed to be coming from the entrepreneur's business sense and not his heart. Santa would have preferred a mix of both. Could he trust the man? Time and a contract would tell. Unfortunately, there wasn't much time, and Christmasville had little experience with legal documents.

# Chapter Four

# Tumbling Idols

No one could advocate harder for Christmasville than Herbert Tuddy. From the moment they entered Quonset Hut Boston Charlie, he babbled incessantly, regaling his Jetsla guests with man-hours spent, widgets produced, and Christmas dollars saved by the various time-cutting measures introduced over the eons. If he hadn't felt a yank on his coat as they entered the manufacturing complex, he would have launched into future plans, too.

"Shh!" Hoho hissed in his ear. "I think you've lost them."

Herbert turned around as Sossaman and his entourage pushed past him and drifted off in various directions. He scurried after them. "To quote projected production numbers—"

Sossaman silenced him with a hand wave and kept moving down the line of elves hammering wooden wheels, and gluing ladders and side mirrors onto little red trucks. At the assembly line's end, he stepped back and watched the whole process, from painting and flash-drying to rolling the finished fire engines onto a conveyor belt, where they were whisked overhead and away to another section of the factory.

Herbert joined him, his chest swelling as he took the operation in. "Something, huh?" Herbert said.

Sossaman responded by leaning in and whispering something to an assistant who caught it in a little black notebook. Herbert shot Hoho a what-the-devil look, but the gentle, exceedingly well-nourished elf quietly cleared his throat and his eyes went south.

"How many rooms like this one?" the assistant asked.

"Currently, twenty-five," Herbert said proudly. When the woman didn't break out into the appreciative smile he anticipated, he quickly added, "But it can vary wildly with the season and product." She grunted and jotted that down, too.

It was more of the same in the Preteen Girls Department, Young Adult Outdoor Living, and the Move It/Wheel It division. Did *anything* make these people happy? Herbert couldn't be everywhere at once, but when at last Sossaman worked his way around to the front of the hut again—and his underlings regrouped around him like metal filings to a magnet—the downcast eyes of the elvish division chiefs seemed to answer with a resounding *no*.

"I suppose you're famished," Herbert said, giving them a bright, cheery elf smile. "We have a buffet set out . . ."

Sossaman smiled for the first time, and Herbert's misgivings melted away. "If only that were possible," he said, tapping his watch. "I need a few words with Mr. Claus, but I'm sure the rest of the crew would love it." He turned to his entourage. "Be ready to go in fifteen."

Herbert sent them with Hoho to the buffet—food was something he excelled at—and conducted Sossaman from the production area. "So, what do you think?"

"Nice."

*Nice?* That was the corporate reaction to a very rare and in-depth tour of one of the greatest production facilities on the planet? Herbert gave him a hard look. What was wrong with this man?

Herbert led him to the command center, where he rapped once on the closed door and entered. Instantly, he pulled back in embarrassment as he realized that the Claus wasn't alone. There were two men sitting before the roaring fireplace: Santa with his big white coffee mug, and Noël Rusk himself, holding a red and white teacup with a reindeer motif—from the expensive, discontinued Tiffany Christmas China collection, if Herbert wasn't mistaken. Santa had rolled out all the bells and whistles for this visit.

"Sorry," Herbert said, bowing low. "Uh, Mr. . . . uh, ahem," he said, humbled to be in the same room with the captain of industry. He stepped aside and waved at Sossaman.

Sossaman, in turn, bowed slightly to Santa. "The tour and refreshments were lovely, Mr. Claus. Noël," he said turning, "if you require anything further, and until you're ready to depart, we'll be talking shop on the plane."

"Excellent," Noël said, nodding. "Have your crew prepare for takeoff. We won't be long here." He looked at Claus, who also nodded.

Herbert escorted Sossaman back to the plane. The luncheoners—still munching on finger sandwiches and decorated Christmas cookies from their rushed meal—were already in line to board. When he ascertained that his services were no longer needed, he hightailed it back to Santa's meeting.

Earlier, he had conveniently failed to close the door completely, so he inched it open a bit more, put an eye to the open slit, and peered in. The two men were still cloistered together, but they spoke in hushed tones. Even with Herbert's extraordinary elvish hearing, catching the conversation was difficult.

"I understand," Santa said. "But I have concerns."

"Hmm," Noël said, sipping from his cup as he leaned toward Santa with rapt attention and politeness. He seemed much more low-key than his lieutenant, Sossaman. He maintained that demeanor until Santa finished speaking, at which point he took a final swallow, draining the cup and setting it down on the table at his elbow. "Well, yes, as I've said before, there are pros and cons to everything. But what can we do? I'm sure you'll agree that failure to act will be catastrophic."

"Yes."

Herbert pulled away from the door. *What* was catastrophic? He repositioned himself with his ear to the crack.

". . . constantly moving ice packs," Rusk said. "Without the permanence of somewhere like Christmasville, all our plans, all our money, and all our precautions . . . Failure will meet us at every turn. We need you. Humanity needs you. Can you truly look at yourself in the mirror at day's end and say it's okay to walk away from so small a request? You give a little and, quite frankly, I can give a lot."

Santa got up and put his mug on the fireplace mantel. "Guilting me, are you? No," he said, shaking his head, "it's not okay to turn a deaf ear to the situation, but to declare what you're asking for to be a *small* request? Hardly, Noël."

Noël also stood up, and Herbert could feel the almost electric power play relaying back and forth between the two men. A slow burn began in Herbert's gut and worked its way up to his face. How dare anyone pressure the Santa Claus? And what the devil? Why would anyone even *try*? He *was* Christmas, for Fudgsicle sakes!

"A trial period, Noël. *Small* scale, *small* numbers with no commitment to extend beyond that—just as you requested. *Small.*"

"Moving all that equipment, people . . ." Noël said. "That will cost me a tremendous amount of money."

"And that's a problem for Jetsla?" Santa said, chuckling.

Noël didn't respond. The mantel clock filled the awkward silence with its steady ticking. Herbert pressed his ear tighter to the door, and it edged open with a squeak. He pulled back from the opening and held his breath. He could almost feel gazes turning his way. Just when he thought he would expire from lack of oxygen, Santa began again.

"We may do extraordinary things with limited resources in our little spot high atop the world," he said, "but reducing further may be more than we can handle. It's a delicate dance here."

"Everyone's dancing, Mr. Claus. What will you do when there is no more music? You've said so yourself: we're almost that far. And once we're there?" Rusk snapped his fingers. "There is no stepping back from the precipice. Global warming is real and on our doorstep. Jetsla can do so much to combat it if you'll just give us this chance to try. And as a bonus, I can provide you with almost immediate relief from your infrastructure problems. Isn't that what you asked for?"

"A trial," Santa insisted. "Four months, at which time—"

"Six."

"Four months, at which time I'll decide whether to continue. And that is separate from the mechanization we need immediately."

The clock began counting again.

"All right," Rusk said, sighing with exasperation. "But I must have carte blanche—"

"With my concurrence. And anything that could pose a threat to my people will be located in a biodome to be constructed outside the big dome."

Rusk's sigh was even deeper than the last. "You drive a hard bargain, Claus, but we have a deal." He picked up the backpack at his feet. "I'll fax you the specifics."

Herbert leaned in just enough to glimpse the two shaking hands.

*Mechanization?* As in automating an assembly line? What on earth would the elves do when Noël Rusk automated them out of their jobs? Herbert scurried off. Santa had just sold their souls to the devil.

Exactly who did one tell when one's world was about to crumble? The best listener? The wisest? Herbert barreled down the hallway away from Santa's command room and turned the corner, where he ran smack into someone with neither of those qualities. Staggering backward, Herbert quickly sized up Hoho, then backed him into a nearby utility closet.

"Say not a word," he hissed to his large, astonished colleague. He delivered his alarming new information in much the same way that a dump truck delivers a load of gravel. When he finished, he studied Hoho's face for some glimmer indicating that information had been received: a murmur of advice, perhaps, no matter how inane, or at least a big, beefy hug.

Hoho's forehead creased, and the corners of his mouth sagged. "Babydoll dresses, tin-soldier uniforms, and little leather boots—a machine is going to make those? Where's the love?"

"*That's* your takeaway from what I told you?" Herbert said, regretting the time he was wasting. "This is cold, hard, business. They don't care anything about us."

"But, but . . ." Hoho closed his mouth and dropped his head.

Herbert felt a surprising rush of sympathy for his uncomprehending friend, and a sudden protectiveness. He patted him on the shoulder and murmured, "Never fear. We'll nip this in the bud. But first, can you do something for me? We need to convene a meeting of division heads, but I can't just blast out a notice without raising questions. So, here's what I want you to do. Personally go to each manager who sat in on our planning meeting yesterday. Instruct them to meet with me in the bunker at two-thirty this afternoon."

"Sure," Hoho said, opening the closet door.

Herbert put a hand on his arm to slow him down. "Nothing else, no extra information. Just the meeting time and place, okay? And don't leave messages. The invitation is face-to-face or not at all."

"Got it," Hoho said. "It's not rocket science."

Herbert watched him hurry down the hall. Quite the contrary. Rocket science was *exactly* what it was. It was high tech versus ancient tradition, personal profit and glory over selfless service, and, yes, Hoho, it was cold, hard widget-counting versus love. Herbert kicked the utility door shut and power-walked back toward Santa's command center. If he intended to foment opposition against Noël Rusk, he needed more information.

## Chapter Five

# When One Door Closes

The door to the command center stood wide open. Claus, surrounded by laptops, monitors, and other blinking, beeping equipment, sat at the main desk scribbling away in a big ledger. Herbert's jaw dropped. The bearded one was more of a get-out-and-press-the-flesh type than a desk jockey. What had Noël Rusk done to him?

"They're gone, sir," Herbert said, quietly sliding into the room as if this were just another carefree day in paradise.

Claus put down his pen. "You have questions, Herbert."

Herbert cocked an eyebrow. "Me, sir? No, sir."

Claus's eyebrows lifted. "Oh. I thought perhaps you didn't catch everything while standing at the door."

Herbert smiled sheepishly. "I thought Noël Rusk wasn't coming."

"A last-minute thing, actually. No one was more surprised than I when the air controllers alerted me to another Jetsla plane coming in."

"But I didn't see him touring the facilities."

"No, no touring," Claus said, loading paper in the inkjet printer. "We spent the time ironing out a few issues."

"Hmm," Herbert said, studying the bell at the tip of his pointed green elf shoe.

"Just 'hmm'?" Claus returned to his laptop and tapped several keys.

26

The printer hummed to life and began spitting paper out onto the floor.

In two quick steps, Herbert beat Claus to the printer. "Issues on what?" he asked, adjusting the external paper tray to catch the printing while Claus scooped up the wayward pages.

"Everything," Claus said. He dropped back into his chair. "Take a look around at how many things in this one room are out of date or flat-out obsolete. That should be a laser," he said, gesturing to the inkjet printer. "And this . . ." he said, picking up the handheld microphone. "Shouldn't an operation as large and complex as ours have a state-of-the-art communication system? For goodness' sake, we're a global command center! The place is falling down around our ears."

Herbert's gaze wandered the room, eventually settling on a sagging curtain rod that was coming loose from the wall. Automating the elves out of their jobs wouldn't fix this.

"If that sounds like criticism for prior Clausian administrations, please don't take it that way. Before I assumed the Sinterklaas mantle, I simply took everything for granted. Now, being responsible for everything, I understand what a truly enormous task it is to keep things rolling."

Herbert nodded. Clearly, the place needed a bit more than elbow grease. When deadlines got tight and the workforce had its nose to the grindstone, no one was available to clean up the side messes. What Santa said made sense. "And Noël Rusk and Jetsla—they figure into this *how*, exactly? It's a worldwide company, and Rusk didn't get to be a billionaire by doing things out of the kindness of his heart. What could we possibly give them in exchange?"

Santa gave him a quick glance and then looked away. The printer continued to swoosh out paper, and the ticking mantel clock filled another awkward silence.

"Claus?"

"It's complicated, Herbert."

Herbert plopped down into another chair. "Oh, dear, what have you done?"

Santa shook his head as if that would make what he planned to say a bit more palatable. "Nothing sinister. He simply wants to lease space from us—the grounds under the far end of the dome and a few additional acres outside the dome. Maybe twenty at most. It's not as if we were using it."

"Why on earth would Rusk want to come here? It's just shifting ice, and the temperature can dip to a horrid minus forty degrees Fahrenheit. We might need a few things fixed, but the likes of Jetsla? Christmasville doesn't need to turn a profit. In the end, isn't all that matters that we spruce up a few things and everyone is happy? Let me contact a home improvement store in Fairbanks, Alaska."

"It's a jurisdictional thing, Herbert. Christmasville holds sovereignty over the biosphere and some ice around it, but no other entity or country owns the North Pole. Rusk can get a lease to do what he wants with no red tape and few restrictions."

"What is it he wants to do so badly that he's afraid to abide by the rules and regulations of civilized nations?"

"He's a brilliant man, you know, the heart and soul of his companies, and he doesn't feel he can cut red tape fast enough to achieve what needs to be done and what he's capable of doing."

Herbert shook his head. "I still don't understand what's in it for us."

"In exchange for less oversight, Jetsla will help us with our immediate need for modernization. They'll redesign us top to bottom. No more wonky assembly lines, a proper shower for everyone—a happy life for elves for eons to come. Every elf deserves that. We'll get what we need to continue our beloved mission, and they will have proprietary rights to the processes that prove successful. If those processes help combat climate change, everyone on Earth wins. Who knows, maybe they will eventually launch a few spacecraft from here. With the atmosphere thinnest at the polar cap, this would be a most efficient place to do it. Wouldn't that be fun?" Santa gave a little shrug. "What can I say? We can't go on like this forever, limping along as we glue and tape things together. Hopefully, in the end, Jetsla will do extraordinary things for mankind and will be richly rewarded for it, and we save our imperiled city. It'll be a win-win-win."

Herbert narrowed his eyes at the Claus. Why was the man fidgeting so? Why such an extreme reaction to a run-of-the-mill lease agreement? "That sounds noble and wonderful. So why do I sense misgivings on your part? The downside for Jetsla is that it would lose money, but as you've already told him, what's a little pocket change to an organization that is worth billions? Why do you think we can trust Rusk? What happens if we elves—the little guy—get lost in the shuffle of a powerful man's dream to become even more powerful? What, pray tell, is the downside for our livelihoods, our homes, future generations of elves?"

"Automation," Claus mumbled, refusing to meet Herbert's eyes.

Herbert's gaze shifted out the door, toward the other Quonset huts and the warehouses full of dedicated elves with aching backs and sore fingers as they worked long hours to provide Christmas joy to billions across the globe. Claus was throwing the elfling out with the bathwater. "And how many will lose their jobs?" he asked, picturing breadlines and bored, out-of-work elves turning to the bottle and other vices as they whiled away their idle hours. Elves were meant for service. Whatever would they do without purpose?

"I can assure you that isn't the intent," Claus replied, and Herbert caught the slight edge to his voice. "Hopefully none . . . er, a few." He shook his head. "I don't have a good idea yet."

Nice. He hadn't even conducted a manpower study? Herbert could almost hear the old Claus spinning in his grave.

As quickly as panic gripped Herbert's chest and threatened to squeeze the breath from him, calm prevailed once again. *Where one door shuts, another one opens.* Who better to fix an impending mess than he himself? "Your old office," he said. "How would you feel about me moving from the bunker into it? Perhaps I could intercept and solve some problems before they get to you. That way, you won't feel as if you have to shoulder everything alone."

Santa's forehead went up as if he had not even stopped to consider who would inherit his old office. "It's a good thought, Herbert. I'll take it under serious consideration."

"Here to please," Herbert said, spreading his arms wide in a magnanimous gesture. And he meant it. It was just a matter of who got the satisfaction.

"There is one thing you still need to take off my back. Have you finished looking into the pilot's license issue?" Santa asked.

"Yes, sir, hopped right on it. A license is definitely required to fly in United States airspace. The first pilot's license was issued in 1927 by Assistant Secretary of Commerce for Aeronautics, William P. MacCracken. Thereafter, your predecessor renewed every ten years for ten dollars. Payments now go to the FAA, which is the successor organization to the original issuing agency, the Aeronautics Branch in the Department of Commerce. I'll cut through as much red tape as I can, and have you airborne again in no time." He put his hand to his lips and pondered for a moment. "If I may say so," he said, "this should never have become an issue. Hoho and I were in a bit of a pickle this past December when we had to fly without Santa. What else could we have done?"

"Nothing," Santa agreed. "I'll leave it in your able hands."

A loud voice interrupted the discussion. "Where would you like this, sir?" a breathless elf called from the hallway as the metal shopping cart he was maneuvering banged into the door frame.

Claus eyed the two-inch-thick stack of paper on the cart. "Perhaps if I knew what it is, Lee . . ."

Lee leaned over and read the transmittal sheet rubber-banded around the paper. "To: Santa Claus, North Pole. From: Legal Division, Jetsla." He raised an eyebrow and waited.

"Jetsla, you say? Already?" Santa came over and lifted out the reams. "I can take it from here. Thank you."

"There's more," Lee said, banging the door molding one more time as he backed out. "But it jammed up the copier. They've got the machine apart trying to figure out where the paper's scrunched up. Hopefully, it won't be long."

"Yes, yes," Santa said, his attention riveted on the paper. "As soon as possible. Call our Xerox representative, Ms. O'Clair. I'm sure she can sort it out."

"Lease agreement?" Herbert asked.

"I suppose so," Santa said. "I didn't expect a document this long. Hopefully, it's standard language, and the review will go quickly."

"Yes, sir. That's a lot of reading, sir. Rusk must have had it locked and loaded, ready to go. I wish I could help you, but unfortunately . . ."

Santa waved him out. "No, you go right along, Herbert. My problem. I have to dig through this myself."

Herbert left the old man to it. He had two hours until his meeting with the division chiefs. That gave him just enough time to pack up for his move into Claus's old office. Though the old man hadn't okayed it, there wasn't a soul in Christmasville who had a greater claim. He secured his prized possessions into canvas carts and measured some rather stylish furniture he had collected over the years. It didn't take nearly as long as he had expected, but with joy in his heart and a bounce in his step, how could he not sail through it? This was turning out to be one of his best days ever. He set off for his meeting feeling invincible.

# Chapter Six
# Wallace to the Rescue

Santa lugged the document toward his desk, then to a side counter before deciding that neither had enough surface area to bear the Jetsla contract. So, he dropped to his knees and began laying out pages across the control room carpet. The beginning was simple and straightforward enough: parties involved, the filtration system, a lease of Christmasville ice property to Jetsla. Santa sighed in relief. This wasn't as overwhelming as it might have been. Then he got to page four. That was where the legal mumbo jumbo kicked in: "therefore's," "parties of the first part unless otherwise noted in sections blah, blah, blah," and on it went. He shuddered to think what would show up on the pages still wadded up in the copy machine!

He got up and hit the green button on the intercom box sitting on the desk. "Department fourteen, I need elf twenty-five in the main office. Repeat. Department fourteen, I need elf twenty-five in the main office right away." He released the button and sat down in his swivel chair. The response would be quick. Having the Claus use the intercom was a rarity. That was what Herbert was for. Lately, though, Herbert seemed to be anywhere but where he should be. And how long did it take to clear up something as simple as a pilot's license? As soon as Wallace, chief of accounting, deciphered the contract, Santa would give the wayward Mr. Herbert Tuddy a talking-to. Santa might not need him for the Jetsla mumbo jumbo, but Herbert could at least handle support work.

Before he could even gather his thoughts on how he would approach Herbert, Wallace skidded to a halt at the center door and offered a crisp salute.

"Wallace, senior accountant, at your service, sir." He held up an index finger, adjusted his fuchsia pompadour, inhaled deeply, and blew the breath slowly back out again. "Sorry. Steps three at a time is a very bad idea. What can I do for you, sir?"

Santa smiled at the elf's earnestness and made a mental note to reward him later. "I need help with *that*," he said, pointing to the papers on the floor. "It's a contract between Christmasville and Jetsla that has to be signed by nine a.m. our time tomorrow."

Wallace looked from the document to the Black Forest clock hanging on the wall. They had less than twenty-four hours, but Wallace exuded confidence and pride. "Paper and pen, sir? In case I need to make some notes . . ."

Santa gave him what he asked for, settled into a chair before the fireplace, and closed his eyes for a few quick z's. No elf liked to be micromanaged, and least of all the numbers people. It was up to Wallace Horatio, son of Lawrence, son of Baylor Winthrop Sizzlebaum. Either Noël Rusk was an honest man, or Christmasville would get royally screwed. If the latter was the case, Santa would at least like to go into the agreement with eyes wide open and a few more concessions.

Santa jerked awake to Wallace shaking him. He was fairly certain he hadn't gotten the full power nap, but the few minutes he did get were deeply satisfying. His eyes went right to the cuckoo clock. Eleven-thirty. "Are we good?" he asked the elf.

"There is good and there is *good*," the elf replied cryptically. "Do you want the good news or the bad news first?"

"Both, quickly," Santa said, wary of long-winded elves (which was all of them, given the opportunity).

"Thankfully, most of this," Wallace said, pointing a toe at the lengthy contract spilling across the floor, "is standard contract legalese. No one writes a contract anymore without including this verbosity."

"Verbosity?"

"Junk language. "

Santa nodded. "And the nonstandard?"

"He will provide a report detailing a top-to-bottom analysis of Christmasville factory processes, equipment, and workflow—that's clearly spelled out—and throw in some 'other upgrades.' But he hasn't specifically listed any of the concerns you detailed in writing. There is no addressing of water quality problems, plumbing issues, or piss-poor communications."

Wallace stopped and cleared his throat. "Sorry, sir, that characterization was uncalled for. I just feel this legal document is so terribly one-sided. It doesn't state that he will hire a plumber, dedicate an IT specialist to write new programs, or bring in new engines to drive our assembly lines or any other equipment—not even a porta-potty to help us through rough times. You won't be able to hold him to giving you anything other than a general analysis. Jetsla, on the other hand, gets free use of our "land" holdings to do whatever they want, whenever they want it, and there is no language specifying an end date."

"No six-month trial period?" Santa's enormous white eyebrows arched until they touched the soft white fur band on his red hat.

Wallace shook his head. "It's open-ended."

Santa began to pace. "I was very specific . . ."

Wallace raised his palms toward him. "Sir, relax. This is the negotiation process. They offer something outrageous that benefits only them, and then we counter to make things more equitable. Most definitely, you should insist on an additional clause specifying a time frame. If this Noël Rusk and his Jetsla prove to be unwanted houseguests, it would be best to show them the door. I can draft something immediately."

"Yes, yes, by all means," Santa said. He took a seat by the fireplace and began noodling through his feelings about proceeding with the whole enchilada. Not even out of the gate yet, and Rusk was already trying to pull a fast one.

## Chapter Seven
# Frankenstein's Brother

Hoho worked best when given a single straightforward assignment with no technical difficulties to divide his concentration, so when Herbert entered the bunker conference room, he fully expected half the chairs around the table to be empty. Surprisingly, all twelve chiefs were present. Herbert gave Hoho a thumbs-up and locked the door. He took the empty seat at the head of the rectangular table and then acknowledged each division chief with a brief salutation. To an elf, he saw confusion in their eyes, drooping smiles, and none of the jovial banter that generally lit up these meetings. Apparently, their single encounter with the Jetsla delegation had done a number on them. Setting them against Jetsla would be easier than he thought.

"Thank you for coming on such short notice," he said. "Rough go with the Jetsla group, huh? Somehow, I don't think they have the first idea about how we run things, and the prodigious amount of product we put out twenty-four-seven, three hundred sixty-four days a year."

You could have cut the silence with a Jim Bowie action figure knife. Herbert felt his face flush. Had his personal feelings made his judgment faulty? Then fiery redheaded Melody, chief of Robotics, nodded in agreement, and the usually reticent Stewart, Fashion Accessories, bobbed his gleaming bald head. Soon, they were falling like a line of dominoes—clack, clack, clack—the division chiefs nodding and agreeing in rowdy tones about what a crock the Jetsla visit had been. They vented their pent-up frustration with angry mutterings and shaken fists. It was great!

"You don't know the half of it," Herbert said. "I want to make sure you get that other half—the truth—before anybody puts a spin on what's going on. Jetsla will be a permanent fixture around here. Done deal between Santa and Noël Rusk himself. All the Claus has to do is put his *Santa E. Claus* on the contract. Jetsla gets free run of Christmasville in exchange for basically telling us what we already know: that the plumbing stinks, the conveyor belts move slower than molasses in January, and yelling across campus at each other is better than our intercom system. They'll tell us that everything is bass-ackward, and point out areas where we can mechanize some things."

Melody's eyes narrowed. "What kind of 'things'?"

Herbert held both palms up. "I can only postulate, but it doesn't take much imagination to picture what mechanization would do to the assembly lines."

A small cry escaped Stewart's lips as the room erupted once more into clamorous shouting and table pounding and even a few unseemly utterances.

"What's the matter?" Melody asked. "Santa doesn't think he can squeeze any more output from us? I suppose he thinks machines can meet his increased production numbers." Her eyes blazed with fury. "They're replacing us with machines, aren't they?"

"Most certainly," Herbert said, not catching everything she said amid the general din, but going with the room's energy.

Stewart searched faces around the table. "Wally? Where's Wally? What does the contract say?"

"Wallace is with the Claus," Herbert said. "I'll snag him as soon as he's done."

"By then it will be too late!" Melody said. "The time to act is before Santa seals our fate with a flourish of his indifferent pen."

"They're replacing us with robots?" It was Lester from Infants. He threw a quick look at Melody. "Not *your* robotics, of course. Well, I think we should strike. Now! Let everything go merrily to heck in a handbasket. Robo, heck no! Robo, heck no!" he said, his fist pumping.

"Robo, hell no!" Melody shouted, springing up with such vehemence, her chair skittered backward. Stewart joined her, followed quickly by the other chiefs taking up Lester's war cry.

"What? Whoa!" Herbert jumped to his feet, but they ignored him and followed Melody to the door, pushing and jostling as they waited impatiently for her to open it. *Santa, Santa, Santa!* It seemed the Claus had created a monster!

Melody got the door open, and the unruly bunch spilled out into the hall, nearly trampling Wallace as he tried to join the meeting.

Jody, head of the lumberyard, grabbed him by the lapels and pinned him to the far wall. "Are you helping Jetsla take our jobs?" he growled, lifting Wallace off his feet.

"No," the wee accountant squeaked, his red-tighted legs bicycling uselessly in the air.

"Put him down," Herbert barked, plowing through the raucous throng. He pried Jody's hands free, and Wallace fell in a heap on the floor. "Pull yourselves together, people. You're punishing the wrong person. And we don't even know if the deal's been inked yet." He drew the numbers elf back up onto his feet. "Wallace?"

"He's still reviewing the paperwork," Wallace said, massaging his neck and glaring at Jody. "The contract is ginormous and he'll be hours at it. In fact," he said, consulting his Dudley Do-Right Canadian Mountie wristwatch, "I've got about ten minutes to grab a snack from the vending machine and then hustle back upstairs. I'm afraid we'll both be long into the night." He shot Jody a guarded look. "I can't do anyone any good staying here."

Herbert nodded. "Wallace is right. And Lester's idea will be more effective than mob violence. We need to hit Santa where it hurts. We go on strike, right in the middle of our midyear push. Fear of a presentless Christmas should concentrate the Claus's mind. Then he'll see it our way."

Jody crossed his massive arms over his chest and stuck his ill-favored mug in Herbert's face. "I say we stop him right now."

"Steady, big fella," Herbert said. "A house divided—"

"He's right," Melody said. She slid in between the two elves. "Violence never ends anything. It just escalates a bad situation."

"Don't blame us," Jody said, pushing his way out of the group. "There's only one person to fix this, and that's *Wallace*. He's the adviser. So advise the Claus to not sign it. Once that happens, it's really a done deal!"

Melody looked at her peers. "We need a show of hands. Who says yea to a strike? Don't be shy because you happen to be management. All we need to do is start the ball rolling, and then we step back and let the unions do the rest."

The division heads, every one a distinguished artisan and village elder, side-eyed one another. It seemed no one was willing to break from the pack and risk ending up on an unpopular side—or, even worse, on the bad side of the burly lumberelf.

"Yea," Herbert said, raising his fist in the air. He looked at Wallace, who did the same. "Melody?"

"Strike," she said, raising her fist, defiance in her eyes. When no one else joined her, she said, "Come on, you bunch of lily-livered milquetoasts. Here's your chance to have your voices heard. If you won't step up now, don't go flapping your gums later. You're not even committing anyone to anything—we still have to take this back to the union stewards. Yea or nay?" she finally screamed. "Yea or nay?"

Eleven other hands shot up, and Herbert nearly wet himself. Melody was a force of nature (and, with her natural leadership abilities, a potential future rival). "Settled, then," he said, trying to reestablish control over the group. "We hit the Eternal Order of the Elves, the Seamsters Union, and the Brotherhood of Animal Maintenance and ask for an immediate strike vote."

Herbert turned to Wallace and said, "You'd best get back. I'll poke my head in later and see how things are progressing." With that, he grabbed the accountant by the upper arm and escorted him away from the division chiefs. "Don't worry about Jody," he whispered. "I'll just cast some doubt on delivery schedules for his yearly lumber allotment. That'll whip him into line. Just concentrate on the Claus."

He patted Wallace on the back, at the same time propelling him toward the steps. If they couldn't get the unions to fall in line, Wallace was their best hope. But no pressure.

# Chapter Eight
# One-Upmanship

Hours passed as Santa and Wallace wrestled with the Jetsla contract. Herbert filled the waiting with pots of hot coffee, constant nodding off, and endless pacing (mostly in the hallway after Santa became annoyed and suggested Herbert go and do it elsewhere). As dawn approached and the Claus and the numbers elf still had not worked their way through the contract, Herbert snorted as his head hit the desk once more and woke him up again.

"Herbert," Santa said, sliding his glasses down on his nose. "Don't you want to call it a night? Or maybe a day . . ." he added as he glanced out the window at the brightening sky.

"But, but you might need me."

Santa's eyes crinkled at the corners. "If I promise that I will summon you before I make anything final, then will you go get some shut-eye?"

Herbert spent a moment hacking his way through brain fog and cobwebs. Finally, finding no downside to the proposition, he nodded wearily. Then he shuffled off to the bunker and drifted into a deep sleep, still clothed in his dress greens.

He awoke on his own, bolting up in bed at precisely 12:20 p.m. Was no news good news? He hopped up from his bed, slowing only briefly to read a note he found taped to his closet door: *Didn't want to wake you. We expect to finish soon. Please return to my office at 12 noon sharp.* Heaven help him, even back in his wildest partying days, he had never slept this late. He skipped changing clothes and raced up the bunker steps as if the sleigh were running late on Christmas Eve.

The control room was a shocker. Empty pizza boxes and coffee cups lay strewn about. But even more interestingly, for the second time in as many days, Santa was entertaining an outsider. Herbert took one look at the long-nosed elf with beady, too-close-together eyes and quietly swore an oath that would make his beer-swilling, poker-playing grandmother cringe in embarrassment. While it wasn't unusual for the Pole to receive visitors, it was unusual to receive elves—or in this case half-elves—who had run away from the Pole years ago, giving up a life of Christmas service to seek personal gain in the world of high finance. Hello, P. J. Foos, the venal traitor who forsook his calling and hopped aboard the Noël Rusk gravy train. Wallace was nowhere in sight. Herbert's eyes flicked back and forth between the Claus and the half-elf. "Uhm," was all he could manage.

"Good news, Herbert," Santa said, rubbing his enormous belly as if he'd just finished his most scrumptious meal ever. "Jetsla and I have worked through the contract glitches. Wallace has gone to download the final document onto a computer disk. We're merely a signature away from getting Christmasville the help it sorely needs."

"Uhm," Herbert repeated. He locked eyes on the visitor and glowered.

"Oh, yes," Santa said, turning to the half-elf, "Herbert, I'd like you to meet Patrick Jefferson Foos. He's our liaison with Jetsla. Mr. Foos, this is Herbert Tuddy, First Assistant in Christmasville."

"Mr. Foos and I are well acquainted," Herbert said, putting out a hand to grasp stubby fingers that could never tie a Christmas ribbon or paint a little red caboose. He squeezed the fingers together, reveling in the grimace that Foos tried valiantly to mask.

"Mr. Foos flew in early this morning to personally answer any questions we might have about the Jetsla agreement. Now that the contract has been sorted out, he will stay on-site to coordinate Jetsla's physical move. With your assistance, of course."

Herbert nodded. "On-site, you say? I'll prepare a place."

"For the time being, he can sit in my old office."

"Your old office," Herbert repeated, grinding out a smile. "No need for him to move twice. I can have someplace else ready in no time." He picked up the receiver on a nearby rotary phone and began dialing numbers.

"Oh, not necessary," Santa replied. "We don't need to deal with everything at once."

"Right," Herbert said. "If you don't mind, sir, a word in private?" He tipped his head towards Santa's private room.

"Mr. Foos—" Santa began.

"P. J., if that's okay with you," Foos said, smiling brightly. "After all, we're in this together."

Santa returned the smile. "Well, then, *P. J.*, if you will excuse us for a moment, your office is right through that side door. Why don't you start making yourself at home while Herbert and I discuss some things?"

Herbert did a slow burn as Foos took possession of one of the only two things in this world that Herbert coveted: that office and the job of Santa Claus. That burn leaped up into a roaring bonfire when the new elf gave him a quick wink just before shutting the office door.

"Herbert," Santa said, ushering Herbert into his room and closing the door, "this isn't permanent, and the location of one's office doesn't make the elf. You're still second in command."

Herbert sighed to himself. He'd seen the accession of three Santa Clauses and never got any further than second in command. Always an elf, never the Claus. "With due respect, Santa, sir, this is a mistake. Perhaps, you don't remember Mr. Foos. When I was selected for the first assistant position instead of him, he deserted us for fame and riches."

Santa retrieved a stubby black pipe from a rack of three on the fireplace mantel and busied himself a moment lighting it. "Oh, I remember him quite well, but here's the thing, Herbert. Where would we be in this world without a little forgiveness? And how far would we get if we couldn't acknowledge that people—even dyed-in-the-wool elves—"

"*Half*-elves."

". . . can change? I plan on giving him a second chance to redeem himself. And you need to do the same. Lest you think I'm an old fool, I do want you to come to me if you think our trust has been misplaced."

"But you didn't see the wink—"

At that moment, a young elf with a million freckles stuck his head in the door. "Boxes for Mr. Foos?" he said to Herbert, talking around the long, thin cheroot hanging out of his mouth. He saw the Claus and promptly removed the cigar. "Sorry, Santa. I'll just put this outside." He left and returned a moment later, reeking of smoke.

Herbert sighed. Arguing with the Claus was like fighting a one-man city hall. Foos would get the office. For now. But only until Herbert could figure out a way to send his overlarge, brown-suited tuchus packing.

"You look dead on your feet, sir," Herbert said to Santa. "Don't you think it would be a good idea to sleep on the agreement before doing anything rash? Sometimes a little distance is a good thing, sir."

"Rash?" Santa said, quirking a bushy white eyebrow. "No, Herbert, I feel very good about this one. Put aside your misgivings. I have no intention of letting Noël Rusk or anyone else put one over on us. With my guidance, Christmasville will be in good hands. I think a good night's sleep on your part might improve *your* perspective, though. Give it time, and trust me."

Herbert nodded. "Well, I guess if we're to get his big influx of Jetsla people, I'd better start the logistics rolling on our end."

"Good man. I knew you would rise to the occasion. I'll expect an update later. For now, I think we both have a lot to arrange. Who knows how fast this will move."

*Faster than you can imagine,* Herbert thought, returning to the bunker. While he might be too late to salvage his office in the short term, he could certainly make Santa keenly aware that the repercussions for passing him over would be severe and expensive.

He looked around at his boxed things. He had no desire to unpack. The faster he got rid of Jetsla and Foos, the sooner he could get into his new office. He booted up his computer, and two new emails pinged into his in-box. The first was from Melody, informing him that the union stewards were onboard and a massive strike vote was scheduled for two-thirty in Quonset Hut Dickens. That was quick, he thought noting that it was now one o'clock. The second message was from the Claus. He was lightning quick, too. Before Herbert had even gotten to complain to anyone that he had been robbed of his prime office, Santa was already sending out a missive directing Pole upper management to muster their staffs for a two-o'clock meeting in Quonset Hut Dickens. Subject: Christmasville-Jetsla Joint Venture (timeline and collocation details). While the head elf might not have handled the assignment of the empty office with any sort of finesse, he wasn't wasting any time putting a political spin on everything else associated with Jetsla.

Herbert headed for Quonset Hut Dickens—the newest structure—

which housed a gymnasium, indoor pool, and conference rooms with walls that could be electronically folded up to form larger or smaller meeting spaces. He stepped onto the sidewalk and a small red projectile bounced off his chest. Solomon.

"No time, fairy. Bigger things on my plate," Herbert said, passing him by with a cursory glance. Solomon and his kind were notorious gossipers. All he needed was intel getting back to Santa about his double dealings. "I think the Claus was looking for you. Something about a game you had scheduled?"

"He said later," Solomon replied, flying backward and keeping pace in front of his earthbound friend. "So right now, I'm all yours." The feathers on his head fluffed up in anticipation.

Herbert dodged around him. "Not now, Solomon. Try Rudolph at the stable. Maybe you can amuse yourself teaching him to flash that nose beacon in Morse code."

"*Try Rudolph at the stable*," Solomon taunted into Herbert's ear as he continued tagging along. "What are you up to, Mr. Big Pants? Methinks you're sneaking around."

"Get lost," Herbert said, shooing him as he might a pesky flying insect. He entered Quonset Hut Dickens and slammed the door behind him, shutting the fairy outside. Solomon responded with mad tapping on the door glass, and something that sounded like a cross between a bumblebee and a buzz saw. He wasn't completely out of Herbert's hair. Sooner or later, the little winged red dynamo would ride in on someone else's coattails, but at least Herbert would have a few peaceful moments, and perhaps Solomon would become fixated on someone else.

Herbert had never seen so many of the Quonset hut's interior walls rolled back, and he was impressed by the sheer number of elves now pouring into the conference room. He busied himself tending to the podium and sound system while trying to put off the division chiefs demanding a heads-up on Santa's presentation. Herbert promised a quiet word before everything hit the fan.

When he finished, the auditorium looked as if all three hundred working elves had taken up residence there. Twenty or so fairies had also joined the multitude, hovering above the elven heads like colorful, exotic fashion accessories. Solomon was not among them. Near the stage, Melody and Stanley stood talking to the three major union stewards. When Herbert verified that Santa still had not arrived, he drew them out in the hallway for a few quick words.

"Fait accompli," Melody said. "Once the vote is over, they're ready to pull everyone off the line immediately. The more artistic are already off printing protest signs. They will be in the Claus's face the moment he joins the meeting, but they'll wait until after he speaks to announce the voting."

## Chapter Nine
# Ends Against the Middle

Santa scooped up his hastily prepared notes for the all-hands meeting. "Not now, Solomon," he said, dodging the fairy for the third time. "You'll make me late."

"Late might not be so bad," Solomon said, hovering between Claus and the door. "Or maybe never. Oh, now, *that's* a clever option. Or maybe even your first radio address. Zoom—a wonderful innovation and excellent use of modern technology, I might add." He flew over to the main computer tower on the command desk and tried with both hands to lever the power switch into the On position. "A little help here?" he said, puffing mightily.

"Don't touch my things," Santa said, pointing a chastising finger at him. "I'll be back in about an hour. Then, if you're up to it, maybe a round of *I see something.*"

Oh, I see something *now*," Solomon said, shaking his head. "Stop, stop, stop!"

"Later." Santa batted him away several more times until Solomon gave up and flitted off. Fairies could be either exceedingly clever or needier than a newborn. With luck, something else would grab his fancy and there would be no need for games later.

The quietness of the day sent prickles up Santa's arms. He heard no soft tapping of hammers, no whistling and singing as he walked to Quonset Hut Dickens. The elf force waited inside to hear about the great things Christmasville would accomplish with Jetsla. Santa smiled, loving the elves' steely focus and dedication. There was nothing the village couldn't accomplish if they put their minds to it.

Wonderful gym, Santa thought as he swept by the weight room in Quonset Hut Dickens. And the heated pool—who would have thought it possible to take a dip at the North Pole? His heartbeat accelerated as he approached the meeting room. What a magnificent sight it would be to see everyone together—one big, joyous family!

He swung the conference room door open and felt his beautifully constructed world come tumbling down like a ton of ugly fireplace bricks. Placard, placard, everywhere a placard: JETSLA, GO HOME! SAVE OUR JOBS! FIRE SANTA! Merciful heavens, why hadn't someone warned him?

Herbert greeted him at the door with an embarrassed smile and then pushed through the nearest protesters to escort him to the stage. The noise piped down a bit, but the protest signs still bobbed up and down like pistons.

"I, uh, don't know what to say," Santa said, surveying the group.

"Truth!" someone yelled from the back.

"Oh . . . always, my brother," Santa said, squinting to get a better look at the elf. "I've walked into the middle of something here that I hadn't anticipated. Since I'm not sure exactly how we got here, why don't we take a step back and start at the beginning?"

A few hecklers challenged that, but the majority of the elves slipped into an uneasy silence.

"I called you here this afternoon to tell you about the new agreement between Jetsla and Christmasville." Hecklers piped up again, but quieted when the Claus raised both hands to shush them. "Considering that I signed the contract less than half an hour ago, I'm astonished to come here and find so much organized opposition to it." He looked askance at Herbert. "As much as we love Christmasville and consider it the perfect place to live, I'm sure we can agree that conditions are far from perfect. Many things are falling down around our ears: communications, transportation, order and delivery systems. If we're honest, we all can see room for improvement, can't we?" He didn't wait for an answer but kept plowing ahead. "Jetsla is a competitive international company with free capital to invest here, and a brilliant CEO, Noël Rusk. Noël and I have personally hammered out the details for a robust plan to upgrade our decaying infrastructure and innovate where possible—"

"Innovate us out of jobs," the same voice yelled from the crowd.

"Certainly not!" Santa said. "As Christmasville's steward, I'm disappointed that you would have so little faith in me. While new robotic technology might someday replace elves at the bench, I give you my solemn word that we will move affected employees to new opportunities. No one—I repeat, no one—gets lost in the shuffle. No one!" he added again for good measure, shaking his head.

"And in return?"

At this point, the audience shuffled as everyone tried to see the bold questioner willing to sacrifice himself for all those who had the same question but were afraid to ask it.

Santa finally zeroed in on the questioner. It was Tocker from Educational Toys. "A livable environment at the Pole—collocation in our biodome. The unused area beyond the runway. But not permanently. There is a four-month trial period, during which we can terminate the contract without penalty should we so choose. And we also have veto power over Jetsla projects that we deem at odds with our mission. There will be some things, however, of a proprietary nature, that we will have only cursory information on, but I have taken a firm stand with Noël on this. We will not hesitate to show Jetsla the door if they do not respect what we stand for and what we do here."

"Any other questions?" Santa asked when Tocker failed to challenge him again. The room was deathly quiet. Even the placards had stopped bobbing. "Please rest assured that this is a good thing. Sometimes the hardest thing in life is change. You might have to get to the lunchroom a little earlier to avoid the longer lines Jetsla people will create. It will be more crowded around here for a while. And they won't all be elves. But you can do this. What is four months in an elf's long life, eh? If you look at the flip side of the coin, not to act now may very well end us. You know, that stitch-in-time thing?"

Out of clichés, Santa checked his audience and found hostile expressions softening. Information had empowered them. They *could* do this. He checked his bullet points and quickly went through the ones he had left, skimming where he thought necessary to keep in his audience's good graces. "Now you know everything that I know," he said when at last he finished. "Jetsla's move into the dome will be quick. Their point man, P. J. Foos, is already on-site. He'll be situated in my old office for the time being. If you have other questions, please feel free to forward them through Herbert Tuddy, and he'll forward them on to me. All right?"

Some in the audience applauded, but most responded with stony silence. Santa sighed in quiet relief. Perhaps he wouldn't be roughed up as he tried to leave—which he should do soon to avoid any second thoughts by unswayed rabble-rousers. "Mr. Tuddy?" he said, tilting his head toward the door. "If you would be so kind . . .?"

Herbert nodded and led him out, giving a thumbs-up to several coworkers as he passed. *Thank heavens for Herbert*, Santa thought. For all his shortcomings, it was a comfort to have him in Claus's corner at the moment. At the first opportunity after things settled down, Foos would have to collocate with the rest of Jetsla. Mr. Tuddy did deserve that office.

***

After escorting Santa out, Herbert circled back inside. He hung around offstage; it would be indecorous to seem to support a strike when Santa had just made clear that Herbert was his right-hand man. The place was still packed with union members busily stuffing their strike ballots into large drums placed on stage in the very spot Santa had stood not five minutes before. The line to vote was dwindling. The rank and file would soon make its decision heard.

When voting finished, the stewards tipped over the barrels, and the counting began. In the spirit of open and fair voting, they did it in front of everyone, but the suspense was awful just the same. Herbert decided to hit the break room. It was empty except for Hoho and his brother Heath, both chowing down on candy bars and non-diet sodas.

"Vote?" Herbert asked, selecting cheese crackers from a machine.

"Twice," Hoho said. "But only one each," he added, swishing a finger between his brother and himself.

Herbert nodded. "Did you hear about Santa's old office? P. J. Foos is getting it. No justice."

"Office doesn't make the man," Hoho said between bites.

"Well, Foos certainly hasn't done anything to merit such a perquisite."

"He's not such a bad fellow," Heath said. "He gave me my first job: sewing baby-doll bonnets."

Hoho dropped his empty soda can into the recycling bin and nodded. "Not such a bad fellow."

Three sharp whistles prevented Herbert from cutting loose in a tirade against Foos. The vote count had been completed. His unopened crackers joined Hoho's Coke can, and he took off at a sprint for the auditorium.

Stewards Nelson (holding the mike), Abercrombie, and Raleigh stood at the podium waiting for the crowd to settle. "No use beating things to death," Nelson said. "You've spoken, and the votes, for each union, are clear. By a two-to-one majority, there will be no strike."

*What?* Herbert replayed what he thought he had just heard. No strike? How on God's winter-white Pole had that happened? He looked out at those still in attendance. Why, they looked serene, almost jovial. They really believed the big guy could deliver on the malarkey he had spouted? Herbert turned and hurried from the Quonset. There was no hope for this group. They were all idiots. Let mechanization sweep them away. He would have to devise other plans to bounce Jetsla back whence it came.

# Chapter Ten

# Meatless Monday

In the next week, Christmasville saw more changes than it had experienced in the previous three centuries. Even though the residences and Jetsla offices were situated at the far end of the dome, the interlopers didn't seem to stay there. Overnight, the village population seemed to double, the noise-level tripled, and the sidewalks needed a passing lane. And when the Jetsla employees and their plant-based diet arrived to share the same lunchroom, even Hoho, Heath, and the bleeding-heart liberals in the 'ville had their loving world knocked off kilter.

Late on AJ (Anno Jetsla) day five, Herbert fell in behind Hoho as he lumbered into the cafeteria. The chubby elf's head was down and his feet shuffled more than usual.

"What's wrong with you?" Herbert asked with his customary lack of tact.

"Nothing," Hoho said, picking up a lunch tray. Then he crinkled his nose and sniffed twice. "What is that smell?"

Herbert's nose soon joined him. "I think something died."

Hoho leaned across his empty tray, looked closer at the neatly sliced brown rectangle in the serving pan, and scrunched his nose up. "Meatloaf Monday?" he asked.

"Meatless Monday," the lunch lady replied. "Tofu." She scooped up the jiggling brownish gel and slid it onto a white plate. "Mashed potatoes?" she said, gliding to the next food warmer, serving spoon at the ready.

Hoho shot a wide-eyed, pleading look at Herbert. "Meatless potatoes?" he asked her.

"Potato potatoes. Yes or no?" she said, waving the spoon. "I've got a thousand hungry elves and Jetsla employees behind you."

"No thank you," Hoho whispered politely. He pressed his empty food tray to his chest and shambled toward the lunch tables.

"Yes to the potatoes," Herbert told her, and he continued down the line ordering double everything that didn't smack of meatless Monday. At the buffet line's end, he loaded up on green molded gelatin salad, grapes, and two granola bars—unappealing, to be sure, but better than Hoho's self-imposed starvation.

He found Hoho in the back of the cafeteria—shoulders and mouth drooping as he stared out the window at the falling snow. Herbert put the laden tray down before him and said, "So we load up on sirloin Sunday from now on. Come on, Hoho. This too shall pass." He looked at the buffet line, which now stretched back out the entrance to the cafeteria. and not one elf. Someone had already broadcast today's menu selections.

Hoho turned doleful eyes on him as a single glistening tear rolled down one cheek.

"It's just food," Herbert said. Telling that to an elf pushing three hundred pounds might be a bit insensitive, but there was so much more to the big guy than just his adoration of food.

When the tear rounded Hoho's jawline, he let out a little sigh and brushed it away. "Where's the love?"

"You've never been out in the big world, Hoho. Profit has replaced love. But try to buck up. They won't be here forever. Before you know it, we'll be back to meatloaf and bacon, all served lovingly by Lucy Lunch over there." Herbert slipped the molded salad onto the next table and covered it with a napkin. "Even she hates slinging this stuff."

Hoho gave him a dark look. "Not *them, me*. What's happened to my goodwill and charity? I hate this place, and I don't like *them*. This Jetsla business is making me a bad person."

Before Herbert could respond, Hoho got up, shoved his chair under the table, and took off.

Herbert let him go and addressed his potato potatoes. He could think of no way they could screw with tamale Tuesday. The big guy wouldn't stay hungry forever.

Herbert would be wrong about tamale Tuesday as well as turkey Thursday and sauerkraut Saturday. By week's end, even he was black-beaned, avocadoed, and cauliflowered out. Hoho was still beating himself up, but his eyes occasionally flashed brighter, and there were fleeting glimpses of a smile. More troubling was his brother, Heath, who was beginning to look gaunt. If he persisted in avoiding the new food offerings, they would soon move him out of his mailroom job, where he had been assigned due to weight-related mobility issues. It would be the delivery beat for him once more.

Herbert, on the other hand, prided himself on being a scrapper. He would stomach what he could, supplement it with his private junk food stash when he could, and talk up Violet Claus's cooking skills in the hope of a private tasting session. And in the meantime, he would keep trolling for Jetsla's weak spot. Everybody had one, and if he sleuthed long and hard enough, he would find it.

## Chapter Eleven
# Itchy Fingers

On the hotness scale, Maybelline Claus was a scorching ten—that is, if one went in for buxom, curvaceous elves with wavy silvery-tipped hair, who served homemade pie for dinner every night and could knit one hell of a green-and-white-striped sweater. From his Peeping Tom position at the open window, Herbert tried to check out her ankles, but alas, her fur-trimmed skirt went the whole way to the floor. No matter, the widow of the recently deceased Santa Claus XII had made it clear that she wanted no suitors and would spend the rest of her years providing quiet, loving support to the Christmasville community. Lonely unattached elves would have to look elsewhere for companionship or one-nighters. Herbert sighed in frustration. What a waste!

Herbert's lust shifted to Maybelline's lunch guest, Violet Flora Claus, an equally fetching elf lady and wife of the new St. Nicholas, Santa Claus XIII. Look at the ankles on that one! He glanced away for a moment to compose himself.

Choosing a new Christmas leader was a rare event, and the installation of his family in the Main House even more so. If old tales be true, the earliest St. Nicholas never married. And the lot of them certainly never had children, in or out of wedlock. Perhaps it was to prevent a false sense of entitlement to a position that traditionally was earned through good work, unimpeachable character, and a smidge of Christmas magic.

"I know I'm late in asking, but do you need help?" Violet asked, bringing Herbert's attention back to the women in the kitchen.

"No," Maybelline said. "It's taken a while, but I can finally say that I'm seeing my way through my grief. I'm settled in the guesthouse, and everything that belongs to me is there. Anything that you have left here belongs here." She put her arm around Violet and gave her a gentle squeeze. "I know it seems overwhelming, Violet, but you'll figure it out. I would be remiss, however, if I didn't warn you about a thing or two."

Maybelline walked over to a small wooden box sitting on the kitchen counter and leafed through the contents. "Yes, this one," she said, pulling out a pink three-by-five-inch index card. "This is the recipe for *Lacrima ambrotos*, which is made from the plant known as Tears of the Angel. Guard this with your life," she said, starting to hand it to Violet. Violet reached out, and she jerked it back. "No one else has it, and it's been handed down through the ages. A gift from the angels, they say. And this," she said, holding aloft a spice bottle containing blue powder, "this is all the ambrotos we will have until the Claus is fully able to replenish the supply. He's the only one who has the authority to make it."

"Rest easy," Violet said, easing the card from her hand. "I'll find a special place for it the moment you are gone."

Maybelline nodded, and her eyes began to fill with tears. She took a slow look around the room. "I guess that's that. Walk me out?"

"Certainly," Violet said. She slid the recipe card under the wooden recipe box and gave Maybelline a big hug, and the two women disappeared through a door into another section of the house.

Herbert waited until their footsteps faded. Then, nimble as a cat, he slid through the window, snatched the recipe from the counter, and slid back out again before one could say *Hey, did you see that?*

Seconds later, he was on his way back to subbing for a sick elf at the toy car shop—just an innocent chap with his hand held protectively over his breast pocket as he hurried down Candy Cane Lane with his fellow Christmas elves.

Three short blasts of the shift change horn atop a pole outside Quonset Hut Boston Charlie sent elves scampering for the shop exit. Herbert waited until they cleared from the workroom, and then took a first peek at his stolen index card. When he'd read the front, he flipped it over to read the back. Every ingredient except one was commonly available, and the one that wasn't—*Lacrima ambrotos*—could surely be found in Violet's cupboard. *Lacrima ambrotos.* The name bounced around in his head for a moment. And *Tears of the Angel*—that one was also trying to ring a bell.

Oh. Dear. Goodness. Herbert's knees wobbled. He sat down on a workbench. This was the recipe for the rarely talked-about secret elixir that created Christmas magic—a recipe so special and so integral to the success of Christmasville that Santa Claus alone was entrusted with making it! Herbert blew out a quick breath, slid the card into his pocket, and checked to make sure no one had seen him do it.

Why on earth had he filched this? Because the thought of something new to eat overpowered his sense of honesty? Or was he acting out merely because the new Claus had given his duly earned office to an interloper? Herbert really couldn't say. Elves were naturally covetous, and he was no different. Regardless, he had something that no one else had, and he wasn't giving it back until he figured out how it might improve his own life. Could it help him get his office back? Or better yet, help him achieve the top Christmasville job that he so desperately coveted? Possibly. So what would be the harm in copying down the secret recipe, returning the original card (while pinching a teaspoon of the ambrotos), and then whipping up a very small batch? To Herbert's thinking, none. He might even regale his buddy Ticker and some others with a little nip. There was an out-of-the-way storage room in Quonset Hut Dickens that would make a great speakeasy. He found a pad of paper on the shift supervisor's desk and began scribbling out the recipe.

Funny how returning what one stole always seemed more difficult than the initial theft. As Herbert approached the Claus house, he couldn't shake the feeling that he was being watched. He altered his route by throwing in a few turns and even a couple of about-faces, but no one seemed remotely interested in whatever he was up to. He was losing his touch, his nerves of steel, the je ne sais quoi that made him Herbert, elf of mystery. Did no one care about him anymore? Just wait until he was offering up *Lacrima ambrotos* on the sly—for a small price, of course. Elves would be dying to cozy up to him. Then they'd see who counted.

The kitchen window was open. He neither heard nor saw anyone in the house, and after a quick look around, he hoisted himself inside and put the recipe back where he found it. Mrs. Claus's spice rack sat where it had before, and he rummaged through the bottles looking for *Tears of the Angel* or some such label.

"Santa?"

Dear me! It was the missus, calling from another room. Herbert shoved the bottle he held back into the rack, jumped the counter in a single quiet leap, and dived out the window. He hit the ground with a grunt and took off like a flushed rabbit, scrambling on all fours until he cleared the corner of the little bungalow. And there he stayed until he heard Mrs. Claus close the window and he could catch his breath.

He looked around again, but apparently no one had bothered to notice him. Good but bad. Without the Tears of the Angel, he was still nowhere. *Settle, Herbert,* he thought, creeping toward the rear of the house to sort himself out. No dilemma was so complicated that old Herbert "Spanky" Tuddy couldn't noodle through it.

He sat down just out of sight of the pathway to the house and, with a nice garden view, put his noggin to work. No other establishment in town would have the tears—certainly none that he could get his hands on. Raybert, the pharmacist, might have it, but he kept everything padlocked and the key on a cord around his neck at all times.

And then he had it! It was staring him right in the face! Across the garden, he spied a patch of the palest blue flowers. The little blossoms were almost waving at him as they danced and bounced on their long, fine stems in the gentle breeze. Mrs. Claus grew her own Tears of the Angel. How splendid!

He didn't check to see who might be watching—someone approaching from the front of the house, a gardener, or Mrs. Claus herself peeking out a rear window. He beat a path through the neatly planted rows and knelt down next to the loveliest patch of flowers he had ever seen. Which was a mistake. How was he to know that the little blue lovelies grew on marshy ground? His tights soaked up the water like a sponge, and he shivered in the sudden chill.

Still he persisted. His shaking hand hovered over the dozen blossoms. How many should he pluck? Too many, and he would certainly be discovered. He closed his eyes and pictured the recipe. *A pinch.* Yes, he could see it clearly. He plucked five blossoms from separate plants and slid them into his shirt pocket. And then impulsively scooped up a whole plant from the squishy soil. Then he bolted for Quonset Hut Alpha.

He locked the bunker door and headed straight for his closet, where he one-handed out clothes, a basketball, and half a dozen other things. Finally, he found the dead potted poinsettia that he had shoved there months ago. He banged out the shriveled root ball into his trash can and potted the stolen flower. Despite its rough handling, the Tears of the Angel seemed happy enough. But could he keep it that way? He tucked the pot away on the top shelf of his bookcase and vowed to water the little blue plant every day.

He turned his attention to the loose blue petals he had stolen. He dumped them into an empty coffee mug, nuked for three minutes in his microwave, and then rubbed the brittle remains into powder with his fingers. When he finished, he guessed the little mound of flower dust to be about three or four pinches. He transferred his precious booty to a clean plastic bag and tossed it up alongside the plant.

Next, feeling quite proud and even energized by his naughtiness, he set off for Sudley Watermiester's Emporium to get the remaining ingredients.

## Chapter Twelve
# Too Hot to Handle

Sudley Watermiester's Emporium stood in the square at the corner of Main and Candy Cane Streets in the West Village, Christmasville's residential section. Because most of the work was done in shifts, the village beat to its own distinctive circadian rhythm. At times, the streets were virtually deserted, their denizens either asleep or busy plying their trade in one of the various workshops. But whenever a shift change rolled around, the residents' comings and goings crowded the sidewalks. Throw in sightseeing Jetsla employees, and what a jam ensued! They moved at a snail's pace in groups much too large and lingered interminably outside every storefront display.

Luckily for Herbert, the shift wouldn't change for three more hours, and he wandered into and out of the Emporium without hindrance. And he would have made it back to Quonset Hut Alpha without incident if he hadn't chanced upon Bumble Frecklesworth, junior comms specialist from Quonset Boston Charlie, thumbtacking a public notice onto the large bulletin board in the middle of the square. Herbert was about to pass it by without further notice—at the moment, social functions weren't big on his agenda—when a nagging thought made him change course and retrace his steps to read over Bumble's shoulder:

*Missing*
*Plant from Mrs. Claus's Garden*
*Please return to house stoop.*
*No questions asked.*

A shiver ran down Herbert's spine. How so fast? Then the shiver reversed course and ran *up* his back. Did the little blue suckers have some sort of homing device attached? Chipped to beep when they were removed from the bog? Dear me, they might already be searching his basement hideaway.

Suddenly, the all-but-empty streets were no longer so empty. Had he really missed the army of service jeeps zooming about? A line of steely-eyed toy soldiers, straight and tall in their red and blue uniforms, marched stiffly toward him. A mere test run by Robotics, or had the think tank released something more menacing to hunt down the Tears of the Angel? Herbert put his head down and pushed past them at a steady pace, sighing with relief as the boots kept right on, tapping out their cadence. The sound receded down the street. False alarm. All he needed now was a pack of toy Waggy Tales bloodhounds to come sniffing his way. And oh, dear Lord, was that baying he heard? He set off at top speed toward Quonset Hut Alpha. They might eventually find him, but by then he would have divested himself of any incriminating evidence

He crept down the basement steps, ready to flee at the barest whisper of activity below. One step, two steps, three steps. He paused. Nothing? Six more, quiet as a mouse. Silence except for his pounding ticker. He scampered down the remaining steps, ducked around the corner, and peeked around the corner. His door was closed, and he still heard nothing.

He sighed quietly, letting out some nervous energy. This sneaking was wrong, so wrong, and it made him look guilty. He pulled himself up and stood tall for an elf, walked up to the door, unlocked it, and swung it open. A cursory glance confirmed that his booty was still on the top shelf and that apparently, no one had paid him a visit. Okay, so maybe he overreacted. He took a deep calming breath. If he just handled things methodically, he was aces.

He dumped his ingredients from the Emporium onto his desk, pulled down the pulverized Tears of the Angel, and set to work. After several minutes of mashing, stirring, and heating, he stepped back and whispered, "Done." Admiring its blueness, he swirled the liquid around in the glass dome that he had borrowed from the overhead light fixture. He stifled the urge to take a sip or even lick the mixing spoon. Again, patience was his friend. He was not a baker, a cook, or even a microwaver of Marie Callender frozen chicken pot pies. No, far better to sample this outside and away from others. At the moment, he couldn't risk being given away by any nasty side effects from an ill-prepared concoction.

Something scraped his door. "A moment?" he called out, mind racing to find a hiding place for the elixir. Before he could take a step, a red blur flashed past his eyes, buzzed like a hummingbird past his ear and behind him, then streaked back again to hover inches from his nose.

"Dabbling?" Solomon asked, hovering.

The fairy was close enough, Herbert could have inhaled him. If he were being honest with himself, he did consider it. He took a step back. "No."

"Imbibing, then?" Solomon fluttered closer to the *Lacrima ambrotos*. His red tunic began to shimmer. "Might I?"

Herbert jerked it away. "Certainly not!"

Solomon chuckled. "So you *are* partaking. Excellent! Just a dribble won't rob you," he said, holding up an index finger.

Herbert shook his head.

Solomon backed up with a hostile squeak, and Herbert, fearing that the pint-size fury would come at his face full throttle, threw up his hand.

The tiny finger began to wave. "*Tsk, tsk.* Spanky Tuddy has been a bad boy. I know what you've been doing."

"No, you don't. Go away. Peter Pan is looking for you."

"No. *You're* Peter Pan. If you don't let me have a quick slurp, I'll tell everyone."

Herbert looked at Solomon's set jaw. How could he possibly know? But what if he did? What if he was the one who had watched Herbert return the recipe? Oh, for crepes' sake, the little fart had him! "Just a quick slurp," he finally said, "but not now. And I'm not copping to anything. I just know how you fairies operate when you decide to be mean." He closed his eyes and began to recite under his breath: "Solomon Grundy, born on a Monday; married on Wednesday.'" He looked at Solomon again. "Come back Tuesday night and I'll have a nice little party favor for you. But come alone because I'm not letting your little friends sip away what I have here."

"Right on, brother from another mother," Solomon said, raising a fist. "Tuesday it is." And he shot away and disappeared under the door.

Solomon had the heart of a showman, and a rep for telling outlandish stories that not even he believed. Herbert's deal was an astute one. It would keep Solomon off his case long enough for Herbert to get himself out of trouble. If Solomon wanted to flap his gums later, Herbert would simply deny, deny, deny.

He placed a thick work folder over the top of the glass container and squirreled it away at the bottom of his bulging dirty-clothes hamper, which hadn't been emptied in several weeks. The smell inside would discourage even the most ardent snooper. Besides, they were only looking for a plant.

He pulled the plant back out, again admiring how happy it seemed to be after getting uprooted from its cozy bog. Pilfering it had been impulsive and foolish. To get out of the mess he had created, he needed to leave the plant on the Clauses' porch, at once. He wrapped it in the latest edition of the *Christmasville Herald* and set off for the bungalow.

That decision lasted about twenty steps. How did he know they wouldn't be watching for its return? He made an abrupt U-turn—not his first today or, he suspected, his last—and slid the plant under his bookcase. Then he plunked down on the floor and put his head in his hands. What did people do with contraband they no longer wanted?

Perhaps he could put it in a box and leave it for Hoho as an anonymous early birthday present. Not a lot of gray matter between those big ears. Herbert's elation quickly evaporated as he pictured the mild-mannered, simple soul sitting in a holding cell crying his eyes out.

If he had more money and power, he might be able to pay someone to make the problem go away. Rich people and politicians could do that. Noël Rusk certainly didn't have to deal with problems like this, not personally. He had people like Stole-my-office-from-me Foos to clean up his messes.

Herbert's head shot up. And why couldn't Foos clean up this one, too? How much would a rich, bright fellow like Rusk pay to buy a shot of lovely blue liquid that bestowed the power of Christmas magic? A pretty penny, Herbert would wager. He pictured Claus sitting in his office suite, and Foos in the office next door—both offices rightfully Herbert's. No, no, no! They could barter. Why not insist on some prime real estate in exchange for the *Lacrima ambrotos* recipe and the Tears of the Angel—real estate as far away from the North Pole as one could get? Then there would be no theft to answer for, or daily reminders of what *he* had been robbed of—one to cancel the other.

Herbert locked his door and went to find P. J. Foos. The turncoat elf would jump at the chance to please his boss. Indeed, it was one of the easiest ways to get ahead. This could be everyone's lucky day.

## Chapter Thirteen
# Bartering

Herbert paused at the door to his misappropriated rightful office. Foos had staked his claim in several ways: a 16" x 20" framed color photo of Noël Rusk and the president shaking hands in the Oval Office (Foos strategically posed in the center of the back row), a large stuffed toy giraffe gazing out the window, a bookcase filled with beautiful leather-bound books that looked as if they had never been cracked open, and a brass nameplate the size of a license plate. What a poser.

"Mr. Foos?" Herbert asked, sticking his head inside the usurper's door. "A moment of your time?"

Foos looked up from his work papers and grinned. "Mr. Tuddy. What can I do for you?"

Herbert felt like a charity case begging for spare change at Christmas. One day, payback for this fellow would be dear. "It's of the upmost importance that I speak to Mr. Rusk. I have a proposition for him."

Foos's grin spread wider. "Well, I can certainly approach Mr. Rusk, but I'd have to know what it's about before I do. Nothing personal, you understand. I triage his contacts."

Herbert seriously doubted Foos was that important. It had been a while since Rusk came on-site, so who ran interference for him elsewhere? Much more likely was someone at his elbow night and day with an electronic tablet. Herbert studied Foos and his everlasting grin. This donkey's pitoot wasn't coming down off his pedestal. It was spill or hit the road, Herbert.

"It just so happens," Foos continued, "that he is flying in tomorrow. But he'll be quite busy, so I'll have to dance a bit to squeeze you in."

"All right, you get me face time, but not here," Herbert said, his eyes darting toward Claus's office. "Somewhere quieter, and I'll see that you get an unlimited lunch pass—"

"A lunch pass?" Foos deadpanned.

Even though Foos had put his touch on things, the office lacked in niceties. "New curtains," Herbert said, indicating the double window that overlooked the reindeer pasture. "A nice mahogany executive-style desk that I've hidden away in storage would look good in here too, and for the cherry on top, the motor pool at your beck and call."

Foos chewed on his lower lip as he studied the decor. "That would certainly be an improvement. This is much smaller than I'm used to. But the exciting work makes up for it. Who knows?" he said, giving Herbert a curious look. "I might even enjoy it enough to ask Noël to make the temporary assignment a permanent one

"Then I wouldn't get too settled, because this office certainly isn't permanent. My things are already boxed up, and as soon as you've got Jetsla's campus set up, we'll have to find you another space. Probably in Quonset Hut Dickens. It's three buildings over—a short hike from here—but as you might expect, office space is tight near the Claus. I'm his right-hand man, so he likes having me within shouting distance."

"And where are you now? Maybe I can slide in there."

"Downstairs."

"As I recall, wasn't that called 'the basement'? That would never do.

My arthritis starts kicking in when I'm in dark, dank places."

"It's no such . . ." Herbert stopped himself. He wouldn't give Foos the satisfaction of baiting him. "I'll let you know what I have available when the time comes. To get back to my proposition, this is for your and Rusk's ears only. If I hear otherwise, I'll take this elsewhere and Rusk will lose out big-time."

Herbert began with as little information and as much intrigue as possible, throwing a bit of chum out and then twitching the line a little. When he saw the bottom half of Foos's grin drop open, he knew he had a chance to walk away with impunity from his self-created fiasco.

\*\*\*

Foos kept his end of the bargain and arranged a meeting at Rusk's suite in the Jetsla office complex. If Santa or anyone else asked about his visit, Herbert would simply lie that he was inquiring after the entrepreneur's comfort and future needs. No one would question the head administrative assistant for Christmas activities about something so completely aligned with his job description.

At half past noon the next day, Herbert and Foos entered Noël Rusk's domain. Herbert expected opulence: Greek statuary and plush cushions in bold, warm tones of red and yellow, but his eyes were met instead by a minimalist decorator's palette of chrome and boring beige. Even in the privacy of his own office, it seemed the billionaire played it close to the vest.

Rusk directed his visitors to a sitting area and several barrel chairs by a picture window. Herbert and Foos took seats, while Rusk remained standing with his hands resting easily on the back of an empty chair. The sleet—an increasingly common weather event—had ceased, and the sun was playing peekaboo through fast-moving clouds. Rusk offered no pleasantries, so Herbert got right to it.

"Mr. Rusk, I, uh, have something you might be interested in procuring—a once-in-a-lifetime purchase." Herbert took a deep breath and tried to settle his fluttering thoughts.

Rusk's eyebrows rose. His gaze shifted to Foos. "I thought Claus and I would be clarifying contract language about our lab. You pulled me into a meeting for *this*? Run it through Grafton in procurement. And please don't call me on my private line anymore. Go through Sherri." He turned to go.

"Wait!" Foos said, standing up. "That was just code, sir . . . To make sure the true purpose of the meeting didn't leak out. Mr. Tuddy has something extraordinarily valuable to share with you."

Rusk looked at his watch and then at Herbert. "What do you have? And please make it quick."

"This," Herbert said, handing him Violet Claus's recipe card and a small vial of blue liquid.

"A cooking recipe?" Rusk tried to give them back.

Herbert kept his hands folded in his lap, laced together in a death grip. "You have in your hands the recipe for the most precious elixir in the world. On that card are the ingredients and steps for creating Christmas magic."

"Say what, now?" Rusk asked, frowning.

"The magic," Herbert said, spreading his arms wide, "that holds all of this together—the secret to all that is Christmasville. I won't give you the long, convoluted story of how it came into my possession."

Rusk eyed him closely. "You do me an injustice assuming that I would deal in stolen goods."

"Oh, no, sir! I have the deepest respect for you. I'm offering you this opportunity because I admire what you have accomplished in your life.

To imagine that your ingenuity and ambition might be enhanced here at the top of the world, with no one to disturb you—the things you could achieve for the good of all!"

Rusk's face remained fixed in a scowl, so Herbert nodded vigorously to assert his own sincerity.

Rusk studied the lined white index card. "*Lacrima ambrotos.* So, every Christmasville elf has access to this?"

"Just the Claus and I," Herbert said.

Rusk nodded, now fully absorbed in the card. "Interesting. And these ingredients—how does one obtain them? All local?"

"Yes. All local."

"Here's the thing, Mr. . . . Tuddy, is it? You say this is an *elven* elixir. How do I know it won't drop me, a mortal, dead where I stand?"

*Noël Rusk, human? Who knew!* "Well . . ."

Herbert shook his head.

Rusk held the vial up to the window, tipping the container just enough to roll the blue fluid gently back and forth. If Rusk had ever coveted anything in life more than he did this, Herbert could not imagine what it could have been. From everything Herbert had read about the billionaire, he liked to push the envelope. A more conservative entrepreneur never would have risked so much money and effort to set up business operations in the inhospitable north. Would he really walk away from the power that the elixir offered? Given Rusk's earlier guilting of the venerable Claus for hesitating to embrace the Jetsla vision, Herbert doubted it. Rusk would never back away from something that inched him closer to what he wanted. Herbert kept his mouth clamped shut and waited.

"I'll take a chance," a quiet voice piped up. It was P. J. Foos. He stood transfixed, gazing upon the *Lacrima ambrotos* as if it were the

Holy Grail. "What I mean is, I'll take the risk for you, Mr. Rusk. If nothing happens to me, you're good to go."

"Feeling a little ambitious, are we, Foos?" Rusk said, continuing to rock the vial. He side-eyed Herbert. "How much?"

"It's not so much about money, Mr. Rusk. I want my freedom, out of this monotonous, freezing place. The Mediterranean? Caribbean? Seychelles? Condo in West Palm Beach? Anywhere that affords me a nice, warm abode—along with the means to keep me safe and happy, of course. Is that too much to ask?"

"Not if this works as advertised. Who could argue with having a wonderfully inviting, multiclimated biodome thriving at the harsh North Pole? With Christmas magic twelve months a year, Jetsla would be limited only by the extent of its imagination." He rocked the vial one more time. "Is there enough in here for two doses?"

"Oh, certainly. Or twenty. Even if you didn't want to make any more batches, you could sell the rest and make back much more money than you will ever spend on me. Of course, I would appreciate you being discreet. Santa and I don't need people beating down our door asking for more. This is a one-time deal." He grasped for the vial, but Rusk moved it out of his reach.

"Tears of the Angel," Rusk said, reading the recipe. "I would assume this grows only within the larger, elven biodome?"

"You would assume correctly," Herbert said.

Rusk shook his head. "Doesn't work for me. What good is the recipe if I don't have the source at my disposal?"

Herbert could feel his dream of a French Riviera life becoming a reality. "I have in my possession one potted plant that will be part of the deal. I, uh . . . I think it seeds, or maybe you can propagate more plants some other way. I—I'm not a horticulturist, but where there's a will, there's a way, as my great uncle, Nigel Tuttle, used to say. Surely for someone of your—"

"Deal," Rusk said.

Herbert sighed in relief. "I suppose we could whip up a simple contract right here."

Rusk shook his head. "I don't think that's necessary, do you? We're talking about something much bigger than we are. If we can't respect that and act accordingly, what's the point? Besides, I suspect you've pilfered this from somewhere, and I don't want any paperwork to surface at some inopportune time in the future and cause me problems. No, if we are to strike a deal, we have to trust each other. You have my solemn word that in exchange for the Tears of the Angel, I will find you a splendid location to live in, and an adequate allowance to support a lifestyle there. If that isn't good enough for you, then we're done here."

Herbert reviewed his options. He could accept Rusk at his word and hope he got what he truly desired, or he could call the transaction off and walk away. Unfortunately, Herbert doubted that he would ever find anyone as powerful as Rusk to strike a deal with, and if the entrepreneur decided to be vindictive, he could report Herbert right now for theft and gleefully watch him go down for the crime. And finally, possession was nine-tenths of the law. Big mistake letting Rusk gain physical control of the vial. Rusk had Herbert over a barrel, and they both knew it. "Deal."

"Not so fast," Rusk said. "Only if it's safe." He crooked a finger at Foos, and when he approached, Rusk offered him the vial. "Game, Mr. Foos?"

Foos hesitated, then took the liquid. "You're fairly sure?" he said to Herbert as he unstopped the vial. "As a half-elf . . ."

Herbert shrugged. "I only know for sure that it works on elf-elves." When Foos continued to hesitate, he added, "Your mother being elvish—that could muddy the waters for Mr. Rusk, but I doubt it. I can't imagine that angels would ever make something that might harm anyone."

Foos brought the heavenly elixir to his lips and took a sip. "Ew," he said, grimacing. He handed the potion back to Rusk, gagging. "That's the vilest . . ."

Rusk stoppered the miniature bottle and tucked it into his jacket. "If he does okay," he said, nodding at Foos, who was wiping his tongue off with a white handkerchief, "and you bring me the plant, we have a deal."

"Today is Tuesday, Herbert said. "Three days should do it. We can finalize things on Friday. I'm certain he'll be fine."

And then he got out of there as fast as his legs would carry him.

*** 

Theft was a tricky business that seemed to go on a tad too long. Would Foos survive the bootlegged *Lacrima ambrotos*? Herbert had no idea, but he had formally consented. And if Foos didn't survive it? Eh, he got what was coming to him.

For the next several days, Herbert kept his head down and lost himself in the big midyear toy production push. He put off Solomon's bachelor party until Saturday by promising that he could bring a few of his friends. When Friday finally rolled around and Foos appeared with a first-class ticket from New York to St. Thomas, and a deed to a beachfront condo, Herbert heaved a great sigh of relief. Then he handed Foos a small potted plant and sent him on his merry way—a win for everyone.

But this didn't put the blue-flowered caper to bed. Oh, no. Herbert still had unfinished business: the second vial, which he had reserved for his personal use. It was time to strut a little of the stuff around, but not enough to empower a rival—just a tease to show who the *real* big man on campus was. He got on his private email server and shot a message to his five closest buddies: Ticker, Tocker, Beltzer, Huban, and Fatty Winkler: *Confidential. Party at Quonset Boston Charlie at ten p.m. on Saturday. Be prepared to stay late.*

Herbert leaned back in his chair as exhilaration swept over him. *Virgin Islands, here I come!*

\*\*\*

They'll tell me I had a good time, Herbert assured himself as he rolled out of bed Sunday morning and his feet hit the cold, hard floor. He couldn't remember much past pouring the first round with his pals in the Quonset hut. His head was on permanent spin cycle, and his tongue was growing dust bunnies.

He threw on some clothes, skipped breakfast, and vowed to do as little as possible for the rest of the morning. Late afternoon would be soon enough to give the division chiefs a heads-up about the Jetsla venture. He could also hold off on giving notice of his departure. He realized he had faults, but disloyalty to the workers on the line wasn't one of them. He would rile his coworkers up, get them on track to improve their working conditions, and then let the chips fall where they may. By virtue of their positions, the Claus and P. J. Foos would be responsible for any fallout.

# Chapter Fourteen

# Suing

Santa stood with Herbert and Wallace on a snow berm outside the biodome, looking out across the Arctic Ocean, its dark surface dotted with ice floes as far as he could see. He cursed the day he was born. The closest ice was blanketed in a layer of unnatural, eerie blue.

"How much spillage?" the Claus asked Herbert.

"Anybody's guess, sir. Jetsla won't give me a figure. Hundreds of gallons? Thousands?" Herbert shuddered in the cold and pulled his hood tighter. The unusual dip back to winter temperatures was bone-chilling.

Santa shook his head. "They've got to go," he said to Wallace. "Tell them that effective immediately, we're terminating the contract during the trial period. And that we will hold them to begin immediate cleanup efforts to keep this pollution from drifting and causing further damage."

"Uh . . ."

Santa turned to face his accountant. "What?"

Wallace offered a feeble, apologetic smile. "Um, I'm afraid there is no cancellation provision during the trial period. The language was struck as a concession to them when they accepted a four-month period rather than six."

"Damn it all!" Santa thundered. "Who agreed to that?"

"Um, you, sir," Wallace squeaked. "But in your defense, it was late and we were running out of time." He looked back across the water. "Who would have thought . . ."

"Get me an appointment with Rusk," Santa growled as he stomped off toward the yellow Snow-Cat. "And, Herbert?"

"Yes, sir?" Herbert said, flipping open a notepad that would soon fill with the orders Santa was barking.

"A complete inventory from the village groundskeeper on what else has been fouled. And alert the herdsmen. No matter how pristine it seems, the reindeer are to be moved away from the creek and given only water from the treatment plant until further notice."

"On it," Herbert said, piling into the snowcat behind Wallace and securing the door. The machine jerked forward before he could even take a seat.

***

Noël Rusk declined an invitation to sit down and waved aside a proffered cup of coffee. P. J. Foos stood a few feet behind him, eyes downcast. "Accidents happen, Nicholas. No one plans these things. We will do our utmost to clean it up."

"I should have known better," said the Claus, setting Rusk's coffee beside his own untouched cup. He walked to the window and tried to calm himself by watching the reindeer, but there weren't any—on his orders, they had been moved to safer pasture.

"Well . . ." Rusk began.

"*Well* is right. Contract provisions or no, I want your operations out of here. Cease and desist immediately!"

"Nicholas, it's not as bad as that. It'll be pristine again in no time.

How could we possibly clean it up if you're kicking us out?"

"Besides," Foos interjected, "we have an ironclad contract that guarantees us four months of uninterrupted operations. Any attempts to interfere with that would be met with Jetsla suing you into oblivion."

"Not helpful," Rusk said. He hiked his thumb toward the door.

Foos hung his head. "Sorry. I'll just be out here in the hallway."

"Perhaps we should sit," Rusk said to Santa, and he sat down in one of the empty chairs by the fireplace.

Santa shook his head and remained standing.

Rusk studied him a moment, the billionaire's eyebrows knitted. Then he continued in a quiet thoughtful voice, his face full of concern. "Technically, Mr. Foos is correct. While his suggested course of action may sound harsh, I can assure you, it would be nothing personal. Business is business. But antagonistic relations never really produce the sweetest fruit, do they? I have great admiration and respect for you, Nicholas, and I don't want us to be at each other's throats. Maybe if I told you about what I want to accomplish here at the Pole, what your generosity in allowing us to be here can facilitate, it would give you a bit of perspective."

Rusk was a tall man. He stretched out his long legs and crossed them at the ankles. It made Claus uneasy. He didn't need the man to wax poetic. He just needed him and his company *out*.

"Wouldn't it be wonderful," Rusk said, "if we could fly conventionally powered aircraft without contributing to carbon emissions? All those airplanes producing net-zero carbon emissions as they crisscross the globe? Just imagine how that would help stave off climate change." He broke into a smile. "It's possible, Nicholas. Scientists at the University of Oxford have successfully converted $CO_2$ into jet fuel, militaries have taken notice, and Jetsla stands at the precipice of understanding how to produce large quantities at a competitive price. That's one of the challenges we're taking up under your biodome. Do you really want to sabotage one of the most promising methods the scientific community has for reducing the level of carbon dioxide in the atmosphere? We can literally save the world with this. We just need freedom from bureaucratic red tape and some additional time."

Claus picked up the fireplace poker and began arranging logs. "I can't deny how impressive that sounds, but as steward of this place, I can't allow you to sabotage its well-being for the greater good. Sacrificing the Pole can't be the only way. We have a contract, and I will honor it. And I will also hold you to cleaning up the kerosene spill. If you can't make it right again, you can pack up and move out at the end of the trial period."

"Absolutely. I have my best people on it as we speak. So if we are seeing eye to eye on this now, I need to leave. I want to personally oversee those efforts. Consider Mr. Foos at your beck and call. He has my secretary's personal number."

"Yes, yes," Claus said. "Do what you can."

The Claus waited until he was sure Rusk was out of the building before he buzzed Herbert and Wallace to join him. "Herbert, please withdraw any of our people from the Jetsla facility."

"With pleasure," Herbert said, beaming. "Jetsla leaving?"

"No, the arrogant fool seems cocksure—insists on sticking it out. Wallace, what does the contract say about Christmasville providing logistical support to Jetsla? Is it simple and clear?"

"Crystal, sir. We provide the acreage at the far end of the dome for Jetsla's use. Nothing else."

"Excellent," Claus said. "Send Halary's crew out there and tell them we're walling off that section of the biodome. We'll see how efficiently

Jetsla can run a bubble at the North Pole without a little Christmas magic to go along with it. Start immediately."

"Yes!" Herbert yelled, jumping up and down on his tiptoes. "That'll show them."

"Settle, Herbert! Let's get it done before we start celebrating."

"Yes, sir, Mr. Claus," Herbert said. He danced out of the room with bells jingling.

## Chapter Fifteen
# Double Dare Ya

Mere hours after Santa and Noël Rusk spoke, a bit of Christmas magic and a few quietly uttered words by Santa had created a separating wall at the end of the airfield, effectively isolating Jetsla in its own minidome. "Let's see him handle that," Santa muttered, and it felt good.

Santa didn't expect Rusk to barge into his office with guns blazing and spittle flying when he learned of Jetsla's new reality. Thoughtful, collected individuals didn't conduct themselves that way. But that didn't mean that the billionaire would take it lying down. Rusk would respond with initial incredulity, followed by guilting Claus about letting down mankind in its hour of greatest need, followed by legal threats. Things would become unpleasant in short order. Well, let 'em rip. The Claus answered to no one. And he was darn-tootin' sure that no court in any land would want to handle the case—or would even acknowledge having jurisdiction, for that matter. Who would want to kill Christmas?

Even so, Claus spent the next two hours hiding in his office, clock-watching and wishing circumstances hadn't devolved to this. When at last Rusk knocked on Claus's door, it was not aggressive, and the man's voice was soft and friendly.

"A moment of your time, Nicholas?" Rusk asked, strolling on in without an invitation.

"By all means," Claus said, standing up. He offered no refreshments. The meeting would be quick and formal.

"At the moment, our communications seem to be muddled, so I thought it best to deal directly. Logistical support for—"

"No muddle," Santa countered, gripping his desk chair. "Christmasville will be following the letter of the law as far as the contract is concerned. You have your space under the dome, but as for any other logistical support, I'm afraid you're on your own." He drummed on the desk with his fingers for emphasis.

Had no one ever told the billionaire baby *no* before? Rusk stood openmouthed and blinking for a moment before he collected himself. "I promised we would clean up the kerosene. There is no need to take out your upset on the billions of people who are at imminent risk from global warming. Quite frankly, how will you sleep at night, Mr. Claus?"

Before Santa could respond, Rusk slipped effortlessly into a new tactic. "You know, there are certain legal ramifications to not providing a *habitable* biodome. After all, isn't a biodome by definition—"

"The dome will continue to provide livable space: appropriate temperature control and humidity, water. But as for anything else— food, postal and laundry services, an airport—you're on your own."

"You . . ." Rusk pinched the top of his nose and took a deep breath. "Our working relationship is spiraling and there's really no need for it, Nicholas. When I left here earlier, I thought we had an understanding. I assure you, we will successfully clean up this misstep. No one will even remember that it occurred. Please don't take out any momentary frustrations on a good cause. Dear God, man!" he said, slamming his fist down on the coffee cart hard enough to rattle the teacups. "We're saving the world!"

Claus shook his head. "And what will you say after the next *slight* mishap occurs? 'Sorry' goes only so far, Mr. Rusk. My decision is final. It was a mistake to let Jetsla come here, and I take full responsibility for that, but you've worn out your welcome. And quickly, I might add. Christmas magic is for Christmas. You can expect no more generosity from Christmasville."

Noël's face flushed, and a vein in his forehead bulged. "This is unacceptable. You may think you've had the last word, but you're naively mistaken. I'll sue your ermine-trimmed red britches right off you. By the time I'm done with you, there won't even be a scrawny donkey to haul your ass to the end of your pathetic little airport, let alone around the world."

Santa cocked an eyebrow. "Until this moment, Noël, I held you in high regard. I felt certain that you would make this world a better place. Unfortunately, though you're a bright and gifted man, you have an inflated sense of your own worth. I fear that you will be the end of us here at the Pole. I'm truly sorry, but if you think I will buckle under your threats, then you are mistaken. In the end, you will destroy your reputation the world over. Think about that before you behave so rashly."

Rush shook his head. "Done thinking, Nicholas. You'll be hearing from my lawyers."

Claus shrugged. "We do have icebreakers visit each September. I'll expect your representatives by early autumn."

Rusk stomped out, slamming the door behind him.

"Wow!" Herbert said, inching his way out from under Santa's bed.

"Get out from under there!" Santa said, "Have you no sense of propriety?"

"I just thought you should have a witness," Herbert said, brushing off a few dust bunnies. "Just one thing is still unclear. Without access to the airport, how on earth will he fly out?"

The Claus chuckled as he pictured pompous Noël Rusk mushing his way across an ice floe on a dogsled. "I told Foos he had twenty-four hours' use of the airport before we pull the plug on that, too. After that, it's not our problem, Herbert."

\*\*\*

Herbert circled to the rear of Quonset Hut Carol, deep in conversation with the only person who seemed able to grasp the situation's gravity and implications: himself. Claus was in high spirits, but if he thought they wouldn't have to deal with the fallout from freezing out one of the richest men in the world, he needed to cut back on the eggnog and double-check what he was smoking in that pipe. Rusk wouldn't sit back and watch a fat man in a motheaten red suit decimate his vision of money and glory. With the power of Christmas magic from the *Lacrima ambrotos,* he would raze Christmasville right down to the ice.

"Yoo-hoo! Oh, Mr. Tuddy." It was Violet Claus, scurrying toward him, fingers fluttering and hair flying in her haste. "My husband?"

"I just left him in his office. At the moment, he's neck-deep in a crisis. Is there something I can help you with?"

"It's the garden," she sniffed, dabbing one eye with a white hankie delicately embroidered with Christmas trees.

"Garden?" Herbert said, engulfed in a sudden hot flash. "What's wrong with your garden?"

"It's all gone," she said, bursting into tears.

"*All* gone," Herbert repeated. "As in somebody stole *all* your plants?"

"Dead," she blubbered. "Soft and rotting." She leaned in conspiratorially. "Even the Tears of the Angel," she whispered. "Not a plant left. Oh, what will Mr. Claus say?" She fluttered past him and hurried on toward Quonset Hut Alpha.

Herbert's mind streaked back to the chemical spill and the bog plants in Mrs. Claus's Garden. Seepage, and it had killed all the Tears of the Angel. Well, all but one, and that belonged to a terribly ticked-off, mercurial billionaire who could deny until the reindeer came home that he knew anything about one measly little blue-flowered plant. And then there was Herbert: the craven scaredy-cat who just couldn't sit on the contraband for even one day without running scared and unloading the ill-gotten goods. If Christmasville was to survive, he needed that plant back!

"Hey, you," he called, waving down a passing service jeep. "I need to be on the Jetsla side as fast—"

"Sorry, sir," the driver said. He pushed his fur-trimmed hat up off his forehead, which left it threatening to slide off the back of his head. "Accounting wants these receipts pronto."

Herbert climbed in anyway. "Santa says otherwise." He hiked a thumb over his shoulder. "That way. Now."

The driver gunned it, slamming Herbert back against the seat and then almost jettisoning him out the side as he executed a tight U-turn. The quick response was commendable but futile. Herbert watched with chagrin as Noël Rusk disappeared into his aircraft, and the door closed. Seconds later the plane taxied toward takeoff. Herbert would never get the plant back now.

*** 

Noël Rusk had his pilot circle the large dome before heading back to Houston. The unspoiled beauty of the Pole awed him—its patchwork of frozen ocean, glowing in a thousand shades of white and blue. Was it possible for anyone but the elves to live here and not destroy it? It had never been his intention to sweep in and put his stamp on the place. Other places? Yes. But the Pole was different. Its loveliness soothed his restless spirit.

He pulled the little blue-flowered plant from its protective box and placed it beside the telephone on the table before him. Was this the key to solving all his current problems? And with a good dose of Christmas magic, could he, Noël Rusk, maintain the great Christmasville biodome by himself? So many questions. He took one last look at the village as the plane banked hard right, and endless white replaced the magical view.

He placed a call. It rang twice before P. J. Foos answered. A diligent worker, that Foos, though not to be trusted too far.

"Seen any villagers with torches?"

Foos chuckled. "No, sir. But I have been instructed by Herbert to move. Considering the source, I'm waiting on the Claus to verify that."

"Just relocate. The Jetsla dome has everything you need, and it's not worth all the back-and-forth."

"Yes, sir," Foos said, and when it seemed Rusk was finished, he asked, "Anything else, sir?"

"No, that will be it. You're still feeling fit, right?"

"Never better, Mr. Rusk. Oh, speak of the devil, here comes Mr. Tuddy."

Rusk nodded. "Excellent. Clear out, and until you hear otherwise from me, carry on as usual." He disconnected the call but kept the phone receiver, contemplating whether he should attempt any more before his pilot chastised him for being on the phone. Rusk usually complied to keep the peace, even though the hazards of using the phone in midflight hadn't been proved to his satisfaction.

Far more troubling was *this*, Rusk thought, pulling Tuddy's vial out of his suit coat pocket. Foos looked and sounded like the picture of health, so why was he hesitating? He had no answer, which disturbed him. Just as he had no evidence that cell phone use disrupted plane instrumentation, he had zero feedback on a mortal ingesting the Tears of the Angel. Was Foos's limited elvish lineage just enough to counteract any ill effects of the elixir?

"Noël?"

Marta stood at his elbow, her voice soft and concerned.

Noël looked into her troubled eyes. God, how he loved this woman! Love, the one thing that his wealth couldn't buy. Attention, yes. Sex, yes. Hangers-on who would trade up from him in a nanosecond if it meant more money in their grasping manicured fingers. But no amount of money could buy Marta.

"What's wrong?" she asked, sliding into the seat beside him.

"Too much potential power and too little humanity," he said, taking her hand.

"You? Noël, if you're struggling with that, I think your humanity is winning."

"Ah, but it's the final decisions and actions that really show who we are, and sometimes, Marta, I fail miserably. My overflowing bank account shows where my decision-making often takes me. Profit, profit, and more profit. But this North Pole venture—it's different. I wish I could make these people understand that."

"You're talking nonsense," she said, taking his face in her hands. "Show me the fast cars, the yachts, and the squandering of your fortune on meaningless nights, awash in booze and mind-numbing drugs. Noël, you don't even own a house, for God's sake. Accumulating wealth doesn't lose a man his soul; *hoarding* does. Your ventures and aspirations are noble. That's what I love about you." She kissed him and dropped her hands.

"I just wish others shared that faith."

"Beautiful plant," she said, gesturing to the Tears of the Angel.

"Yes," he said, never taking his eyes off her. He unbuckled his seat belt, followed her to the bedroom in the rear of the plane, and closed the door. Together, they would shut out the world and create a lovelier one of their own. His lovely Marta. How had he ever lived without her?

*** 

Foos clicked off his phone. "Well, if it isn't Mr. Tuddy, esteemed assistant to Santa Claus," he said as Herbert approached his desk. "Come to gloat?"

"Certainly not," Herbert said, though his wide grin suggested otherwise. "Seeing as how Jetsla is on its own for all those little niceties that Christmasville has been providing, Santa Claus wants me to pack you up and send you on your merry way. Empty shipping boxes will be in shortly."

Foos looked wistfully around his office. "I don't think so. I've kind of grown accustomed to the place."

Herbert shook his head. "You're out! Go. No one wants you here."

"Oh, I don't know," Foos said, leaning back in his desk chair. "Santa might appreciate hearing what I know. Future Jetsla plans, little blue plants . . ."

"You slimy little—"

"Careful with that, Tuddy. I think we both would agree that I could nail you to the wall with what I know."

"And I you."

"That's about the size of it. But if we both keep our mouth shut, we'll both get what we want, won't we? You get the Virgin Islands, and I get a nice place to ride out this ridiculously boring assignment. Look at the bigger picture, Spanky."

"First of all, no more *Spanky*. I had enough of that growing up. Second, yeah, it looks like we'll both be satisfied, but so help me, if I catch word of you screwing over any of my friends here, I'll send the Claus a nice chatty note that gets you canned, and you can bet your pointy shoes that I'll mail it from a position of safety in the sunswept Virgin Islands. Got it?"

Foos grinned. "Sure. Now, get out. And send those boxes back. P. J. Foos has people to impress."

## Chapter Sixteen
# Dropping Like Sinkers

Santa locked his sitting-room door, popped in the earbuds, and cranked up "Jingle Bells" to full blast. If his hearing went, fine. He couldn't bear any more. First, the chemical spill, and now the Tears of the Angel, lost. Had any Christmas Keeper in the history of Christmasville ever seen such calamity and woe?

Santa's cell phone vibrated in his pocket. It was Elliot from Exterior Snow Patrol and Transport. "Yes?" Santa asked, feeling himself tense.

The connection was bad, and Elliot's voice crackled back at him in bits and pieces. "Santa . . ." followed by static crackle, gibberish, and then ". . . another one."

Santa reached over and turned off the Christmas music. This would be the death of him. He slid his heavy brown leather coat on, pulled a fur-lined cap down low over his ears, and turned out to meet the latest—though probably not last—catastrophe.

The old yellow Bombardier snowcat, looking more like a jack-in-the-box on tank treads than an efficiently designed snow vehicle, tracked along the biodome's perimeter on its final approach to the air lock on the far side of the airstrip. Santa studied the tarp-swathed cargo lashed to its top. The mission had been effective, he noted with a sigh. Would that it were not so. But it could have been worse: to have found no body out there in an environment where no elf could survive for long. Now, at least, the remains could get a proper send-off and burial.

He left the Quonset hut window and headed to the airfield to oversee removal of the body to the makeshift morgue in Quonset Hut Boston Charlie. His heavy black boots shuffled across the ground newly covered in a thick glaze left by freezing rain. Who would have anticipated building a mortuary in a land of happy, singing, carefree immortals? Not one but *four* dead elves, and two fairies, in the span of eleven hours made it a reality. It broke his heart. How many more ceremonies would he preside over before someone figured out what was afflicting his staff? Had Jetsla dumped something in the food or water? No, everything had been tested, and passed with flying colors. A viral or bacterial pestilence? Negatory on those also. Were the later elven deaths possibly copycats of the first? Right now no one could answer that. It was as if the outer world's insanity had invaded the North Pole and poisoned the very air they breathed. Was this the last death, or would there be more? Santa shuddered to think of it.

The snowcat proceeded through the air lock and lumbered toward Santa and the elvish honor guard waiting at the tarmac's edge. The guard stood at attention, their clothes of darkest green without bells or insignia, their heads bared and bowed in respect, their expressions pinched in grief and disbelief. In a land dedicated to good cheer, how many more of these must they bear?

Santa bowed his head and followed behind the honor guard carrying the bier, while a small band trailed behind him playing a dead march. Six months on the job, and the Pole was hemorrhaging workers. And the fairies—how could one replace the fairies? In the past 287 years, the Pole had lost but one elf, and that involved a worker who froze to death after accidently becoming separated from the rest of his crew.

Donning the red Christmas suit and hat did endow the wearer with extraordinary insight and abilities, but omniscience certainly was not among them. Was the current Santa the problem?

Once inside the mortuary, Santa sent the band off with a wave and paused for a moment at the morgue door. He would let Dr. Dash, the medical examiner, do his thing. And if he could shed no further light, Santa would be forced to concede that ending this unfolding horror show was beyond his ability. He required outside assistance.

As he returned to his quarters in the command center, he stopped briefly in the corridor and admired the portraits of the Sinterklaases who had come before him. To the hurried or the unobservant, they might look the same, but as he perused them, he noted the distinct turns of nose and the slight differences in laugh lines around the eyes, and the sparkle within them. He studied his own reflection in the glass of the last picture frame, and scrunched up his nose when he realized how little his picture resembled his predecessor's. The Claus mantle might convey the title, but it did not make a man honorable. He was quite sure that none of these men and women had pursued the mantle. Indeed, it was quite the reverse. And somehow, the mysterious process had always got it right, and the glorious North Pole tradition had flourished for centuries. So, what, dear God, had gone wrong with *his* selection process? One day, his own visage might resemble the rest, but some trials must still await him before he became worthy to fully wield the Christmas magic. If things got any worse, he'd never make it. He made a vow right then and there to tighten production schedules. By the end of the business cycle, he would have some numbers to show, by golly!

Back at the control room, he jotted a few notes outlining new quarterly projections. Then took to his bed to go over everything besetting the village, but the warmth or the weariness—maybe both—soon overwhelmed him, and he rolled over and gave in to sleep without any further insight into his boatload of problems.

His naps were never long enough. The ME soon sent word that he had finished his autopsy. Santa threw on his heavy coat and returned to the morgue.

One look at the good doctor told him it wasn't as he feared. It was much worse, if he was reading the examiner's expression correctly. The ruggedly handsome doctor's face looked unusually creased and aged. Santa followed him to the stainless-steel gurney where the body of the elf called Tocker reposed, his beautiful elvish face unblemished even in death. Santa closed his eyes a moment and offered a silent prayer. "What happened? And no sugarplum coating, please."

"The same results as Ticker, Beltzer, and Huban," Dash said, shaking his head. "Death by drowning."

"But why?"

Dash shrugged. "I don't know, but something drew them to the water—a sort of hydrophobia in reverse. He seemed to ponder this. "Is there such thing as hydrophilia? Anyway, we don't get a handle on it, it will kill us all. Any elf worth his salt knows to stay away from the water. We can't swim, and we drop like fishing weights."

"Well, at least there were no fairies this time."

"Unfortunately, there were," Dash said."

Santa's eyebrows shot up. "Truly? There were no reports."

Dash flipped down a corner of the cloth covering Tocker's torso, revealing a stoppered vial filled with a bright yellow powder. "We found it in his pocket."

"In this?" Santa asked, picking up the vial and tipping it. The powder slid from one end of the tube to the other.

"Just the dust. "I can only conjecture that the fairy was alive and in his pocket before, before . . ."

Santa nodded and put the vial back on the gurney. "The fairy deaths and the elves—you believe they're related?"

"It would seem so. The time of death for each individual may be the same, but with just the fairy dust, there's no way to tell."

"Who is the fairy?"

"A definitive identification will come only with further testing, but family and friends have reported Fincher as missing."

"Solomon's brother?"

"Mmm." Dash withdrew a folded cloth from a cabinet near the gurney, billowed the diaphanous pale-yellow fabric over the deceased elf, and let it fall in a delicate shroud. Then he rolled the whole table into a small walk-in refrigerator, lined it up beside the other three, and closed the door. "Whoever will decide, just let me know how you want to handle the ceremony."

"Yes, by the end of the day," Santa said as he headed for the door. He paused when he reached it. "Dash," he said, turning to find the coroner watching him closely, "I feel so helpless. What else can I possibly do?"

Dash shook his head. "Don't beat yourself up, Claus. I'm asking myself the same question."

## Chapter Seventeen
# Getting One's Reindeer in a Row

Herbert hurried along the brick pathway stretching from Quonset Hut Boston Charlie to the stable. He glanced over his shoulder before breaking into a jog. No witnesses, and everyone immersed in the midyear toy push—he wouldn't be missed for a while.

"Herbert?" It was Gustav, the chief herdsman, decked out in red waders and a green polka-dotted stocking cap. He carried a metal bucket in one hand and a pitchfork in the other and was walking a path that would soon intersect Herbert's. "Out for some exercise, I see."

Prickles ran up Herbert's arms, and he hadn't even done anything wrong yet. "Well, can't have anyone confusing me with Hoho, now, can we?"

Gustav gave him the once-over. "Be at peace, brother elf. I think it will be a while."

"In that case, I'll walk to dinner tonight." Herbert pointed to the bucket. "Just beginning to muck, or finishing up?"

"Oh," Gustav said, "just putting this stuff away. Everything's neat and tidy like the Claus likes it. The boys will be good until late afternoon, when they start grunting pitifully for their evening meal. No, I'm headed back to clean myself up and then off to a delightful bowl of vegetarian something or other. But first, how goes the Jetsla mess? Rumor has it that the whole north side's been fouled."

"I think not giving the swill a name is better," Herbert said, falling in step with him, "but our vegetarian days are over. The lunchroom is changing back to regular fare. Too long a story," he said, anticipating the question forming on the herder's lips. "Regarding the spill, your rumor has it half-right. While I'm not at liberty to discuss everything that is going on, I can give you a little something that will keep you up at night. An industrial spill has contaminated thirty acres of ice floe. Once we pointed it out—"

"Oh, dear."

"Oh, dear, yes, and its discovery came down to our diligence, not theirs," Herbert said, puffing out his chest. "They're all over the problem now, and I have to admit, the landscape is significantly improved since our first visit. But then, you can't always see impurities, now, can you? Don't worry too hard on it, though. I aim to keep them on their toes until it's put right again."

Gustav gave him a kindly smile. "You're a good man, Herbert."

"I do my best," Herbert said, beaming. "Between the two of us, we'll keep this place humming, right? The Claus says your marching orders remain unchanged. Until further notice, you are to keep the herd away from the creek and see that their water comes from the filtration system and not the pasture. How are the herds? You're managing to keep them watered without the creek, and no evidence of sickness?"

"Aww," Gustav said, waving him off. "Not difficult. Everybody's happy. Rudolph has already put on five pounds in the off-season. But it's Jetsla that has me worried. How didn't they see that coming?"

"Gustav, I can't answer that without getting myself in hot water. For now, we just take things one step at a time. Anatoli will inspect the entire dome for contamination. Until then, we safeguard the reindeer and I'll keep leaning on Jetsla."

"You got it. Now if you'll excuse me, I have some washing up to do."

"I won't get in anybody's way," Herbert asked, "if I say a quick hello to the team before I head back?"

"Help yourself," Gustav said over his shoulder. "And if you don't mind, would you close the stable doors when you're through? A little quiet time is good for the boys."

"Not at all." Herbert wandered into the barn. It smelled of fresh hay and leather and was immaculate. Two rows of stalls ran the length of the building—four on one side, five on the other—with a shiny brass nameplate tacked to each door. *Cupid, Donner, Blitzen . . .* Herbert went methodically down the left side, sweet-talking and caressing Rudolph's teammates as he waited for one of Gustav's grooms to leave. When at last the elf disappeared, quietly singing some unfamiliar German carol—Herbert found Rudolph's harness and dropped it inside his stall. "Bet you'd enjoy stretching your legs a bit, wouldn't you?" he said, stroking the big guy's nose. "I'll be right back." And then he left to find a willing accomplice.

He found the stout but gentle elf beelining for the cafeteria.

"Where's the fire, Hoho?" Herbert asked.

"First in, first out," Hoho said. "At the front of the line, I can choose from the normal food. How can anyone exist on tofu burger and sprouts?"

"Well, then, you'll be pleased to know that I've fixed that. It wasn't easy, but effective immediately, Jetsla employees will no longer be eating with us."

Hoho skidded to a halt. "No more awful-smelling, strange-looking burgers, Brussels sprouts, or runny substitute-egg products?"

Herbert shook his head.

"I love you," Hoho said, and he wrapped Herbert in a bear hug.

"Enough," Herbert gasped, fumbling to peel himself free. "The joyous look on your face is reward enough."

Hoho released him, but he was so energized, bouncing and grinning, that Herbert took a step back in case he came in for a second rib-crushing.

"We have something important to take care of. So, grab a burger—or two—and meet me at the stable in twenty minutes."

Hoho took off again as if someone had announced early closing of the lunchroom.

"Hoho!"

Hoho wheeled around. "Yes?"

"Top secret mission, okay? Not a word to anyone."

Hoho gave him a soldier's salute and then burned fat toward a rapidly growing buffet line.

Herbert passed on the food. What he did need was a fast way to get the attention of the only person he knew who could battle larger-than-life Noël Rusk: the indefatigable Hamelin Russell. The immortal soul runner could handle the entrepreneur with one hand tied behind his back. A simple tap, a touch, a mere caress from the soul runner, and Rusk's dark soul would be hurtling toward the hellish afterlife that he deserved, and Christmasville could return to normal. And while Mr. Russell was at it, it would be nothing for him to scoop up that damn plant and leave it on Mrs. Claus's doorstep, with no one ever the wiser about the little adventure it had been on.

## Chapter Eighteen
# It Doesn't Work That Way

Hamelin Russell, soul runner extraordinaire, stepped out of the Weigh Station's afterlife portal beside St. Anthony's Catholic Church in downtown Nevis, Maryland. Since the overhaul of the transportation system after Nemie, son of Coeus, had screwed it up all the way to hell and back, travel to and from the hereafter couldn't be finer. Missions to Earth, including this one, were closer to target and tended not to wander over time.

He turned his back on the church and looked across the street toward the boardwalk and the sparkling Chesapeake Bay. In five minutes, the soul of soon-to-be-deceased Maury Dennison would be waiting for pickup near the public swimming area. That meant crossing to the Dairy Freez, a short walk past Orphan Annie, (a small, single-story 1920s vacation bungalow that had somehow escaped modern-day renovations), then a quick left onto Bay Avenue and a leisurely stroll past Second Street to the corner of Bay Avenue and Third. Not too far past that, he would find the Sunrise Garden—a delightful miniature oasis of koi ponds, oriental footbridges, and driftwood sculptures—and just beyond, his thirteenth soul pickup of the day. After that, it would be a quick trip for Mr. Dennison to the pearly gates, and then back again to Fredericton, MD, for a crab imperial take-out order from Stoney's restaurant. Life was good.

"Cross here, Nemie," he said to his fellow soul runner, taking advantage of a break in the traffic through the small resort town. "It's not far."

"I *have* been here before, you know," Nemie said, hurrying to catch up. "That dreadful Anacostia Delta concert you dragged me to."

"If I recall correctly, you were stalking me at the time. There was nothing wrong with that concert except the mayhem you created by trying to screw with one of the musicians. But then again, that was just the sort of lousy scoundrel you were at the time."

"And now I'm your bestie," Nemie said, cutting his eyes at Hamelin.

"*Pfft.* One more disparaging word about Anacostia Delta music, and when I go to fetch the next transportee on the list I'll leave you stranded here by yourself."

"Feel free. I don't need coddling."

Nemie might not need coddling, but the Weigh Station powers that be weren't so sure about his ability to fight off a couple of old-school demons prowling for him by order of his adoptive father, hell's second in command. Months after Nemie had rejected a life in hell for one filled with heavenly promise, highly placed afterlife sources reported that teams from Hades were still on high alert for information on his earthly whereabouts. It made sense. Beelzebub Number Two wasn't going to watch his only son switch sides without one hell of a fight. Hamelin shuddered to think what would happen should the bub ever get his hands on the young fellow.

As they passed Orphan Annie, Hamelin took a casual look around to be sure that no one was following them. Even if he discovered a tail, there would be no fight—Hamelin and Nemie would simply flee to the nearest Weigh Station portal and live to tell the tale, so to speak. "Left," he said, satisfied they were alone. "We'll be a little early, but that's okay."

As they turned onto Bay Avenue, a chubby sandy-haired boy of perhaps ten approached carrying a basket of red, white, and blue pinwheels. "Jesus saves," he said, reaching out a hand. He dropped a red plastic disk the size of a quarter into Nemie's hand. One side read *Jesus saves*, and the reverse read *John 3:15*.

"Bless you," Nemie said, but the boy had already moved on down the street to the next soul in potential need of saving.

"Coin?" Nemie asked, offering his to Hamelin.

"No thanks," Hamelin said. "You keep it. It might come in handy some dark and dreary night."

As they passed the koi ponds at Sunrise Garden, something caught Hamelin's eye—and his sixth sense. He threw a quick protective arm in Nemie's direction and turned toward the motion. The small garden was abuzz with activity: strolling couples, darting children, bounding dogs. He scanned quickly to the left and then back in the opposite direction. What the devil? Then, there in the middle of the garden, he spied the most pompous, self-serving elf he had ever had the displeasure of meeting: Herbert Spanky Tuddy.

Hamelin stood riveted as Herbert climbed up into the biggest tree in the garden and flung himself out into midair, his arms spread out like bird wings. As he plummeted to Earth he chanted: "Hamelin, Hamelin, Hamelin."

Hamelin heard an "*Oh, dear God*" as the elf hit the hard ground with a thud, and then he watched in amazement as Herbert returned to the tree, shinnied even higher, and did another swan dive. There were no postjump utterances this time. Tuddy remained motionless, his face firmly planted in the soft earth. There may have been quiet crying.

Hamelin walked over and nudged the top of Herbert's head with a black high-top Converse sneaker. "You do realize that it takes a lot more than that to do in an immortal, don't you?"

Herbert staggered to his feet, spitting grass. "I knew you'd come," he said, grinning broadly.

"You thought that if you offed yourself, I'd pick up your soul?" Hamelin shook his head and sighed. "You're an idiot, Herbert. Just because I once tried to take you into the afterlife doesn't mean I'll be assigned indefinitely to come get you."

Herbert shrugged. "It worked, didn't it?"

"No. We're here together by sheer coincidence. What's the matter, not having fun anymore in the regime of a new Santa Claus? He revoke your "I'm a big operator" license?"

"I'll try to assume that was a joke," Herbert said, his grin fading. "The Pole is fine; the new Claus is fine. I, uh . . ." He shut his mouth and studied his shoes.

"Hurry up. I'm getting old here, elf." Hamelin's gaze shifted to Hoho, who gave him a friendly smile. "Hi there," Hamelin said to the portly fellow. "I don't suppose you could add anything."

Hoho shook his head.

"Nothing is right," Herbert wailed. "The new Claus is stupid, a rival is making my life miserable, and by this time next year—if we even still own the place—we'll all be out of a job. And worst of all, I seem to have made a very bad business decision." He sat on the ground blubbering.

The weight of Hamelin's soul-running manual in his coat pocket tugged at his sense of duty and fleeting time. His on-time statistics were impeccable this month, and no unhinged Christmas elf was going to screw with that. "What do you expect me to do?"

"Stop them!"

"Stop who?"

"A deal has been made with the devil."

"Devil? Okay, now we're entering a realm I might actually be able to effect change in." Hamelin sat down on the ground beside the despairing elf. "Is it Bub Number Two again?"

"What about my adopted father?" Nemie asked, drawing near.

Herbert's tears stopped flowing. He hiccupped once and shook his head.

"Some other demon?" Hamelin was beginning to have his doubts. Demons weren't exactly snow-loving, North Pole types.

Herbert wagged his head on that one too. "It's Noël Rusk. Santa has made a deal with that crazy gazillionaire chief executive of Jetsla. In exchange for updating systems at the North Pole, Santa struck an agreement to permit Rusk to use Christmasville as a base for his business operations. They're planning to mechanize our jobs and take us commercial. They've already poisoned our water, and soon they'll be suing our asses off. And on top of that, Rusk has in his possession . . ." An emotion that Hamelin couldn't quite decipher swept the elf's face. Herbert began beating his breast, and the wailing kicked in once more.

Hamelin shifted his gaze to the heavens. ". . . seven, eight, nine, ten." A bit calmer, he looked at Herbert again. "Where's the sleigh?"

Herbert gave Hamelin a blank stare. "What?"

"I don't play twenty questions," Hamelin said, narrowing his eyes at both elves. "Last chance. How did you get here?"

Hoho beamed at him, rose up on his toes, and pointed to a little stand of dogwoods at the garden's edge. Above the heads of a cluster of ten or twelve noisy children, Hamelin saw a pair of antlers.

"You *stole* Rudolph?"

Hoho, who wore his guilt like a neon sign, cast his eyes to the ground and bit his lip. In contrast, Herbert locked eyes with Hamelin and stuck his lip out. "The word is *borrowed*, and a little jaunt out and about never hurt anyone. The boy likes to fly."

"Mmm," Hamelin said, eyeing the tree Herbert had been jumping out of. "I'm sure you'll figure it out. Best do it before the coppers arrive. They might be nasty folk if you tell 'em that whopper. My advice is to get on old Rosy Nose over there and blow this town before you get thrown in the clink and Santa himself has to come bail you out." He got up, sidestepped around the two elves, and hastened toward his pickup on the public beach.

"Wait!" Herbert called after him. But it wasn't the elf's heart-wrenching, pleading tone that set Hamelin back on his heels. Confound it! Runner Operations had just changed his soul pickup. He yanked his manual out of his coat, ripping stitches around the pocket as he did so, and fanned until he found the page with his soul transport list. A soul pickup in *Christmasville* in ten minutes? It wasn't Herbert Tuddy's, and he didn't recognize the . . .

Hamelin whirled around. "Don't touch me," he snarled, finding Herbert's hand within inches of his coat hem. He wouldn't let this fool of an elf play Russian roulette with his ability to transport a soul into the afterlife with a single touch.

Herbert snatched his hand back. "Sorry," he squeaked. "I, uh, *we* need your—"

"The reindeer—go get him," Hamelin said. "Now!"

Though Hoho was about the size of a refrigerator, he could move with surprising speed when he had the bejeezus scared out of him. He darted to the dozen children admiring Rudolph, politely excused his way into the middle of the throng, and led the reindeer back to Hamelin.

"Here's the plan," Hamelin said, motioning both elves closer though not within touching distance. "I want you to lead the animal around the corner and away from prying eyes. As soon as that happens, scoot back to the Pole. I'll be right behind you."

"Promise?" Herbert said, his eyes wide with trepidation.

"Solemnly," Hamelin said. He shooed off the children still staring from a distance and watched the departing elves disappear around the building with Rudolph.

He called over Nemie, who had gravitated to the children. "Did *they* ping you?"

"No," Nemie said, his eyes filled with caution and maybe a little fear. "Are we involved with my father again?"

"No, misunderstanding on my part. I've taken care of it."

We're wanted elsewhere?"

"North Pole."

"Bub Two is making a mess up there?" Nemie asked. "Tell me truthfully."

"No. It's nothing of the sort. The elf was just using an expression 'a deal with the devil.'" And then, seeing Nemie's blank stare, he added, "Never mind."

As if drawing a line that he did not want to cross, Nemie scuffed the tip of his boot along the ground. "Uh, not to be questioning your authority, but maybe Christmasville is not the wisest place for me to be right now. I treated those people horrendously. If they figure out who I am, they'll be tossing me right back out of the dome again. Santa would be alive and well today if my father hadn't sent me there to make trouble."

"I think they understand that you were not a willing participant."

"That's where you're wrong. I went willingly, to make trouble.

When I was young and didn't understand—"

Hamelin put his hand on Nemie's shoulder and shook him gently. "Because you didn't know any better; you were taught to hate. But then you grew a conscience and did what you could to stop the attack on the Claus. You've since made your amends, and your service to humanity and the afterlife has been admirable. Besides," Hamelin said, releasing him, "the Weigh Station wants *me* there, not you. You take this pickup and then return to the Station, where they'll either pair you up with someone else or send you out to rejoin me. Trust them; they generally get it right."

When Nemie still hesitated, Hamelin added, "I can hang around for a few minutes. Let's go see what's what with Mr. Dennison."

The two runners crossed the street to the boardwalk and followed the flow of people flocking, as they always do, to a tragic public death. On the beach, Mr. Dennison, the transportee, was stretched out his on back while another man performed CPR and a third knelt close by, talking into a cell phone. Hamelin sensed inevitable death despite their frantic measures.

He stopped short of the beach. "Go on. I'll keep an eye out for any hellizens so you don't have to keep looking over your shoulder."

Nemie, now invisible to the growing crowd of gawkers, moved quickly through the crowd and settled on the sand beside the man still valiantly performing CPR. He put his hand on Dennison's. Nemie had the gentle touch, Hamelin thought, watching the young runner immediately become absorbed in that sacred moment of death and soul transfer. How someone could so quickly and easily cast aside the influences of growing up in hell was beyond Hamelin. Truly, Nemie had a good soul.

The transfer ended smoothly and quickly. A moment later, Nemie gave Hamelin a thumbs-up and began retracing his steps back to the transportation portal outside St. Anthony's. Hamelin watched him until he turned right toward Orphan Annie and disappeared from view. Normally, Hamelin wouldn't let Nemie wander off by himself, but there was little chance of hellizens nabbing him in the short distance he must walk.

Why had the Weigh Station algorithms suddenly changed his transportation list? Hamelin wondered. Or maybe it wasn't a random, computerized change. His gut feeling was that meeting the elves wasn't by chance. Someone wanted him in Christmasville. Now.

# Chapter Nineteen
# Life According to Fatty

Hamelin exited from a portal system painted in drab shades of gray and army olive drab, into the enchanted, sparkling, snow-filled and icicle-decked red, white, and green wonderland known as Christmasville. A broadcast French noël played quietly from a speaker mounted to a nearby pole, and if he listened carefully, he thought he heard someone off in the distance singing in German. He had been here once before, but the visit wasn't for pleasure, and he'd had little opportunity to take in its magic. This too would be a brief visit. One quick pickup and he would be gone again.

He ducked into the closest building, which was a reindeer stable painted dark green with a red roof. He hadn't been in one of these in ages, and it was everything he hoped to avoid: dank and smelling of fresh manure. Yet here he was, nodding at the North Pole's nine finest grunting, honking, earth-pawing reindeer and wishing he were anywhere else.

"I was beginning to think that you'd changed your mind," Herbert said, stepping out of Comet's stall.

"A promise is a promise," Hamelin said. "But give me a minute or so. I have business, and then I'll be right back." He opened his soul-running manual. *Fatty Winkle, North Pole* sat at the top of his transport list, and the countdown clock beside the name indicated two minutes until pickup. Hamelin tucked his book away and proceeded past the rows of stalls and out another set of double barn doors, into a barnyard. To his surprise, he wasn't in the enormous biodome that housed Christmasville, but in a smaller adjacent dome. And no matter which direction he turned, open pasture and grazing reindeer surrounded him. How the tundra plants thrived this far north was beyond him. Christmas magic?

He began walking again, heading for the ribbon of stream that lay not far ahead. As if sensing something amiss, the cluster of reindeer ahead of him parted and allowed him passage. "Shh. S'all right, s'all right," he soothed as he moved through them, then slipped through the gate on the other side of the field. He walked a little faster as he saw the mist hovering over the shallow stream, and reached the water just as a green-clad elf, kneeling at the water's edge, tumbled face-first into the slow-moving stream. Hamelin dropped quickly to his transportee's side and took his hand. It was cold from exposure. Fatty Winkle's life force immediately began flowing up Hamelin's arm. Hamelin closed his eyes and watched the elf's life flash by in a series of still and moving pictures as Fatty's lovely soul song played out the soul of an elf life well lived. Lovely except for the squeak or two. And the buzzing like an enraged hornet. What was happening?

Hamelin adjusted his hold on Fatty, and a flash of crimson light shot out from Fatty's chest and smacked Hamelin square in the face.

"Oof!" shrieked the little red fairy as he slid down Hamelin's nose and landed in a tiny feathered heap on the ground. He stood up immediately and set a course parallel to the stream, staggering dangerously close to the water only to course-correct at the last minute and reel in the opposite direction, toward safer ground.

"Come back here!" Hamelin yelled as the singer paused Fatty's song.

The fairy executed a clumsy about-face and began retracing his steps. When he reached Hamelin, he snapped a sloppy salute and said, "Solomon Grundy reporting for duty, sir. Born on Monday—"

"Died on Friday," Hamelin mumbled as he watched the fairy sway. "It's midweek, so you've lucked out there. Come, now, though. I don't think you're well. Why don't you sit over there and when I'm done, we can go inside the stable and let them take a look at you."

Solomon pointed toward the stable and raised an eyebrow.

Hamelin nodded. "But I wouldn't advise flying. I can walk with you if you'd like, but you'll have to wait."

Solomon shook his head and staggered off in the general direction of the stable—his zigzagged walking interspersed with quick hops and a few fluttery attempts to take flight, none of which panned out.

Hamelin sighed. "I know only what I need to know," he muttered, "and fortunately for you, Mr. Grundy, it is not your day." He waited until the little guy meandered into the barn before he took up Fatty's hand again and let the life review finish: Herbert's party, the illicit elixir, the poisoning. When the song ended, he reverently released the dead elf's hand. Fatty Winkle had been a gracious, goodhearted elf. "Don't worry, Mr. Winkle, I'll have you safe and sound in no time. Soon you'll be lost in an everlasting life of love and joy."

Hamelin started back across the pasture, making sure the gate was shut so the reindeer would stay away from the stream. Oh, Herbert Spanky Tuddy, what mischief have you wrought? he thought. No wonder you're at rope's end.

He made directly for Herbert, who sat on a large wooden tack box waiting for him as others ministered to Grundy. The fairy had made it as far as the stable before collapsing. The scowl the elf shot Hamelin suggested Herbert had no clue that Herbert had poisoned a good friend. Hamelin would change that shortly. At least four other elves appeared in Winkle's life review. How many of those had not yet died? Soul-running statutes prohibited him from interfering in the lives of others, not even to save a life, but that didn't mean he couldn't plant a seed in Herbert's selfish noggin to save any surviving friends.

"About time," Herbert said with a huff.

Hamelin said, "Time is of the essence for me. Who else was at the party?"

Herbert's eyebrows shot up. "What party?"

"*Your* little party. It seems your feeble attempt at usurping one of Santa Claus's greatest responsibilities has poisoned Mr. Winkle. Who else was at the party?"

Herbert slid off the tack box. "I've done no such thing. I should have known you wouldn't lift a finger to help me. Have a nice trip back, *friend*."

"I'm nobody's friend," Hamelin said, using his considerable height advantage to tower over the four-foot elf. "But if you want to protect your friends from the same end as Fatty, you'll tell me who else was at your get together. You shouldn't care as much about what others will think as about what will become a part of your last judgment review. Herbert the indifferent *murderer*, or Herbert the compassionate *lifesaver*? Be quick, idiot. Who else might you have poisoned with the *Lacrima ambrotos*?"

Herbert lifted his eyes to Hamelin's. They were swimming in tears, and his lower lip trembled. "Poisoned?" he whispered. "Are you sure?"

"Quite. Who else?"

"Ticker, Tocker, Beltzer, Huban, Fatty—th-they were all at the party. All poisoned?" His voice rose into a panicked "Oh my God!" Every head in the stable whipped around, and Hamelin had to shush him. "I'm the only one left." He turned away and wiped his face on his sleeve, the bell on his cuff jingling softly.

"I do not know your fate, Herbert Spanky Tuddy, and I cannot intervene here. If there is any faint vestige of reason in that pointy head of yours, you must tell them everything. Don't force me to come back and do for you what I just did for Fatty Winkle."

Herbert sniffed. "I know, but it's messier than that."

"Life is messy," Hamelin said. "You make your choices, and I guess people like me come along and clean them up." He turned to Solomon, who was presently sitting in a tub of water with several herdsmen ministering to him. "Now, not to be impolite, but I'm in the middle of a job and I don't have time for this. Isn't there a friend that you can confide in who can help you sound this out? Hoho, perhaps?"

"Hoho? Really?"

"Okay, so no friends," Hamelin mumbled. He put his hand to his chest, feeling the growing discomfort that always attended the carrying of another man's soul. "Whatever mess you've gotten yourself into, it must be a doozy if it affects your sense of self-preservation. I will indulge you for exactly two minutes more to sort this out with me, and then I must transport."

"Two minutes wouldn't begin—"

Hamelin raised two fingers.

Herbert heaved a deep sigh. "Okay, I'm sort of lying," he said. "On the night of the party, there were other, um, things we might have imbibed, and I'm not a hundred percent sure that I drank *any* of the elixir. Memories are a bit fuzzy there."

"And you're certain that no one else besides you and your friends had access to your concoction?"

Herbert opened his mouth to speak, then shut it abruptly.

"*Who*, you little weasel?" Hamelin said, coming within inches of poking his index finger into the middle of Herbert's chest.

The elf's eyes grew wide, and he gave a panicked *oh*. "I, uh, might have sold some elixir, along with the recipe, to Noël Rusk."

"Oh . . . my . . . God," Hamelin said, punctuating each word with a finger poke in the chest. Herbert closed his eyes and shuddered. "You've poisoned one of the richest men in the world, and you're futzing around as if you thought you could *hide* it? I'm curious, Herbert, how does something like that feel?"

"Not particularly warm and fuzzy," Herbert said, retreating from Hamelin's forefinger. "But I'm rectifying the situation. That's why I came looking for you. You can fix this. It's just another day's work for you."

"Herbert. I transport souls of the newly deceased. Nothing you've said remotely touches on that."

"Yes, it does! All you need to do is dump Noël Rusk's evil, black and sulfurous heart in hell, and this goes away."

Hamelin sighed. "Sorry, Herbert, you dark and damaged soul of an elf. This intrigue bullshit isn't remotely in my professional repertoire. I can't make unauthorized pickups. Someone needs to give it to you straight—me, I guess. Put away the animosity you have toward the new Claus and accept that he legitimately got the gig over you. Don't try to draw others into any vendettas you're hatching. It just makes you look sm—"

Herbert's eyes flashed a warning.

"Er, petty."

"You have no idea what it's like to work so hard for so long and never get anywhere. I don't get the gig, I don't get the office, I don't get the respect—"

Hamelin put a hand up. "You're preaching to the choir, bro. I've been at the Weigh Station for hundreds of years. Suck. It. Up!"

"Well," Herbert sniffed, "I'm doing better than I was. Actually, based on everything you've told me, what I now need from you might be less than what I imagined. We just wait until the poison kicks in and, voilà." He gave a little hand flourish for emphasis. "Then all you need do is help me get back the Tears of the Angel and the recipe so no one can cause any more inadvertent harm."

Hamelin frowned. "Say what, now?"

"Tears of the Angel. It's a plant, an ingredient in *Lacrima ambrotos*. I, uh, unwisely and impulsively stole a plant and, uh, sold it to Rusk."

Hamelin chortled. "Ah, so now we're at the heart of the matter, and the Herbert I know so well. You've screwed up spectacularly and are in need of extensive CYA. Sorry, *Spanky*, just fess up and get it off your chest. As someone who has witnessed millions upon millions of life stories, I can assure you that confession is good for the soul. That's one true thing you *can* take to the bank. Okay, your two minutes are up and I really must go."

"No, no, no, no!" Herbert cried, following Hamelin. "It's more complicated than that."

Hamelin kept walking. "Everything in your life is complicated, elf."

"Stop! Listen! The pollution from the Jetsla facility killed every last Tears of the Angel plant in Mrs. Claus's Garden, and if I don't get the one remaining live plant back from Rusk, Christmas magic will disappear. Christmasville as we know it will be gone, and the Earth will see no more visits from Santa Claus."

"Oh, well, that's just show biz, I guess," Hamelin said. He stepped into the portal and left the irksome elf stewing in his own problems. Death was nothing more than a door to something else. For the good ones like Fatty, something wonderfully better. For damaged cases like Herbert? He shuddered thinking about what would happen to Herbert when it came time for him to pay the piper.

## Chapter Twenty
# Rooting for the Little Guy

Santa sat in his armchair and fretted, stood at the window and stared, left scuff marks on the wood floor where he paced. Christmasville simply wasn't equipped to deal with medical emergencies, and hours had passed since Gustav took charge of Solomon Grundy's fate. Could the fairy hang on long enough to be diagnosed and saved by a veterinarian? Santa prayed fervently on it. And he would gladly accept the hostility that a healthy Solomon would throw at him for entrusting his health to a reindeer herdsman. What else could they do?

"There's hope," Herbert said, coming quickly and quietly up behind him. "Gustav says Solomon's stopped talking nonsense and his glow is bright and steady now."

Santa released a long, slow breath. "Praise be to God. For all the annoyances he causes . . ." He stopped and shook his head. "The last thing we need around here is another death."

Herbert hung his head. "Yes."

"I'm sorry about Fatty. I remember how the two of you worked the Lego division when it first stood up. Long hours shared make for great friendships, don't they?"

"They do. He hasn't been gone a day, and there are already a thousand things I want to say to him."

"It seems to go that way, doesn't it?" Santa said, patting him on the back.

"Don't celebrate too soon," Gustav said as he entered Santa's study and sat down in the small straight-backed chair beside the bed. His ubiquitous polka-dot cap was missing, and circles darkened the skin below his eyes. "Solomon is stable, but he still has a long journey before he's out of the woods."

"As if you could keep a good fairy down," Santa said smiling. "What happened, Gustav? Jetsla pollution? Something else he got into? Tell me so I can ensure the safety of everyone else in Christmasville."

"Something," Gustav said, lifting one shoulder. "He looked drunk, but since fairies aren't given to overindulging . . . He seemed dehydrated, but an IV was out of the question. Do fairies even *have* veins? Maybe, but I doubt that I could get even my smallest needle in one. So we stuck him in a bath of warm water and kept him there until he sobered up and whatever it was wore off, flowed out . . . I have no experience in treating those little guys. He definitely got into something. And my guess would be that it's also what killed Fatty— probably the other elves, too."

Herbert nodded, then clasped his hands behind his back to keep them from shaking.

"As soon as he can hold a conversation," Santa said, "I must speak with him and find out what got him into this unfortunate situation." He moved out into the control room, sat down at the main desk, and pulled a writing table out of his wooden in-box. Despite his best efforts, he couldn't find a pen or pencil anywhere.

"Let's not rush things," Herbert said, taking a mechanical pencil from a drawer and handing it to him. "If we push him too hard after such a terrible fright, who knows how far we might set him back."

"Mmm," Santa said, nodding. "Who's with him now?"

"Dimitri," Gustav said, rising. "I told him I would be right back. I just thought you'd want straight information before it ran through too many people. By midday there will probably be half a dozen explanations for what happened."

"Thank you, Gustav. I'll put out a memo and nip that in the bud. More people with the right information means less chance of illness and fatalities. I'll also check with the Weigh Station, see which soul runner they sent . . ." His voice drifted off into an uneasy silence. "At any rate," he said, scrawling on a notepad, "we need all the information we can get, to stop these unfortunate occurrences from happening again."

When Gustav had excused himself, Santa turned to Herbert and said, "You look a little pale. Please don't tell me that you're ill."

"To be perfectly candid," Herbert said, clutching at his stomach, "I think I've been overindulging ever since the tofu pizza went away."

Santa grimaced. "That food was dreadful, was it not? Thankfully, once the cafeteria runs through the last of their Jetsla larder, we won't be entertaining any more of that. Go home, Herbert, and put your feet up for the rest of the day. I can't afford for you to go down for the count. If I need something, you can be sure that I'll summon you. Better yet, I'll ask Mr. Foos for help. In spite of the tension with Jetsla, he's volunteered to stay here in his office to keep things running smoothly. Efficient elf, that P. J. Foos."

Herbert quirked an eyebrow. "Okay. I am feeling a bit woozy, but is there anything I can do before I go? I'd hate to overwhelm Foos with my duties."

Santa gave him a thoughtful look. Another dedicated public servant. When things settled down—should that ever be possible again—he'd waste no time moving Herbert into the office currently occupied by Foos. "I would be ever so grateful if you would get Noël Rusk on the line—"

"Mr. Foos, sir?"

"No, *Noël Rusk*. I don't want any middlemen slowing this conversation down. Tell him I need a face-to-face immediately. And if he can't accommodate that, tell him I'll be soliciting help from others who are way over his pay level. And I'm not bluffing."

"Wise choice, sir. Foos is just too far down on the totem pole to trust with anything important. Dime-a-dozen worker bee." Herbert picked up the phone and began dialing.

"One thing more, Mr. Tuddy."

"Yes?"

"Feel free to be as persuasive as you deem necessary to get him here. I'll give him a second dressing-down once he arrives. He has to pay dearly for the loss of these innocent lives."

"It would be a pleasure, sir."

"I thought so. Then, make yourself scarce—your house, not your office. I'll send Hoho around later with some chicken soup."

Herbert smiled feebly. "Much later, if you don't mind, sir."

It took Herbert the longest ten minutes in memory to get a call to Rusk and have him agree to return to Christmasville. Then he hustled off, sweat rolling down his temples. He made it as far as the nearest trash can outside and vomited. Ticker, Tocker, Beltzer, Huban, and Fatty Winkle, dead. Herbert's closest friends and their fairy drinking buddies—how had Santa not put it together? The man was too trusting. If Herbert weren't still in perfect health, he would swear that Hamelin wasn't jerking his chain—that something had gone terribly awry when Herbert made the *Lacrima ambrotos*. Why wasn't he dead, too? Surely, he must have imbibed. He leaned over the trash can and hurled again. Would the poison soon claim him too? Maybe that would be a better option than Hamelin Russell spilling his guts to Santa about the whole sordid affair.

He wiped his mouth on his sleeve and took off again for his bungalow. If he was dying, he'd prefer to have it end while he was handsomely tucked into bed in his best red plaid smoking jacket, rather than hanging over a garbage can full of his own upchuck.

Herbert spent several hours staring at his bedroom ceiling. Truth be told, he felt sick about his friends, but he didn't feel any more infirm than he had last week or the two before that. If his home brew killed Fatty and the rest, either he was immune to the poisonous effect of the tonic he had created, or he had, in fact, never ingested it. He just couldn't fill in the gaps in his party memories, but he suspected that the latter was probably the case and, moreover, that he should get himself up and deal with his mess.

He rolled out of bed. Hamelin wasn't his only problem. If Solomon started yapping about the party, again the jig was up. His only consolation at the moment was that fairies seldom let a good deal pass them by. If Herbert could make Solomon an offer that charmed his little black boots off, the fairy's lips would be forever sealed. And then Herbert would set his sights on Rusk. That billionaire couldn't leave Christmasville without Herbert getting his plant back. He mused about the harsh sound of words like *theft*, *blackmail*, and *extortion* . . . Whatever worked. Hamelin Russell was in a league of his own. As much as Herbert hated to admit it, the soul runner could outwit him at every turn, and as much as he might claim Hamelin as a friend, he knew deep down that it wasn't so. Hamelin played by his own rule book and would not risk his own bacon to save someone else's. Best tread lightly with that one.

# Chapter Twenty-One
# Bribes and Promises

Santa ushered Noël Rusk into his command center and invited him to sit on a hard metal chair. There would be no tea, no small talk, no coddling. "Mr. Rusk, I believe you have met my assistant, Herbert Tuddy?"

Herbert kept his gaze on the floor. Surely, the billionaire wouldn't admit to side dealings with Santa's underlings.

"Briefly," Rusk said, keeping his eyes trained on the Claus. "I would prefer a more private conversation, if you don't mind."

"Actually," Santa said, "I do. Herbert is an invaluable member of my team. Having him here will reduce paperwork and additional explaining." The big man stood behind his massive desk filled with beeping, blinking electronic equipment, crossed his arms, and said, "Thank you for returning, Mr. Rusk. Although I must say, I was surprised that you left Christmasville. When last we spoke, you gave me the impression that you would personally handle the kerosene spill. Since that time, half the plants in my garden have died, and we've had five elves perish under mysterious circumstances in the past week. That's four more than in the past *five hundred years!*"

"Deaths?" Rusk said, looking surprised. "Oh, that genuinely pains me. My heart and the hearts of all Jetsla employees go out to your community on the loss of your loved ones."

"Give me one good reason why I shouldn't send Jetsla packing right now." Santa cocked his head and gave Rusk a cold, hard stare.

"Because the Jetsla mishap didn't cause those deaths. We conducted a thorough inspection. Mr. Foos reports that the spill was limited to the ice floe and was successfully cleaned up, with no leaching into the surrounding area. And let's be frank. This was a fluke. I can personally guarantee that it won't . . . can't happen again. The spill was caused by the inadvertent opening of a shutoff valve on the flow line between the kerosene reservoir and the testing chambers. Engineers have installed a double set of pressure valves—if one fails, there is now a backup safety valve. And those valves are inspected twice daily."

"Our experts suspect otherwise. And quite frankly, even before the domes were separated, you weren't acting in good faith. From the moment you sent over the contract without the trial period we both agreed on, you've been trying to have your own way no matter the cost to Christmasville."

"God help humanity," Rusk said, running his hand down the back of his hair. "You think I'm not sincere, that I'm only in this for the fame and profits that will come from our discoveries? No businessman will deny wanting those things; they are the lifeblood of industry. But to suggest that we don't have feelings, that it isn't possible for someone like me to work for the greater good . . . Why, your loss of trust is shocking, Nicholas. I really do care what you think, and I don't want you doubting my motives. Truly, something else is at work here. And that's even more reason to take down the wall between the two domes. If there is something dangerous in your environment, let Jetsla help you identify and get rid of it. We need closer communication, not separation."

Santa shook his head. "It's a little late. You have already created irreparable damage to the Pole, Rusk. A small flowering plant that grows here? Tears of the Angel? I'm certain you've never heard of it."

Rusk blink several times and his jaw tightened. "Tears of the Angel?"

Rusk was a hard one to read, but for the very first time, he seemed rattled. Herbert was certain the entrepreneur would sell his mother if there was a dollar in it for him, and he would spill the dirty Tears of the Angel deal and leave Herbert high and dry if it helped Jetsla keep its foothold in Christmasville. Herbert's head began to throb. Whatever had he seen in this man to hold him in such high esteem?

"Its pale-blue flowers," Claus continued, "are harvested several times a week by a specially appointed elf and carefully dried by Mrs. Claus for future use in something called *Lacrima ambrotos.* It is essential to Christmasville's survival. Imagine our shock and dismay upon finding the plants dead and rotted, and the nearby water fouled by your little mistake? How do you suppose you'll make that up to us?"

"I'll hire the world's best botanists—"

"To reanimate the dead? Noël, it's too late. As we speak, I have elves on their hands and knees in our garden, trying to find a viable seed that can germinate."

"Nowhere else on Earth?"

Claus slowly shook his head. "Not that we know. According to Christmasville legend, the very first Santa Claus brought a single plant with him—a gift of the Keepers, of which he was one."

"These Keepers—can't you go back to them? Name the place, and I'll send a team . . ."

"A realm where you and I cannot venture. Even your money cannot arrange a trip into the afterlife and back. I am the last of the Keepers on Earth, and I know of no such plants anywhere else."

126

Herbert could almost see the gears in Rusk's head cranking. He would give the plant back!

"But if you could find one—even just one plant—would that be enough to set things right? Does it self-pollinate or could it be propagated by cuttings?" This was a determined man.

"It self-pollinates, but as I said—"

"Settled, then," Rusk said, standing up. "I will not rest until you have this plant back in your care, Nicholas. All my resources—people, contacts, and personal wealth—will be marshaled to restore what has been taken from you." He thrust out his hand. "You have my word as a gentleman."

"All this out of the goodness of your heart?" Santa said, looking askance.

"You must remove the wall."

*Barter the plant back? Son of a bi . . .* Herbert almost fell out of his chair. The man had no shame.

"Ah." Santa ignored the hand and walked to his window. The pasture was still empty—no reindeer today, and certainly not tomorrow. He couldn't see the other Quonset huts or the elves who toiled therein, but he could picture them as they bent over their work, and he could feel their dedication in his heart. Without the Tears of the Angel and its magical powers, he couldn't maintain this wonderful place. It would fade into memories of what used to be and thoughts of what might have been. Why, oh why, must the saving action come from this driven man who would stop at nothing to fulfill his own ambitions?

Santa turned back around to Rusk. "It seems we need each other, Mr. Rusk. I will remove the wall after you find me another Tears of the Angel. Those are my only terms. Accept them or get out."

"Agreed," Rusk said.

For the first time since arriving, Rusk shot Herbert a look. A warning? Reassurance that he would not reveal Herbert's wheeling and dealing? Herbert kept his mouth shut. Rusk could go ahead and play his hand. When the time came—yes, soon—Herbert would play his too. It would be a royal flush, and Rusk would have to fold and go home.

# Chapter Twenty-Two
# Free-Range Herbert

Herbert ached to tell his corpulent leader how diabolically he had been played, but first assistant at the Pole hadn't risen to his position by being bold or impatient. Oh, no. A stealthy elf was a wealthy elf. Herbert kept his mouth shut and followed Santa out to the far end of the big dome to watch him remove the wall sealing off the Jetsla facility. It wasn't a lengthy process—no teams of elves and reindeer straining to pull down the thick, sound-deadening fabric separating the domes. Santa mumbled a few words, and the curtain sparkled away into nothing.

Flush with the hope that his imbibing of the bootlegged *Lacrima ambrotos* might give him similar magic at his fingertips, Herbert longed to try his own hand at it, but that would just invite questions leading to more questions and a whole lot of trouble.

Herbert's next order of business involved pinpointing the billionaire's private rooms in the Jetsla compound. They were there somewhere; he'd seen the personal furniture carted in. With the aid of an extra emergency skeleton key—Herbert's rank did come with certain privileges—he borrowed blueprints from Santa's office and located Rusk's suite within an hour of the entrepreneur's shameful performance.

Herbert's survival kit included more than just a master key to

Clausian documents, however. He had a face that everyone knew, and it, too, opened many doors. For his second task, he would waltz into Jetsla as if he owned the place and check out the suite. Every lock at the Pole opened with the master key. Claus required it. With any luck, Rusk wouldn't be there, but the Tears of the Angel had to be gracing a windowsill somewhere. After all, how many people would let a ticket to untold power and success out of their sight? He was betting bedroom.

Happily, even a billionaire needed no elaborate security measures in a place as remote as the North Pole. Herbert nodded to the petite receptionist with the button nose and tightly permed lavender hair and waltzed onto one of the Jetsla elevators. No badge, no escort, not so much as a gentle admonition to confine himself to certain areas of the building. It was free-range Herbert with a simple, fool-proof, plan.

He got off on the third floor, the top, and stood for a moment staring at the only door—straight ahead and unmarked. Two quick paces put him at the door. He felt a cold lump in the pit of his stomach. If caught, Rusk would never believe the reason Herbert had concocted for being there. He ducked back in the elevator, hit the button to close the door, and began hyperventilating. And if Rusk needed to ride the elevator down? A trembling finger bypassed the lobby button and pushed the button for 2. Herbert needed a moment. The elevator eased to a stop and the doors rolled open. Complete silence throughout the elevator bay. No one had answered his knock. Rusk wasn't home. Herbert stabbed the Close Door button, got off again at 3, and entered Rusk's apartment with his master key.

The entryway opened into a cozy living room, which Herbert quickly passed through. To the right, an efficiency kitchen, and on the opposite side an extra room piled high with boxes. Stooped low and stepping cautiously, Herbert crept along the short hall, toward the master bedroom at the end. The door was open. He stopped and listened: the tick of a clock, nothing else. His eyes swept the room: unmade bed, nightstand, easy chair, but no Rusk or anyone else. He leaned in a bit farther and checked the double windows on the far side of the room. There in the pale Arctic light sat the Angel Flower, still in its cheap plastic poinsettia pot, modestly exposing its chaste blue petals and yellow stamens. What a lovely sight. Herbert made a dash for it.

"Ahem." The voice behind him was quiet but authoritative.

Herbert whipped around, still clutching the plant. Not ten feet away stood Noël Rusk, his wet hair plastered to his head, a fluffy bath towel wrapped around his waist.

"I suppose an explanation wouldn't do?" Herbert said, quickly averting his eyes.

"Oh, I know the explanation," Rusk said, walking toward him. "You make poor choices, each one creating a need cascading to the next one." He reached out and grasped the pot.

Herbert yanked it free and slid a step closer to the bedroom door. "Um, you know you can't keep this, right? You heard Santa. It's the last of its kind."

Rusk scoffed. "Well, that sounds like poor planning on your part, doesn't it?"

"Actually, no," Herbert said. "If I hadn't removed this from Violet Claus's garden, there would be *no* plants left."

"Why, how misguidedly noble of you! But I'm afraid we've already made a deal. I get the plant and elixir. You get a one-way plane ticket to the Virgin Islands and a condo with a killer beach view. Put the plant back."

Herbert shook his head. "A deal that is just as easily unmade. I've never used my end of the arrangement, and you just need to graciously stop trying to bite off the hand that is feeding your obsessive need to be free of oversight." Herbert tried to gauge his chances of a successful run for the front door: chairs he could overturn, objects he could swing, a paperweight to hurl . . . "When you consider it, this will be a better deal than the one we first struck. You get the *Lacrima ambrotos* for free."

"But forgo the millions upon millions that I could reap by making and selling more?"

*Exactly.* And Herbert had only one comeback for it. But to tell Rusk that there was something more to the recipe than just mixing the ingredients, that any *Lacrima ambrotos* the billionaire produced would most assuredly kill the people he sold it to? Fatal mistake, and perhaps not just for the imbiber. Herbert would have to admit that his own concoction had already killed other elves. Oh, what Rusk could do with that information!

Rusk moved a step closer.

"Stay where you are," Herbert countered, moving back a step and holding the pot as far away from Rusk as his arm would reach. "And stop being ridiculous. You already have more money than you could ever run through. This is more about control and one-upmanship."

The billionaire was on him in three steps, yanking the pot free and shoving Herbert just hard enough to bump him up against the wall and bang his head. He fell like a brick.

"Okay, okay," Herbert said, rising painfully and slowly. He rubbed the knot rising on the back of his head. "Now that we've settled that you work out and I don't, we should talk. I, eh, didn't want to, but I see I need to come clean with you. You will never succeed in making the recipe. The elixir in your possession is a failed experiment—literally poison—and whoever you sell it to won't live out the week. Those dead elves that Santa mentioned? All felled by one sip of that beautiful crystal-blue liquid."

Rusk's eyebrows drew low over his eyes. "It's a nice story, but Claus was clear—"

"Because he doesn't know about the ambrotos that I made. Any reasonable person would blame Jetsla."

Rusk ran his hand down the back of his wet hair. "I need to change. Go sit in the living room. If you slip out before I join you, I'll take the plant straight to Claus and repeat what you just told me." As he returned to the bathroom, Herbert thought he saw someone move away from the door inside the bathroom. Rusk wasn't alone, and now they, too, knew the full story about the ambrotos—a second person who could rat him out and he couldn't even identify them. A wife? Lover? Perhaps if he knew . . .

Herbert sat down in the chair closest to the entry door. He wrung his hands. He was losing his touch, and Rusk was a master—with no scruples. Who could trust someone like that?

The elixir was no good to Rusk, and only a fool would use the plant to make more. So, what could the man do to an elf who might momentarily have veered off the straight and narrow but was now trying to do the right thing? Either run straight to Santa, or blackmail Herbert to get more favorable arrangements in Christmasville. That's what. But fat chance with that. This new Santa Claus was coming into his own, and he wouldn't be pushed around. What little pull Herbert did have wouldn't sway him in the least.

Herbert wrung his hands a while longer, tapped his foot, and crossed the living room as he assessed Rusk's present state of mind and location. His guess: still in the bathroom primping in the mirror and doing what Herbert himself was doing: working out how to work this situation to personal advantage.

If Rusk got to Santa first, he would poison the well, spinning the Tears of the Angel story to his advantage and punishing Herbert for setting him up in a bad deal. That left Herbert only one choice. He had to get there first and add a little elvish spin of his own. It would be a hometown elf's word against an outsider who had long since worn out his welcome.

Herbert slipped out quietly, rode the elevator, and crossed the Jetsla lobby at a casual stroll. Once outside, however, he broke into a sprint, commandeered the first service vehicle he saw, and directed the driver to Boston Charlie.

# Chapter Twenty-Three
## Spinning Tales

The once-jolly Santa looked as if someone had skewered him through the heart with an ice-fishing spear. Herbert felt ready to throw up.

"Sit," Santa decreed, sending him to one of the fat man's fireside chairs. "Too many details and moving parts to take in at once, Mr. Tuddy. Tell me again, a little more slowly this time."

Herbert breathed deeply, double-checked that the door was locked, and started over. "Noël Rusk has a Tears of the Angel plant. I saw it with my own eyes as he entered the Jetsla building. There is also information—God forgive me—that I have been withholding from you. I didn't do it out of malice, but with the intent to shield the reputation of someone else. But," he said, hanging his head, "I'm afraid that I now must let the chips fall where they may."

"That's what we should *always* be doing," Santa said, settling on the edge of the other chair. "Tell me."

"The elves who have left us for whiter, fluffier snows: Ticker, Tocker, Beltzer, Huban, and Fatty Winkle—I believe I know what killed them. Last Saturday, each of us received an invitation to attend a drinking . . . uh, party in a private room in Quonset Hut Boston Charlie at ten p.m."

The logs in the fireplace shifted, sending out a shower of sparks as flames attacked a patch of wet wood. Santa leaned forward in his chair and interlaced his fingers. "Whose invitation?"

"I'd rather not say. To malign the character of someone who cannot defend himself would be despicable. Suffice it to say that it was one of the individuals who attended, and let's leave it at that."

"For now," Santa said, glaring.

Forever, Herbert thought, but Santa might think he doth protest too much. He nodded in agreement. "Honestly, I'm ashamed to admit that I don't remember much after arriving. All I can say definitively is that there was quite a bit of booze."

"Hmm."

"And there may have been some shots of, er, …" Herbert squeezed his eyes shut, his mind casting wildly about in one last, desperate attempt to salvage his career, his reputation, his everything. A moment passed before he heaved a defeated sigh, and whispered, "*Lacrima ambrotos.*"

"*Lacrima ambrotos?*" Santa said, pulling back with wide eyes. "That's impossible. Exactly how drunk were you, Herbert?"

"Ten sheets?" Herbert responded weakly. He expected a sanctimonious lecture to follow on the virtue of moderation, but Santa remained silent, stroking his beard as his deep blue eyes tried to read Herbert inside and out. Even a good chewing out would be preferable to the sad, thoughtful eyes that studied him now.

"I'd say so," the Claus said at last with a hint of a smile. "Be at peace, brother elf. I think you're letting your imagination run away with you. I'm the only one with the recipe and authority to make the elixir, and I haven't made any since becoming the Claus."

"I believe it was bootlegged batch, sir."

"Oh?" Santa said, rising out of his chair. "Dear me. This is wrong on so many levels. There is much more to *Lacrima ambrotos* than the mere mixing of ingredients. There are commands, incantations that I alone know. An illegal batch of ambrotos could be lethal."

"That's exactly my point, Santa."

Santa shook his head. "But think about it, Herbert. If everything you're telling me is true, why are the rest of them dead and you seem the picture of health?"

Herbert came out of his chair and fell to his knees at Santa's feet. "You've got to believe me. Someone at the party *made* the ambrotos. I—I can't remember drinking any of it. But I meant to." Herbert wiped a tear from his eye.

"Herbert, please get up. This story is wilder even than anything Solomon has ever made up—which is a sobering thought." Santa reached out and, with his large, gentle hands, coaxed Herbert to stand. He also leaned into the elf and sniffed. "Have you been *communing with the spirits,* as it were?"

"Heavens, no!" Herbert said, pulling away. "This is a workday, sir. If you don't trust what I'm saying, go ask Solomon. He'll verify what I'm telling you; there were fairies at the celebration. Solomon was there."

"I wish I could," Santa whispered. His gaze shifted to the window.

Herbert went pale. "Dead?"

"No, but . . ." The round man shook his head. "Our little Solomon isn't doing well. He's comatose and giving us no insight into what happened. He doesn't even know about the death of his brother, Fincher. His remains were found with the most recent, uh . . . If he regains consciousness . . ."

*If? Heavenly hemlock!* Herbert was killing all of his friends. "But he was ambulatory the last I saw him."

"Tough little guy," Santa said, nodding sadly. "It would seem that you are the only living witness to an event that all the stricken victims attended. Noël Rusk—he was at the party, too?"

"Oh, no, sir. But he definitely has a Tears of the Angel plant," Herbert said, nodding fiercely. "I firmly believe that Mr. Foos snuck into your garden like a little Peter Rabbit and snatched a plant when no one was looking. He'd do anything to get ahead with his boss, including lying and stealing. He hates us, sir. I tried to warn you."

Santa shushed him with a finger to his lips. "Mr. Tuddy, you are terribly unforgiving, which is unbecoming an elf, especially one of your elevated status. Your accusations are damning. You have proof?"

Herbert shook his head. "But Rusk definitely has the plant. I snuck into his room—"

"Herbert!"

"—about half an hour ago and it was sitting on a windowsill."

"Herbert! What's wrong with you?"

"Stop being so nice!" Herbert yelled. "Get with the program! The bully billionaire has the only existing Tears of the Angel plant, and you're wasting time throwing indignation at me for trying to save Christmasville. We've got to go get the plant before he destroys it!"

A polite tap on the door halted their heated exchange like the bell at a boxing match. Santa walked to the fireplace, lifted a poker from its stand, and poked aggressively at the logs. "Leave a note, Patterson," he called. His face was flushed, though not with its customary rosy glow.

There followed a moment of silence, after which young Patterson, newly assigned in the office, replied, "Mr. Rusk here to see you, Mr. Claus. He says it's urgent."

"If he doesn't have the plant, don't let him in," Herbert whispered. "Unless you want to keep him occupied while I search his room again."

He eyed the window. It was his only possible avenue of escape.

"Out," Santa whispered, pointing the poker at the window. "But NOT anywhere near the Jetsla compound, is that clear?"

"Okay," Herbert muttered. "But you're making a doozy of a mistake."

They slid open the window, and Herbert slipped out, immediately disappearing feet first into a drift of fresh-fallen snow.

\*\*\*

Santa checked Noël Rusk's hands as soon as Patterson admitted the entrepreneur into his private room. One was clenched as tightly as his jaw, while the other carried a green canvas backpack that didn't seem big enough for a potted plant. Santa ground his teeth together. Why would any other Claus tolerate a loose cannon such as Herbert?

"What can I do for you, Noël?"

"Fire Mr. Tuddy, your first assistant. I found him wandering around my apartment this morning. As there were no visible signs of a break-in, I would assume that he let himself in with a key. Most unacceptable on both accounts. I have Mr. Foos changing the lock as we speak."

Santa's jaw dropped as he feigned surprise. "You have my deepest apology. No one here in Christmasville, no matter what their station, is exempt from displaying respectful, honorable behavior. I will call him in at once."

"In addition to handing him his hat, you should also ask him about the plant he was carrying around. He said it was an Angels Tears plant, but if I recall correctly, you told me those were all destroyed. He babbled on for quite a while but made little sense. Before he beelined for the door, I was under the strong impression that he planned to hide the plant somewhere in my apartment. Truthfully, Nicholas, I can't work in an environment where I have to worry about my personal safety—or the integrity of the people I'm in business with."

"I agree, and you can rest assured that this won't happen again. The idea that Mr. Tuddy would have a plant in his possession and not relinquish it forthwith is puzzling. Very puzzling," Santa said again, shaking his head.

A sudden draft of cold air turned the Claus around. Herbert's window of escape hadn't closed. "Oh, dear, a little airing out is fine, but this …" He walked over and pulled on the lower sash. The window refused to budge. He tried a second time with the same result.

"If I may?" Rusk asked. "I learned the trick to it in my first flat which, by the way, was quite a dump." Before Santa could protest, Rusk was at the window. He gave the sash a hard push upward and then pulled it closed. "The weights," he said, tapping the window. He put his nose up to the glass pane for a moment, then reached up and locked the window. "I think you may have a peeping Tom," he said, pointing outside. "Best keep this locked."

Santa put his face to the glass and noted a series of footprints walking away from the beaten-down snowdrift under the window. "What is *wrong* with people?" he asked as he drew the curtain.

"You seem to have more than one security problem. Would you like me to have some of my people conduct a safety assessment for you? No charge. Neither of us should have to deal with creepers in our personal quarters."

"Thank, you, but I'll handle it—and the issue with Mr. Tuddy."

"Excellent," Rusk said. "I'll get out of your hair now and leave you to the rest of your day. Sorry to have thrown a wrench in your schedule by barging in. And thank you for your prompt removal of the wall. For my part, I have already reached out to find us the best horticulturalists. Don't worry. I'm going to solve your problem."

"Thank, you, Noël," Claus said, walking him to the door. "And I do appreciate the heads-up about Mr. Tuddy."

Rusk lingered at the door a moment. "If I may ask you one question about the Tears of the Angel? Acquisitions clerks are a breed all their own, and I've never known one who didn't create a personal stash of supplies—to barter for other supplies when times are tight, dole out sparingly to office allies, or sell on the black market for their own gain. That sort of thing."

Santa nodded. "Oh, Tuddy isn't any different. He thinks it's secreted away and that I don't know, but 'he knows if you've been bad or good,' right? I don't mind his little maneuvers. They're generally benign, and his actions have always benefited everyone, so I turn a blind eye."

"Really? Even with a plant as powerful as the Tears of the Angel? Just think of the price he could get for it in an underground market."

Santa's naughty-versus-nice senses began to tingle. Rusk's pronouncement struck him as more of a fishing expedition than a statement of fact. "Anyone who pays or barters for Tears of the Angel would be a fool. Making *Lacrima ambrotos* is its only use, and I am the only one on this Earth who has the ability to unlock its magical properties. Without me, it's just a lovely plant."

"A lovely plant," Rusk repeated, nodding. "Well, let us hope that if Mr. Tuddy has the plant, he's not fool enough to try and peddle it. That would be most unfortunate."

*Definite naughty list*, Santa thought, watching the billionaire sweep out the door. Herbert was telling more truth than tale about Rusk, he suspected. Santa hurried back to his window and flung up the shade. As nearly as he could tell, Herbert had beaten tracks toward the lunchroom. Not a bad idea if he feared an uncomfortable face-to-face with Rusk. "Patterson!" he shouted.

"Sir?" Patterson asked, appearing immediately.

"I need you to find Mr. Tuddy and have him report to me."

"Yes, sir."

"And, Patterson?" he added, catching the eager young clerk right before he disappeared. "Top priority. Don't return until you've personally escorted him back here. Understood?"

"Right-o," he called over his shoulder, and was gone in a flash.

# Chapter Twenty-Four
# Man of Stealth, Lady of Mystery

Herbert ordered the driver out of the first service vehicle he saw, and burned rubber across the tarmac. Rusk wouldn't just hand over the plant. He would create a much more elaborate charade before giving up the only leverage he had in Christmasville. Dollars to Christmas Stollen, the plant was still in the apartment. The only question: *Is the mystery woman there?*

He didn't hesitate this time—elevator up, key in lock, entry gained. He swept through the first two rooms of Rusk's suite. No plant. He stopped and listened before entering the bedroom. Not a single sound. He leaned in the door. The Angel plant on the shelf bloomed back at him, and a beautiful woman with long dark hair, sitting in a chair, stared at him in openmouthed surprise. She dropped the book she had been reading, and stood up, tightening the sash on her robe.

"D-don't scream, please," Herbert said, raising his hands in reassurance.

"You!" she said, putting the chair between them. "You were here this morning, fighting with Noël."

"Not fighting. We just disagree . . . on so many things. It's okay now. We're good now, and he said that I could come get the plant. So if you don't mind . . ." He moved carefully toward the window.

"Stay right there. H-h-how did you get in?" she asked, her eyes flicking toward the front of the apartment. "Mr. Foos changed the locks."

"There's not a lock made that can resist this baby," Herbert said, showing her his skeleton key. "But everything's copacetic, miss . . . Noël has okayed this. I'll just take the little blue guy and be gone. That way Santa, Hamelin, and everybody else can stand down, and things can go back to normal."

"Hamelin?" she said frowning.

"Russell—Hamelin Russell. A friend who's been helping me."

"An elf?"

"Oh, heavens, no. He's a soul runner."

"Hamelin Russell is here," she said, moving toward him.

"He was here, and he's due back in a few hours for a one-on-one with the Claus," Herbert said. "But don't worry, you don't look as if you're ready to expire anytime soon. He's only interested in the short-timers, if you know what I mean. Now, if you'll excuse me," he said, pointing at the plant, "we'll just be on our way."

"No." She picked up the plant and hugged it to her bosom.

What *was* it with these people?

"Sit," Noël Rusk's woman commanded him, indicating the chair. Then she sat down on the edge of the bed. "What's so important about the plant? Tell me, and then I'll decide whether to hand it over."

Herbert wanted to tell her that her boyfriend could fill her in later, but the steely look in those expressive brown eyes suggested she would argue the point. He sat down. "This is a Tears of the Angel plant—the last of its kind, thanks to the Jetsla fuel spill. When used correctly, it creates Christmas magic. If your boyfriend leaves with it, this Christmas wonderland will wither and die."

"And no more Christmas," she said, staring at the plant.

"Yes." Herbert relaxed a bit. This one had a heart. She would do the right thing.

"Does he know—"

"Absolutely. And honestly, if you'll excuse my bluntness, the man doesn't have a soul."

"If you knew him as well as I do—"

"Lady, he will use the plant to leverage a better position for Jetsla."

Her eyes narrowed. "I thought you just told me he said you could have the plant."

Oops. Herbert hung his head and slowly shook it. And then he said something that he swore he would never admit to anyone. "I stole the Tears from Santa's garden and sold it illegally to Noël." Oh, dear God, he had never been good at talking to stunning members of the opposite sex. "I need to return it to clear my own conscience," he said, bumbling on. "And save my people, too."

She looked down her fine Greek nose at him. "I see. So, it's Christmas *and* self-preservation."

"Yes," he whispered, his mind frantically casting about to shift the conversation. "You seem like a nice lady. Why on earth are you with a man like him?"

"Noël is a good man. And he's brilliant. You have no idea how much he gives to others in his own quiet way. Not everybody needs to be thanked with a public pat on the back." She stared at the plant for a moment. "You elves live a long time, don't you? Just think of what he could achieve with a long life and Christmas magic."

"He's a jerk, lady. And no one except Santa Claus can draw forth the type of power found in the *Lacrima ambrotos*. The plant is of no personal use to Noël. Don't end up on the wrong side of this. Now that you know the importance of the plant, please give it back to me. We don't even have to let Rusk know that it was you who gave it to me."

"No."

Now he got it. He was mistaken about the "nice lady" part. Birds of a feather . . . She was as devious as her beau. He threw his hands up in the air. "What will you take in exchange for the plant?"

She thought a moment—a tactic to squeeze better terms out of him, Herbert guessed. Well, he had nothing left to offer. He waited as long as he could stand. "I have—"

"A meeting with this Hamelin Russell," she said, cutting him off. "He will be impartial. That's the only person I'll give the plant to. Arrange it."

"Okay. We're friends," Herbert said, lying through his teeth. "But you'll have to do your part too. How will you keep the plant safe until I make arrangements?"

As she thought it through, Noël's woman massaged an Angel leaf between her thumb and forefinger. At last, she said, "You just get Mr. Russell to meet me at the stable in two hours, and leave Noël up to me."

# Chapter Twenty-Five
# Just Tell Me

Forty-five soul pickups in six hours—if Hamelin weren't already deceased, this pace would put him six feet under. The mental and emotional burden of experiencing the life reviews of the dying and then transporting their souls into the afterlife was heavy. The trips to heaven weren't bad, but the ones to hell did a wicked number on a soul runner's psyche. He and his fellow runners could only hope and pray that the virus sweeping the Earth would soon ebb and return runner schedules to something more manageable.

As soon as he had a gap in his schedule, Hamelin headed back to the Weigh Station to regroup. Upon stepping out of the transport portal, he found himself surrounded by a noisy crowd of stationers waiting to port out. No doubt, a major conference had just ended. Gridlock wasn't an unusual situation in the White Corridor. Most offices, conference rooms, and anything else needed to administer the Station's myriad responsibilities as an intermediary organization between life and death, heaven and hell, were located here. The elders lived here too, but the residential area was strictly off limits for soul runners, leaving Hamelin to imagine their creative use of the corridor's ubiquitous white color scheme in their bedrooms.

"Yo! Hamelin!" called a tall, strapping man, bearing down on him.

"Luke!" Hamelin shouted over the top of the milling crowd. "I was just coming to find you."

"Consider me found," Luke responded, punching Hamelin in the shoulder. "Long time no see. You've time for a cold one, right?" He spun Hamelin around in the other direction. "Then I'm off to an oh-so-important meeting with some top dogs."

"Really?"

"Yes, to the top dogs," Luke whispered, and "no to it being different from any other time-wasting session."

"You could always return to running souls. One word from me and consider it done."

Luke laughed. "Thanks, but no thanks. One word from you and I'll be on a street corner grinding an organ with a monkey on my shoulder." He steered Hamelin toward a nearby door. "New shortcut. Gets us there in half the time."

It did. If anyone at the Weigh Station was more connected, Hamelin hadn't met them, and he'd been around long enough to know pretty much everybody. Luke had turned away from his lackadaisical days as a soul runner and wouldn't be calling the Station home for much longer—destination heaven, for sure. Hamelin sighed. If only he could maintain good behavior long enough to straighten up and fly right like his friend!

In minutes, they reached a tiny refreshment stand tucked into a niche in a quieter, less frequented side corridor. The three tables sat empty, and no one was waiting for an order. Luke ordered two of something and joined Hamelin at the table in the corner.

So, what's the word?" Luke asked, flicking some of the foam from the thin head atop his drink.

"It's a war zone out there," Hamelin said. He stretched his legs out, closed his eyes, and enjoyed the rare moment of downtime. "At the rate we're going, if this extends into next year, there may not be any Earthlings left to transport."

"No problem, they'll just shift you over to the Andromeda galaxy. I hear it's quite different, but very nice."

"Pass," Hamelin said. "I'm too old for something new." He took a swig of his drink, was surprised that Luke opted for root beer, and drank half of it down anyway. "I need help sorting something out."

Luke set his glass down. "I don't like the tone of that. Why don't we settle for you describing the wonderful sights you've seen, and then call it a day?"

Hamelin checked around for eavesdroppers. The woman manning the stand seemed to be occupied moving bottles around; otherwise, they were alone. "I just had a disturbing pickup—"

"Oh, dear God, you're getting me in trouble again, aren't you?"

"No! No, no! I transported and everything went smoothly, but I'm having a bit of a moral crisis."

"Read your soul-running manual, dude. Everything you need to know, including all moral stands, can be found right there. Don't go getting yourself into trouble by going rogue."

"No rogue," Hamelin said. He downed the rest of his drink and pushed the glass aside. "My question is simple. Based on the information you witnessed in a life review, have you ever subverted a tragic future death?"

Luke spat a mouthful of drink back into his glass. "Ha! You're joking right?"

"Uh-uh."

At that moment, the quiet little refreshment kiosk suddenly got busy. Neither runner said a word as two stationers queued up to place orders—both to go, much to Hamelin's approval. When they disappeared down the corridor, Luke said, "Section two, paragraph one: 'Under no circumstances will a runner interfere—'"

"Yes, but have you ever *done* it?"

"Hell no! That goes for heaven, too!" Luke said. "And I'll pretend that you never asked me that question." He wiped his mouth with a napkin and stood up from their little round table. "Nice chatting with you, Hamelin, but I've got to go."

"Come on, Luke. The fact that I'm bringing this up shows my good intentions. I'm still dealing with the Santa Claus crowd, and I'd like to protect the institution of Christmas. That's it."

Luke sighed and dropped back into his chair. "You can have the best intentions in the world, Hamelin, but it isn't your role—or anyone else's here at the Weigh Station—to interfere in the conduct of a mortal's life. Or an immortal's, for that matter. You have a good heart, but leave it alone. Just transport 'em. Right?"

"Yes, but it's hard."

"Hard tasks make good men, and that's what we're striving to become. Buck up, okay? Now, I really do have to go to my meeting."

"Sure," Hamelin said. "Thanks for your time."

Luke looked at him and hesitated. "Don't do that. You haven't lost your best friend. I'm just telling you because you need to hear it. Someone has to paint a clear picture for you."

"I know."

"Better yet," Luke said, digging into his pocket, "I'll leave you with this." He placed a thick silver coin on the table. Later, bro."

Hamelin picked up the coin and chuckled. Staring back at him was the relief of a walking angel. Pesky flyboys were the last thing in this world he needed. He pocketed the coin and headed back to his room, though not to sleep—no one needed forty winks in the afterlife. What he needed instead was some quiet time to consider his options. Maybe he could meditate his way out of his dilemma.

Soul runners resided in Building 25—an apartment building that resembled a Holiday Inn—only there was no pool or room service, and once one left, there was no rebooking for subsequent visits. The quickest way there was by the portals on the main corridor. Hamelin retraced his earlier route with Luke.

The White Corridor was now empty. Hamelin hopped the portal and arrived at Building 25 in less time than it took to walk to the portal. He got off on the first floor, which housed the more senior runners, and entered the first apartment on the right: number 7.

As the door closed behind him with a soft whoosh, he froze midstep. If he had known he had company, he would have passed on the meditation. "Miguel," he said to the flyboy sitting at his kitchenette table. "What are you doing here?"

"*Hello* would be more inviting," Miguel said, rising and bowing slightly.

"It looks to me as if you've already settled in," Hamelin said, taking in the card game laid out meticulously on the table. "I should have known Luke would summon you." He fished around in his pocket and retrieved the angel coin. "Here," he said, and he tossed it on the table, where it landed on the jack of spades. "Nice trick."

"Nice landing," Miguel said, studying the coin's placement. "I believe it would translate as—how do you say it?—a rebel with intellect." Then he chuckled. "Who says I can't keep my own tabs on my favorite people? Keep the coin, Hamelin. It didn't summon me."

Hamelin stretched out on his bed. "Nor did I. Now, if you'll excuse me, I have some thinking to do. You know your way out."

"Cheer up," Miguel said. "It's not as bad as you think. Not all is yet lost."

Hamelin snorted. "Being an angel, you can say things like that. I suppose you know exactly how things will end."

Miguel smiled. "Would that it were so, Hamelin, but I'm afraid angels are not as omniscient as you might think. Just as you are fond of saying, we know only what we need to know."

"Which puts you way ahead of the rest of us," Hamelin said.

"Well, yes, I suppose so," Miguel said, nodding. "But that doesn't mean we can just sweep in and solve a world of problems."

Hamelin propped himself up on his elbows. He might as well let Miguel have his say because it didn't look as though he was going anywhere until he did. "So you're not sweeping in here to interfere and solve all my problems? How very un-flyboy of you."

"I have faith that you can solve your own problems, Hamelin, but what's wrong with a little guidance along the way? Save you some time, bro."

"Okay, Miguel. I'll bite. Here's my first question. I would assume that you are sometimes privy to things that you are not allowed to act upon or share with others?"

"Yes. We keep it pretty close to the vest."

Hamelin nodded. It was one of the angelic traits he found most aggravating. For some reason, flyboys seemed to relish standing smugly around as things went to hell in a picnic basket. Hamelin had never considered it a matter of what they were allowed to say and do, but more a matter of what situations they chose to exercise power over. "Regrets?"

"Regrets?" Miguel repeated as if trying out a new word.

"Yeah, you know, did or didn't—"

"I know what it means," Miguel said. "Absolutely not. We're God's angelic host, and free will doesn't figure into that. His mission is our mission." He studied Hamelin a moment. "And *your* regrets?"

"Oh, no," Hamelin said quickly. "We are also part of—"

"No, my friend. You're the perfect example of someone who has free will tripping him up at every turn. To speak freely, in earthly vernacular, why are you feeding me such . . . *tonterías*?"

Hamelin laughed. "And that, Miguel, is the sole reason that I'm still here conversing with you. You're the only angel I know who doesn't play games. It's so refreshing. As you said, there is a soul runner saying: I know only what I need to know."

"Yes," Miguel said, nodding. "And it is a good one."

"Yes, until now. During my pickups in Christmasville, I learned something troubling, something that may lead to other deaths. And before you start," he said, throwing up a hand, "I know well the prohibition against interfering in the lives of mortals. But this time, it's different. It involves immortals, and if things play out as my information suggests, there will be catastrophic repercussions."

"Death does not come often to that village."

"No, this was my first pickup there, but I fear it will not be my last. What should I do?" Hamelin asked. "Have I learned this because I need to know it? Because I need to take action on it?"

"You can't act on what you know. That's a slippery slope. So all you need do is ask."

"I *am* asking," Hamelin said, wishing he hadn't engaged Miguel. He had been mistaken. On second thought, Miguel was just one more idiot flyboy playing at God.

"But are you asking the *right* question, Hamelin?"

Hamelin rolled his eyes. "Forget it, flyboy. I should have known you wouldn't help me." He pointed toward the door.

Miguel formed his thumb and index finger into the shape of a gun and pointed it at Hamelin. "Now you're talking."

"Huh?"

"All you had to do was ask for help. As it happens, I am in between things, and I would be glad to help. Tell me, Hamelin, what have you learned that is so troubling? Leave nothing out."

"I would suppose you've heard the details about the deaths of the elves and fairies in Christmasville?"

"Yes."

"Well," said, Hamelin. "The Pole has not been able to determine what caused the deaths, but when I picked up the latest soul—during the life review—I saw the link between them. It's *Lacrima ambrotos*, an elixir that only Santa Claus is authorized to make."

"Yes, from the Tears of the Angel."

"And why does it have that name, Miguel?"

Miguel leaned toward him and whispered, "I'd have to kill you."

"But I'm already dead," Hamelin said, chuckling. "So please, be my guest."

"Need-to-know."

"So it won't help me here?"

Miguel shook his head.

"It seems one of the Christmas elves bootlegged the concoction, fed it to his friends, and killed everyone but himself. That I can deal with. What I'm worried about is the brew getting into anyone else's hands. Should I tell the Claus the whole story? It's a complete violation of the bond between runner and transportee."

"Yes, he should be told, and no, you should not go down that path. As a matter of fact, other players in this scenario are already beginning to take responsibility for their actions. But there is yet a role for you to play. So, perhaps you are still asking the wrong questions," Miguel said. He cocked an eyebrow and waited.

Hamelin raised an eyebrow and tried to outwait the angel, although he knew it would be futile. Flyboys taught lessons the hard way, and Miguel apparently intended this to be one of those. "I give up," he said at last.

"Too soon," Miguel said, folding his cards into a side pocket. "Check in with the Runner's office and ask them to clear your schedule on my behalf. Then meet me at portal six. This shouldn't take long."

Dropping Miguel's name worked like a charm. The Weigh Station's Runner Operations immediately cleared Hamelin's visit to the North Pole. It was the baggage they were forcing on him that caused a problem. The last thing he needed was to have Nemie assigned to him again.

Elder Timothy, Hamelin's immediate superior, sat across from him in his office in Runner Operations. Timothy ran a tight ship—his desk was clean of paperwork, his bookshelves meticulously ordered by color and size, and the outer office similarly tidy. It was an amazing feat considering the current tidal wave of souls to be picked up, and runners to be assigned to do it.

"Activity will be short and sweet," Hamelin said to him. "No need to go in with a show of force. Nemie can tag along on another trip."

"It's not up for negotiation, Hamelin. Nemie should go and show a contrite face at the North Pole for the evil he participated in."

"But he is contrite."

"Well, then, it shouldn't be a big chore for him. At the rate elves are dropping dead, we can't afford to have any of our runners on the outs with Christmasville. Repentance will do his soul good."

"But getting entwined—"

Timothy got up, walked to his door, and opened it. "Report back here when you're done. You can tell me all about it."

"Yes, sir," Hamelin said, having no choice but to exit. Nemie was already sitting in the outer office waiting for him. Hamelin jerked his thumb toward the outer door and said, "I'll fill you in." He gave a nod to his former coworker Ruth and left wondering what Miguel would think of their tagging along.

Miguel was already waiting for them at portal six, and Hamelin detected no change of expression when their eyes met. Nemie's presence didn't seem to make a difference. But then again, you never could tell with a flyboy—except for Eli of the Twelfth Angelic Corps. Eli was the closest thing to a bully that the Angelic Corps could produce. He and Hamelin had tangled a few times, and as far as Hamelin was concerned, if they never met again it would be a swell world. That feeling, no doubt, was mutual. Fortunately, Miguel was at the opposite end of the spectrum from Eli, and maybe Nemie tagging along truly didn't make a difference.

"Elder Timothy insisted that—"

Miguel interrupted him with a raised hand and nodded at Nemie. Then he stepped into the portal. Having the flyboy as a point man would make things run much smoother at the Pole. Having him not flap his gums about what was going on there was an added bonus.

# Chapter Twenty-Six
# Repercussions

Santa stood before his official portrait in the Sinterklaas hall and searched for some reassurance. He found none. The face that by now should have begun to magically resemble the other Sinterklaas stared back at him as unchanged as the day the picture was taken—no Santa wrinkles, no eye twinkles, no features that made him appear like his predecessors. That despite the problems that he was adequately juggling at the moment: elven deaths, loss of the Tears of the Angel. Surely, none of his forebears could have been more challenged or done more. Hadn't he been firm enough with Rusk? Exactly what did he have to do to be accepted around here?

"Santa, I have news," Herbert said, interrupting his soul-searching.

"Of the good kind, I hope," Santa said, prying his eyes away from the troubling picture. He turned to Patterson, who was standing quietly behind Herbert. "I was beginning to think I would have to send out a search party for the two of you. Thank you for your efforts."

Patterson chuckled. "Sorry, sir. It just took me a while to work my way over to Jetsla. Will there be anything else, sir?"

"Jetsla?" Santa asked, shooting Herbert a look. "No, Patterson, just follow up on whatever is in the in-box."

"I can explain," Herbert began.

"No, you can't, Mr. Tuddy," Santa said, heading back to the central command room. "I gave you specific instructions not to go near Jetsla. That's insubordination, if I'm not mistaken. You've wasted my time and Patterson's. Give me one good reason why I shouldn't suspend you. Fourteen days is sounding pretty good right now."

Herbert closed the door. "Because I know where the Tears of the Angel is," he said, "and I've arranged to get it back."

"The Tears?" Santa said, breaking out into a beatific smile. "Rusk has it? I'll send security to pick it up posthaste—not another instant in the hands of an outsider. That plant rightfully belongs to Christmasville, and I won't play games with the welfare of hundreds of elves."

"I'm afraid it's a bit more complicated than that, sir, but the problem is solvable. It seems that Hamelin Russell is the only person who the keeper of the plant will pass it off to. When is he arriving?"

Santa's countenance darkened. "That's ridiculous. Just give me a name. I'll send someone—lots of someones—over for the plant. No more pussyfooting around. Who has it, Hamelin?"

"Um, *nada* on that, sir. Let me just tell you that it's no longer Rusk. The safekeeper is in a precarious position, and I guaranteed their safety in the handover."

"Mr. Tuddy! That was not in your authority to promise." Santa leaned over and flipped on a microphone sitting on the desk. "Mr. Patterson, please report to the control room. Patterson to the control room."

"Would you like me to hunt him down? Turnabout, fair play?" Herbert asked, edging toward the door.

"Stop!" Santa said, pinning him in place with a pointed finger. "I have the sinking feeling that you're playing games just like Rusk. Even if you aren't, I can't constantly be searching for you and wondering what commands you're issuing behind my back. Until that plant is safely back in my hands, Mr. Tuddy, and I have a complete accounting of what's going on, I am suspending you. You are to report to your residence—in the village, not the bunker—and remain there until you receive further word from me."

"But—"

"Patterson," Santa said as the clerk entered the room, "please craft an email immediately, announcing that Mr. Tuddy is taking an indefinite leave of absence from his assistant position. Run it by me before it goes out."

"Oh, how terribly sad," Patterson said, his hand touching his breast in a sympathetic gesture. "Right away, sir. And Mr. Russell has just arrived. Should I send him in, or keep him otherwise occupied for a while?"

"Bring him right in," Santa said. He directed Herbert out with the same finger he'd used moments before to hold him. "What I said, Herbert. While you're there, compose an email with the particulars of your unauthorized agreement. If I agree, I'll share them with Mr. Russell."

"Oh, but you have to," Herbert said. "It's a foolproof—"

"No!" Santa said, raising his hand. A sudden revelation hit him, He pulled his hand back and flipped it over to study his palm. Christmasville's problems were in his hands, but his grip had no strength. He was a reactionary, and he'd totally lost control of his staff. His predecessor never would have been having such an inane conversation as this. He tightened his hand into a fist. "Who is the Santa Claus?" he quietly asked.

"You, sir."

"Correct answer, Mr. Tuddy. Not you, not Noël Rusk, not the individual who has the Tears plant. Somehow, things have gotten off track around here, and I'm about to rectify that in the most painful of ways. From now on, you'll toe the line, Mr. Tuddy. No sneaking behind my back to organize protests. Did you think I didn't know? No stealing knickknacks. No. More. Nonsense! It's not your job to fix all things. If I find you subverting my position one more time, I will consider the punishments at my disposal, up to and including banishment. Do I make myself clear, *sir*?"

Herbert stood slack-jawed and wide-eyed. He nodded and walked out with his head down.

***

Herbert fought back tears as he stumbled through the hall of the Sinterklaas. How had things gotten so topsy-turvy? So close to having everybody's problems solved and getting dressed down like that? He smashed his fist into the picture of the current Claus as he walked by his portrait, sending a shower of glass to the floor. "In your face," he grumbled.

"Sir?" It was Patterson, escorting Hamelin Russell and two other individuals toward the command center. Herbert's eyes were drawn to the shorter of Hamelin's companions. The man was wrapped in an ethereal glow and moved with a peaceful elegance. Angel or otherworldly being of some other sort? Herbert could feel the probing energies of the three immortals as they studied him back.

"Fine," Herbert said, brushing aside the clerk and his concern. "I'm feeling a bit dizzy, that's all." He suddenly wheeled around. "A moment, Patterson. Santa wanted me to fill in Mr. Russell on something before their meeting. We'll just be a moment." He motioned for Hamelin to step away from the rest of the group and led him farther down the hall.

"You have that look, Herbert," Hamelin said. "You haven't come clean yet, have you?"

"Take your holier-than-thou–ness somewhere else," Herbert snarled. "I have a solution to our dilemmas right at my fingertips. Just listen, for a change."

Hamelin's eyes narrowed. "Insults are never a good opening statement, Herbert. You have one minute to whine about *your* dilemma. Go!"

"I need you—"

"Nope!"

"To serve as a go-between with the individual who has the only remaining Tears of the Angel. They didn't take it—"

"You're right," Hamelin said, shaking his head in agreement. "We both know who took it."

"Irrelevant," Herbert snapped. "She's promised to give it back, but only to you. So I need your presence at the stable for like five minutes. No more elves poisoned by illicit *Lacrima ambrotos*, and a chance to ensure that citizens of the globe can Christmas for many generations to come. Too much for you, Mr. Smarty-pants? Because if it is, then maybe that angel—or whatever he is—is more capable of understanding how important the next five minutes truly are?"

Hamelin raised an eyebrow and drew back. "There's bite to the elf. Who knew? Just one question: why does she want me? Do I know her?"

"I have no idea. Personally, I don't see the fascination. I simply mentioned you were coming to see Claus, and she hopped right on it. So are you coming or not?"

"Go in without me," Hamelin called to the others. "I need five minutes." He turned back to Herbert. "Now or never. And if this is just more of your foolishness, I will make sure that your life is a living hell. I know people."

***

Herbert led Hamelin out a back door of Quonset Alpha. "She thinks you'll be impartial, so while it may be a stretch, please try to be pleasant. She's Rusk's main squeeze, and she's taking quite a risk."

"I can't believe you gave the plant to Rusk. Smooth, Herbert. How on earth did you ever think you would come out in the black with one of the biggest wheeler-dealers this side of Vegas? What, pray tell, did you get out of it, besides a boatload of trouble?"

Herbert mumbled something unpleasant, which Hamelin chose to ignore.

The hairs on Hamelin's arms suddenly stood up, and he turned around to make sure Nemie and Miguel had not followed them. "Elf, what are you up to?"

"Huh? Nothing, I swear. This was her request, not mine. I would just as soon she fork over the plant and the affair be done with. Why are you hesitating? Say what you want and I'm on it. I'm your wingman. Let's just get this done."

Hamelin looked at the needy elf and wondered how he had ever attained a position of authority. He was a jackass of all trades and master of none—a Walmart superstore of ticky-tacky products in an enchanted land of mystery and magic. Hamelin didn't get it. And at the moment, Herbert's earnest expression indicated he wasn't getting things either. "How long do you think the others will be with the Claus?"

"Not sure," Herbert said. "Santa sent me off with something else to do. Want me to go get them?"

"Absolutely not!" Hamelin said, his arm shooting out to bar Herbert's way. "Should I not be back by the time they are finished, I need you to intercept the flyboy and the runner and keep them busy elsewhere. Whatever you do, don't let them come this way. Got it, *Spanky*?"

Herbert gave him a frown and a nod at the same time, then trotted off.

Noël Rusk's woman was standing at the opposite end of the barn, looking out across the pasture. She was statuesque, and although he could not see her face, he found her attractive. As he entered, she turned as if she'd heard him coming, but Hamelin knew that his silent footfall had not given him away.

"You've been here before," she said, smiling shyly.

"And you," he replied, walking slowly toward her. "How could you ever have considered me impartial, Marta?"

"It got you here, didn't it?" she said, still smiling. "The first time I ever toured this barn, I could feel your presence."

Her steady gaze went right through him. "And I should not be here now. I'm not alone."

She looked past him, but her eyes registered no alarm. "It's time," she said, offering him the Tears of the Angel.

He took it from her. "Thank you. Now, if you'll excuse me, a flyboy will be waiting—"

"I waited for you," she said. The pain in her voice cut him to the quick.

"They watch now," Hamelin said, avoiding her eyes. "It would not have turned out well. *This* will not turn out well. I have to go."

"Transport me," she said as he turned from her. "My time is long past due. This is painful without you."

"Noël Rusk?" he scoffed. "You seem to have done quite well for yourself. What could you possibly want?"

"You," she whispered.

"I can't have this conversation here . . . now." He began walking.

"Then when?" Marta said, and she followed him as he walked away from her. "What's the value of an immortal life if you can't fill it with the things that you care about, that have meaning? I want you to transport me into the afterlife, as I should have been years ago. Please reverse this unjust and ill-conceived decision."

"I can't," Hamelin said, circling around so that he was behind her now. If he had to leave by the back door and draw her away from Quonset Hut Alpha, he would choose that. "I fear for your soul. To kill a man is a mortal sin, Marta, and it's doesn't bode well for your eternal destination. I could not transport you *there*."

"I have repented, and repented, and repented yet again. I'll take my chances, Hamelin. If you can't transport me, then have pity and let someone else do it." She watched him a moment, then said, "I forgive you." Then she turned and hurried toward the stable doors, toward the Quonset hut and an earthly escape that Nemie would readily give her.

Hamelin didn't chase her. If her mind was made up, who was he to interfere if a mulligan wanted to give a second life back? "Don't do it this way," he called after her. "I'll give you a date."

That brought her to a halt just inside the doorway. "Name it."

"After Christmasville quiets down. When the angel and the other runner are far from here. Otherwise, they will sense the energy as your soul releases its earthly ties. If you go to them now, there will be questions . . . that will be difficult for me to answer. When they find out that I failed to transport you and gave you a second chance at life, there will be grave repercussions for me. If you have any feelings left for me, please let me end this *injustice*, as you call it, in the subtlest way possible. Otherwise, I will most certainly be damned to hell."

When she didn't respond to his plea, he added, "Unless that's what you seek. It is a funny love that would desire the damnation of another so as not to be alone in eternal torment. I have been there, and you won't find any solace in me being consigned there forever. I am truly sorry, Marta, for the pain I have caused you."

A shrill, clear whistle blasted out from Quonset Hut Alpha. It was Herbert, at the front door, waving his arms wildly as he hopped up and down.

"No need to rush away," Hamelin said. "They will be here soon enough. Everyone has a choice, Marta, and I understand if this is yours."

"Not here," she said, backing away from the door. "Will you keep a promise to come for me soon? Here or elsewhere, you can find me?"

"I promise, and yes, I will know," he said, motioning her to follow him out the rear stable doors. She ran for him, reaching out for his hand, but he tucked it behind his back and jogged out the double doors without touching her.

"I'm sorry," he said, stopping when they were hidden behind the barn. "I can't go any farther. Jetsla is that way," he said pointing. "Follow the path until it intersects with the next Quonset hut. From there, your way should be clear. Please don't try to contact me again. I'll find you. Okay?"

She nodded, her eyes welling with tears, and trembling lips replacing her earlier smile. "I love you, Hamelin. Please don't break your promise."

"I promise," Hamelin repeated. "But I want you to consider one thing in return. Leave him. Separate yourself from a despicable human being. That's all I ask."

He left her. Not for the first time, but for one of the last. Marta, the love of his life, had issued an ultimatum he could not ignore.

# Chapter Twenty-Seven
# RIP

Herbert took the Tears of the Angel from Hamelin. "Sweet relief," he said, cradling the plant as if it were a newborn elf.

"Where are the others?"

"Still inside," Herbert pulled a yellowing leaf and the last of its blossoms from one of the branches. "Chop, chop, Hamelin. Let's put an end to this drama."

They found Santa, Miguel, and Nemie huddled at the command center's main table, speaking in low tones and looking as if someone had died. Patterson sat unobtrusively in a corner, pulling on his scraggly beard and taking notes. "Merry Christmas!" Herbert said, sweeping into the room.

Santa's enormous white eyebrows shot up from where they had been hooding his eyes. "Dear Lord, you have it!" he said. He rushed forward and swept the plant from Herbert before the elf could launch into the heroic story of its recovery.

"And it's not too much the worse for wear," Santa said, holding it aloft for the others to admire. He touched a yellowing leaf and sent it fluttering into the pot. "Nothing that Fermier and his boys in the garden can't fix with a little care and a lot of affection."

Santa turned to Patterson. "Go tell the main cottage that we have the plant back."

"Yes, sir," Patterson said, reaching for the pot.

"Just bring Fermier back to fetch it," Santa said, drawing the plant closer to his voluminous belly. "From now on, he'll be babysitting it day and night." He returned to his seat and nestled the poinsettia pot between two notebooks in the center of the table. His face suddenly returned to the pensive expression Herbert had seen upon entering.

"I thought you'd be happy," Herbert said, sensing distress not only from Claus but from Nemie as well. The angel was impossible to read.

"It's not that I'm not," Santa said, a slight quiver in his voice. "Truly, Christmasville is grateful, Herbert. It's just that things continue to tumble from bad to worse." He fell silent a moment, then said, "Six elves reported to sickbay this morning. That makes seven when you include Lucky Larry. He was admitted last night, and they don't . . . they don't . . . well, maybe not so lucky." He dabbed his cheek with the back of his hand. "I'm sorry, I need a moment." He walked into his bedroom and closed the door.

"So we still have problems," Hamelin said to Miguel.

"I would say so, Hamelin. Unfortunately, when one fire is put out, another one pops up. And temptations are everywhere. Still, having the Tears back will solve one. The Claus can handle the rest, I think."

Miguel turned to Nemie, who couldn't seem to take his eyes off Hamelin. "I must go. Fill Hamelin in?"

Nemie nodded.

The door to Santa's bedroom creaked open, and although he looked a bit haggard, Santa emerged with a composed expression. "Herbert, please sit down."

"Yes, sir," Herbert said taking a seat at the table. Delivering the Tears made everything better. Santa would reconsider his rash decision to suspend him.

"Hamelin, if you'll join us too," Santa said. "You have my deepest appreciation for your role in getting the Tears of the Angel back."

"Sit here," Nemie said, patting Miguel's empty chair. "I can't wait for you to regale us with the details."

"I'll stand, if you don't mind," Hamelin said, and he moved to the single window on the far wall and leaned against the sill.

"Merciful heavens," Santa said, dropping his coffee mug. Coffee and broken china flew everywhere. "How did that happen?"

All eyes turned toward the command desk, and the group watched in horror as the last leaf on the Tears of the Angel detached from the plant and floated into the bottom of the pot to join the rest of its mates. Herbert bit his lip and groaned. Master Gardner Fermier's expertise would no longer be needed. This plant was officially dead.

The office door swung open, and Patterson stuck his head in. "Sorry to interrupt, sir, but I did knock. Dr. Dash said to fetch you. Solomon is awake and he's talking."

Herbert felt every ounce of energy drain out of him. The little guy would blab everything, and just like the Tears of the Angel, he would soon be a goner.

Nemie caught Hamelin's eye. "May I have a few words with you outside?"

"Plenty of time to talk later," Hamelin said, holding the door for Santa. "Visiting Solomon is next on my agenda. You stay here and wait for Fermier."

# Chapter Twenty-Eight
## Singing Like a Fairy

Santa hurried into Boston Charlie and entered the hastily constructed sickbay just off the hastily constructed morgue. At the rate things were developing, he might have to dedicate a whole new Quonset hut to the village's ever-growing health crisis. He almost bowled over Dr. Dash as the ME came out of the unit.

Santa shuffled backward three steps. "Please don't tell me we've had more," he said.

"No, no, status quo," Dash said. "Being the only doctor, I'm on double duty at the moment. I have no idea what this new malady is. And honestly, there isn't a lot I can do except make the patient comfortable. They'll either get better, or to be somewhat coarse, I'll have to switch over to my ME hat."

Santa shook his head and sighed wearily.

"But good news," Dash said as he pushed two fingers into Santa's shoulder. "Something is going our way. Your chatty little friend Solomon is wide awake and *ready to blow this joint*—his words, not mine. And that would be wonderful, because he's driving Nurse Kelly crazy. What a lady's man."

"Hmm. Then let me at the Casanova, and maybe we can all be better soon. You've done yeoman's work here, and you have my undying gratitude. Who would have thought that when we sent you to medical school to learn about anatomy in order to build more realistic action figures we would have to pull you off the design board for this, huh?"

Dash shrugged. "Service is service. Hang in there, Claus. I'll let you know if anything changes."

Inside the infirmary, Santa and Hamelin walked past three curtained-off patient areas before reaching Solomon Grundy. When Santa peeked around the last curtain, he found the fairy sacked out in a pink Barbie doll bed with a matching nightstand and plastic chair close by. For heaven's sake, couldn't they have found something a little more GI Joe–ish? The little guy could become ferocious when ridiculed.

While Hamelin remained outside the curtain, Santa pulled a sitting chair up beside Solomon's bedside table and prepared to watch him snooze for a while. However, his ample rear end had barely begun to warm the seat when Solomon snapped awake with a buzz and a flutter that brightened his feathers from dull maroon to vibrant scarlet.

"I thought you had forgotten me," Solomon said, sniffing dramatically. "It took you long enough to work your way down the row."

Santa chuckled. "Actually, I started at this end. Dr. Dash says you're on the mend. How do you feel?"

"Mended. So if you bring me my clothes, I'll be up and about, doing something useful."

Santa couldn't recall Solomon ever contributing anything of worth, but he did sorely miss his company. "I'll arrange it on my way out—right after we talk about what happened, so I can spare others from going through what you've endured. Any ideas how you were poisoned? New diet? Visit somewhere outside the dome? What?"

Solomon put his hands to his head. "*Oy vey!* Worst *Lacrima ambrotos* ever. How do you drink that rot gut?" He stuck his forefinger in his mouth and made upchucking noise.

"Ambrotos? Where did you get the ambrotos?"

Solomon's finger hovered just outside his mouth. "Uh . . ."

"Who gave you the ambrotos, Solomon?"

"Mmm . . . Was someone bringing my clothes?"

"*Solomon!* No answer, no clothes! Out with it, Mr. Grundy!"

Solomon began to quiver, and his bright glow disappeared as a darker shade of red appeared on his chest and chased his scarlet coloring down to the tips of his feathers, where it vanished in silver sparks. He threw the bedsheet up over his head and moaned, "Herbert."

"Herbert Tuddy. You're sure? Where?"

The bed sheet emitted a long, slow hiss. "At his party: Ticker, Tocker, Beltzer, Huban, Fatty Winkler. We thought it was terrible stuff. For all his boasting, Tuddy could never be worthy of the Santa Claus mantle. He's a terrible cook. I had my doubts as soon as I caught him with that little blue plant. And it started out so well: party ice cubes, strobe lights, techno music, and a few loose wom—" Solomon began a fit of coughing.

Ticker, Tocker, Beltzer, and the rest—dead now. And the plant too. Santa stood up. "I've got to go, Solomon. I'll have them get your clothes. Try to take it easy, okay?"

"Am I in trouble?" Solomon asked from under the covers. The bedsheet was quivering, but Santa couldn't decide whether Solomon was having a relapse, or shaking in terror.

"Oh, there's trouble in River City, all right, but you don't trouble your precious head about it."

As Santa and Hamelin passed the duty nurse on their way out, Santa said, "Please tell the good doctor that I need to speak with him in Alpha immediately. Whatever I'm in the middle of, he should interrupt. Oh, and Mr. Grundy is asking for his clothes."

Now, where is that lying, inept Herbert Spanky Tuddy?

## Chapter Twenty-Nine
# Anything But the Naughty Book

Herbert sat down on the curb outside Sudley Watermiester's Emporium at the corner of Main and Candy Cane Streets. As much as he'd like to dig a hole and hide in it, that wasn't really possible in a land of floating sea ice. He couldn't think of anywhere that Santa couldn't find him. Once word got around about what a loser he was, every elf and his brother would be looking down on him. Behind him, a black speaker attached to the building's soffit blasted out a jolly rendition of "Here Comes Santa Claus." Herbert got up, yanked up one of the oversize red-and-white plastic candy canes lining the walkway, swung it hard at the music box, and pulled the wiring loose. He was rewarded with instant silence. He returned to the curb to await whoever would come to get him. It probably wouldn't be the Claus. He had more meaningful things to do than fool with an underutilized and underappreciated elf with no job title and occasional bouts of bad judgment.

Of all the ways he had pictured being apprehended, Herbert never imagined this one. One hundred or so feet down Candy Cane Street, he saw P. J. Foos rapidly bearing down on him—coming on behalf of Noël Rusk, no doubt. The set of his jaw and the clench of his fists suggested a meeting not to Herbert's benefit. He scrambled to his feet. How in the world had the double-dealing twerp tracked him here? Out of the corner of his eye, Herbert also noticed Sudley Watermiester peeking out of his doorway. Son of a gun, the businessman had sold him out!

"Spanky!" Foos called.

"Herbert!" It was Patterson, coming from the other direction down Main Street. Judging speed and distance, Herbert reckoned that if he remained stationary, both elf and man would corner him at the same time. Should he throw himself on the mercy of the tool of a mercurial, sinfully rich man whose scruples shifted with his desires, or should he throw his lot in with his own kind, who had him dead to rights and would certainly stick him where it hurt?

Herbert bolted for Patterson and, reaching him, kept sprinting. He could swear he heard the pounding of feet behind him, but despite the earnest pleas from both pursuers to hold up, he didn't stop running until he reached Quonset Hut Alpha and scooted safely inside the door. He could sort it out with Patterson later. He hoped never to face Rusk and company again.

He hit the communications room in a rush and flung open the door with a little too much force. It slammed against the wall and rebounded. Santa, Hamelin, and Nemie looked up, startled. Herbert wouldn't dispute Solomon's admission about the party. It was time to suck things up and take his lumps. Ultimately, his punishment would be in Santa's kind and fair hands.

"Solomon's given you the full story?" Herbert asked, dispensing with the niceties.

"I would expect so," Santa said. He closed the oversize notebook lying open in front of him and slid it back into place on the shelf behind him. It was the Naughty Book. Oh, boy, the little feather duster must have sung like a canary.

Herbert cast his head down, not in an act of feigned humility, but in true mortification. He had always thought that the loss of prestige would be the deepest blow one could suffer, but he was wrong. Without the respect of one's peers, one had nothing. How could he ever face the rest of Christmasville? His mind raced back to the airplane ticket Foos had given him. Was it possible that it hadn't been canceled yet? "Would you like me to elaborate on anything?" he asked. Knowing that he no longer had a seat at the table, he took the chair in the corner—a witness stand of sorts.

"Yes, and without a longwinded story defending your actions. I have a sickbay full of elves. You made *Lacrima ambrotos* without authority to do so?"

"Yes."

"Who else had access besides your fellow partiers? I'd ask the others, but with the exception of Solomon, they are all dead."

Herbert hung his head and nodded.

"No! Look right into my eyes, Herbert Spanky Tuddy, and tell me who else. Who else might have been exposed that we can potentially save?"

Herbert wiped his tearing eyes and dragged them back up to meet Santa's steely gaze hovering above two steepled hands. "No one. The party was an intimate gathering of a tight-knit group of friends. That's it. Except for the fairies. Solomon horned his way in when he found out about the ambrotos. He brought some buddies. And that was it. I swear. If anyone else is sick, I don't see how it could be from the elixir. That's the honest truth, sir. Cross my heart and hope to die," he said, making the sign of the cross on his chest. The intensity of Santa's eyes forced his gaze floorward again.

Santa shifted in his chair. "I'll accept that for the moment. Now, what else have you stolen, Mr. Tuddy?"

Herbert's eyes suddenly darted to one of Santa's bookcases—the one with the metal mouse figurines sitting on top. There were recent additions—some of his most cherished acquisitions, including the twelve-inch-tall yellow-and-black plastic Mr. Peanut; the majestically rearing plastic palomino horse; the metal mouse he had *borrowed* earlier, several elaborate knobs; and half a dozen other pilfered oddities. Bad move on Herbert's part. When he glanced back at Santa, the Claus's eyes were not on him, but on the shelf. How had his things moved from the bunker to here? He could see it now. They would nail him for every indiscretion. Talking about piling on.

"So that's where Sawyer's peanut bank went to," Santa said. "As I recall, we looked high and low for that one. Still have money in it?"

Herbert cast his eyes to the floor. "Yes, sir. It, uh, wasn't about the mon—"

"And if I'm not mistaken, isn't that Trigger, the first-in-a-series Roy Rogers action figure that Ebony Maris has been crying about for going on two years? Thank heavens you found it. She'll be so pleased."

"Yes, sir," Herbert said, wishing he could disappear under the table. "She'll be so happy when I return it."

"Oh, yes, Herbert, you'll start making amends by returning everything."

"Yes, sir."

"I just have one question," Santa said, sliding his cheaters down his nose as his crystal blue eyes locked on Herbert. "What the hell is wrong with you, son?"

"H-h-hell?" Herbert said. Never had he ever heard a Claus stoop so low as to use profanity. Had Herbert fallen that far that he needed to be spoken to so harshly?"

"Yes, you heard me, and maybe you should have heard it a long time ago. You've known nothing but privilege your entire life—your father a shop steward and your mother a gifted seamstress. You moved right to the head of the factory table. No struggles or jockeying to be noticed." Santa threw his hands up. "Too much, too soon? What? Tell me, Herbert, why are you just so . . . so *naughty*?"

Herbert recoiled. Naughty? As in the Naughty Book? His knees began to knock. "I don't have an answer. But I'm trying very hard to change my ways. Like the Tears of the Angel. Yes, it was wrong to take it. But look at what I did to get it back. I'm trying, I'm really trying."

"And I forgive you, Herbert."

"Whew," Herbert said, his body deflating as he released bottled-up tension. "I wasn't sure that—"

Santa held up a meaty hand. "But my personal forgiveness shouldn't be confused with societal forgiveness, which will be extended to you after you make amends for the atrocities you've committed against your fellow elves."

"Oh, I shall, I shall. Just tell me when and where and I will wholeheartedly apologize, sir."

"In accordance with the laws of Christmasville and my authority as established therein," Santa said, reading from something on the desk in front of him. "I am ordering you to be held in detention forthwith for the next seven days until a jury of your peers can be convened to address your violation of Elven Statutes Six, Eight, and Thirteen: murder, theft, and fibbing."

Herbert's jaw dropped. Santa walked to the door and opened it to three hefty poker-faced elves dressed in red peacekeeper uniforms, standing at attention on the other side. "These gentlemen will see you to your temporary quarters in cottage three, where you will remain until the jury is ready to hear your case. You can also request a representative of your own choosing to speak for you. Is there anything else you wish to add before you leave?"

"They don't need to handcuff me or anything like that," Herbert said as he left the room. After all, there was absolutely nowhere he could run to, and the humiliation would be unbearable.

"Cuffing won't be necessary," Santa said to the elves. "Good day, Herbert." And he closed the door, shutting Herbert out.

Herbert walked ahead of the uniformed elves; he wouldn't suffer the indignity of being led away to house arrest. He kept his head down for fear of the looks he might already be receiving from other villagers. Information traveled fast in a small town, and they were probably already talking about him. He just hoped that they had heard of his valiant effort to retrieve the Tears of the Angel. That should count for something. It certainly had Noël Rusk out to get him. Fear flashed through Herbert. Where was Foos, and exactly how secure was cottage three when it came to keeping unwanted guests out?

\*\*\*

Santa cradled his head in his hands and tried to rid his memory of the woebegone expression on Herbert Tuddy's face. Would Christmasville *ever* be filled with joy again?

"I know exhaustion when I see it, Nicholas." It was Dr. Dash standing at the door of the control room. He looked at Hamelin and Nemie, and they exchanged polite nods. "Nicholas, shall I come back, or would you prefer to come and find me?"

Santa dropped his hands and smiled wearily. "No, it's fine. I know that we will eventually find our way out of this. It's just so hard." He directed the good doctor to the empty chair beside Hamelin. "Dash, meet Hamelin and Nemie. They've been sent from the Weigh Station to help. I wanted to tell you that Solomon said something that may answer some of our questions. Apparently, Herbert bootlegged *Lacrima ambrotos* and that's what has been sickening and killing our villagers."

"Ambrotos?" said the doc. "But how? You're the only one with the authority, the recipe, or the main ingredient."

"Well, precisely. And that's why it's poisoning everyone. The ones who died ingested it at Herbert's party. Solomon verified that. I'm not sure yet how your current patients got hold of it. We'll keep digging. In the meantime, does this help your treatment plan for the ones we have in sickbay?"

Dash shook his head. "At least it's something. I'll do my best."

"That's all I can ask," Santa said.

# Chapter Thirty
# Correcting False Assumptions

As Solomon dozed in the warmth of the desk lamp, Santa studied the fairy's profile: a fluff of scarlet feathers tumbled down his forehead to a petite upturned nose, and lips that were parted in gentle snoring. Oh, sweet oblivion. Santa could use a nap like that about now, only he might choose to sleep far too long.

Herbert was safely secured in cottage 3, and it was just a matter of time before all Christmasville turned topsy-turvy over the whole unfortunate affair. Santa's gaze floated around the control room, finding little comfort in the cold gray metal furniture, black plastic log books, and beeping equipment. Some elves aspired to be elevated to Claus—Tuddy, for instance—but he never had, and that made it even stranger that he had been anointed. Well, that hadn't turned out, had it? For how could the Claus separate the naughty from the nice when he clearly had no special insight into people? He was still very much Ethan, an unremarkable elf who enjoyed whittling pieces of black walnut into heirloom keepsakes.

He looked at the Tears of the Angel plant still sitting shrunken and bare on the control room desk. He picked up the dead husk. "Well, that's the end of it," he said to Hamelin and Nemie, who were sitting on opposite sides of the room. There was a coldness between the two that Santa couldn't decipher. "Who would have thought it—the last of the Tears of the Angel? It had a good run. I just wish it hadn't ended on my watch. Fermier said it would have survived its little adventure if it had remained in an elf's possession. Herbert, Herbert, Herbert, what were you thinking?"

"Last?" Nemie said, pushing up in his seat. "Who told you that?"

Santa frowned. "N-no one. It's just one of those things I know— like how to launch the sleigh or circumnavigate the world in a single night. The Claus *knows*." He paused and thought about it. It seemed he *had* acquired some unique Clausian skills.

"Well, Mr. Claus," Nemie said, "apparently not everything. There are others."

Santa's eyebrows lifted. "You've seen them?"

Nemie shot a quick look at Hamelin and something unspoken passed between them.

"Nemie," Hamelin said, "is the son of Coeus, Titan of inquisitiveness and intellect. Sometimes, we're surprised by what deep and sudden insight he has. His knowledge can be astounding."

*Insight?* Santa brightened. Nemie, raised in the chaos of hell, for the moment a yin to his peaceful yang?

"Tell us," Hamelin said.

"It was Caina on Cocytus, the frozen lake bordering hell, where my foster father, Beelzebub Number Two took me as a little boy. I remember plants such as this growing on the far side of the lake. They were of rare, blue loveliness in such a desolate place, and I wanted to cross and pick some." He rubbed his left cheek and laughed ruefully. "That request didn't go so well."

"Well, I can make everyone happy," Hamelin said, rising. "Just draw me a map, Nemie. Nothing fancy. I'll take the portal there, hop out long enough to grab a plant or two, and be back before you know it. Your troubles will be over, Santa, and we can get back to transporting souls. The world sorely needs us at the moment."

Nemie shook his head. "You're not going there alone. It's too accessible to hell. I'm coming with you."

"The Weigh Station would have my hide if I let you anywhere near hell. Your father's spies are everywhere."

Nemie rolled his eyes. "Yeah, like they would pass up a chance to shanghai you again if I weren't there. It's either both of us or neither." He crossed his arms and thrust out his chin.

"Ahem," Santa said, clearing his throat. "I'm afraid it must be all for one and one for all. If we've learned anything, it's that unless the Tears is in the possession of an elf, it will not survive. I'm coming with you." He swept the pile of papers before him into a ragged stack and sprang to his feet in a nimble move that belied his size. "I will just need a few minutes."

"Whoa, Hoss," Hamelin said, raising both hands. "We have a problem. You can't ride the portal system. Only the dead . . ."

"Oh," Santa said, his face falling.

"He can take the sleigh," Nemie said. "It's okay to do that this time of year, right? I can ride shotgun, if you want."

Santa shook his head. "Bigger problem."

"Only at Christmas?" There was a note of disappointment in Nemie's voice.

"Oh, no, it's not that. It's just . . ." Santa paused a moment, shifting his weight from one foot to the other. "The Clausian license to drive the sleigh, er, ah, seems to have lapsed with the passing of my predecessor. I had Herbert working on a renewal, but I don't think that's gone through yet. We're six months out from needing it, so I guess we figured no rush."

"Surely, there is someone else you trust to go in your stead?" Hamelin said.

"There is only one other elf who has the authority to drive the sleigh, but I don't trust him."

"Who?" Hamelin asked. "Nemie and I can put the fear of God in them. Trust me, and I can assure that you will be able to trust *him*."

Santa ran his hands down his neatly trimmed white beard, trying to wipe the weariness from his face. He couldn't even make himself utter it.

Hamelin groaned. "It's Herbert, isn't it?"

The Claus closed his eyes and nodded. "One simply doesn't forgive and forget all the mischief that misguided elf has created—the source of the very mess we're scrambling to clean up."

The room fell silent.

"Got it!" Hamelin said, a huge grin suddenly split his face from ear to ear. "I've been known to tool around in some pretty sweet rides in my time, and I've ridden in the sleigh once. Driving it didn't seem to be so big a deal. How about teaching me?"

Santa shook his head. "Same problem as me, Hamelin: no license. While a traffic ticket may not mean anything to you, I'd hate to risk them getting ticked off and impounding the sled."

Hamelin's grin vanished.

"So it's Herbert," Nemie said. "That's if he has the appropriate legal documents."

"He does," Santa said without enthusiasm. "But—"

"If he's all we've got, there are no buts about it, Santa," Hamelin said. "Beggars can't be choosers. Herbert drives, and you'll go to supervise. I doubt he'll need much oversight. After suffering the indignity of house arrest, I suspect that Herbert will be most amenable to playing by the rules. I'll go spring him."

"Right behind you," Nemie said.

\*\*\*

Three quaint A-frame chalets stood three hundred feet behind the Quonset Huts. As Hamelin understood it, the Claus lived with his wife, Violet, in the nearest and biggest, the wife of the recently deceased Santa occupied the midsize guest cottage, and tucked behind those two stood a second and smaller guest quarter where Herbert Tuddy was cooling his jets.

As they approached the residences, Hamelin cut his normal walking speed in half. "Nemie," he said pointing opposite the cottages, "maybe you should hit the stable and give Gustav a heads-up about taking the sleigh out. It will take a while to hitch the team up."

"Sure," Nemie said, keeping an even slower pace behind him, "but we need conversation first. I want to know what happened in the barn earlier."

"Nothing dramatic," Hamelin lied. "It's a barn with manure, smelly animals, and lovely oiled leather. What were you expecting? The woman gave me the plant without any sort of protest or bargaining. Short and sweet, let's eat."

"No reminiscing?" Nemie asked, staring intently. "She asked for you, so you knew her, right?"

"Our paths have crossed."

"Where?"

Hamelin quirked an eyebrow. "Is your life so boring that you need me to bore you with mine, too?"

"Oh, come on, Hamelin. I may not be centuries old like you, but I certainly wasn't born yesterday. I felt the energy. I felt the vibes, and they were all wrong."

"Vibes?"

"Don't you trust me?"

"Of course," Hamelin said. But that was a lie, too. He trusted few, and Nemie was still an unknown quantity. The new soul runner might be on his acquaintance list, but he still hadn't moved—and might never make the jump—to trusted-friend list. He kept his gaze on Nemie, but his thoughts traveled back to Marta as she left him to return to the Jetsla compound. If she did as he asked, there would be no further troubling vibes.

"Don't bother to deny it, Hamelin. A soul was begging to be picked up. What the hell went on in there, and why didn't you transport them? Or call for someone else to do it? What game are you playing?"

"No game. I have my instructions, and as they say, it's way above your pay grade. Occupy yourself with something you can make a difference at." When Nemie opened his mouth to respond, Hamelin glared at him. "Case closed. Got it?"

Hamelin got no buy-in. Nemie walked away from him and studied three elves pushing laundry carts across the tarmac to a blue jet. Nemie was too sharp for Hamelin's good.

"I'll go talk to Gustav and then I'll meet you back at the command center," Nemie said. He walked off without giving Hamelin another look.

Hamelin let him go. Chances were high that the young runner would report the incident as soon as they returned to the Station, but bad vibes were a matter of interpretation, and who said a newly minted soul runner—even one as gifted as Nemesis, son of Coeus—excelled at that? For the good of everyone, Marta would need to be transported sooner rather than later, before someone started an inquiry. Hamelin would never forgive his partner for interfering.

The peacekeepers posted at cottage 3's front door parted and let Hamelin enter. Either security was very lax, or they didn't care who visited Herbert, as long as he didn't accompany the visitor on the way out. Hamelin found the disgraced elf hunched over a writing tablet at the kitchen table and chewing his fingernails.

Herbert's face blanched when he saw Hamelin. "Where's Santa?" he said, his eyes darting to the front door. He got up and put the table between them. "I'm not going with you without a fight."

"Herbert, do you actually think that a table would keep your soul away from me if I were set to take it?"

Herbert brandished his pen. "I'll fight you."

Hamelin's eyes crinkled in amusement. "Mightier than the sword, but another time, okay? The Claus sent me to fetch you, so listen up because I'm not one to repeat myself. Where is Santa's new license to drive the Santa-mobile?"

Herbert frowned and lowered his pen. "He's complaining about that now, is he? At a time like this? The application is on my desk in the bunker. For heaven's sake, we're still six months out from Christmas."

"No, he's not. I'm just checking. You must have been born under a lucky star, Herbert, because you're getting a very gentle reprieve. If there is no license, then you must be the one to drive the sleigh. Come on, let's get cracking."

Herbert raised the fountain pen into fighting position again. "Uh-uh. There's no need to fly the sleigh in June. I don't trust you."

"Nor I you. But if you're as smooth an operator as I think you are, you'll seize the opportunity to be helpful in a difficult situation. I think you call them brownie points."

Herbert cupped his hands to his mouth and yelled, "Guards!"

Two wide-eyed peacekeepers immediately burst into the room. "Sir?" said one, looking back and forth between Hamelin and Herbert.

"False alarm," Hamelin said, waving them back out. "By Santa's orders, Herbert and I will be walking back to Quonset Hut Alpha. If you need to confirm—"

"Yes, sir, already confirmed, sir," one of the peacekeepers said. He clicked his heels together, and the two disappeared to resume their watch.

Herbert began shaking his head. "Why should—"

Hamelin raised an index finger. "Please close it, Herbert. Don't blow this with stupid questions and thoughts of what's in it for you. It seems there are other Tears of the Angel plants in this world. You and Santa will fly the sleigh to their location and bring some back. It will undo some of the damage you inflicted by stealing one in the first place."

Herbert hesitated, mistrust still reflecting in his eyes.

"As much as you don't deserve it," Hamelin said, "when once it's done, you might actually be considered a hero."

Herbert headed for the door. "Well, then, what are we waiting for? And where are we going?"

"Helldale."

"Say what?"

"The suburbs of hell. Don't get the notion that this is will be a cakewalk. We'll be close enough to hell to hear the screams."

"Oh, dear God."

"Good move. A few prayers couldn't hurt. Now, hurry up. I've been uncharacteristically patient with you."

# Chapter Thirty-One
# Crossing Lines and Dialing Codes

Just when Herbert had begun to despair of ever walking free again, he inexplicably found himself not only sprung from a prison of his own making, but in a commanding position on a mission that just might save his tuchus and restore his position in the Christmasville hierarchy. However, Hamelin was wrong with the bit about the lucky star. Excellence would always out.

When Herbert and Hamelin arrived at the command center, the Claus was all smiles. Herbert expected no less. It was the nature of the Clausian beast to be bright and jolly. It worked nicely in Herbert's favor. If he ever assumed his rightful place as Santa, he'd have to fight that inclination. It left one wide open for manipulation. The cheery fat man was already formally dressed in his fleecy red working suit, and was gamely fighting his enormous belly as he leaned over and yanked on his big, heavy, black boots.

"I can have us out of here within the hour," Herbert said. "Just give me a few GPS coordinates. We'll be back before lunchtime."

Santa shot Hamelin a look. "Did you tell him?"

Hamelin nodded. "I did. I told him we were visiting Helldale."

Santa arched an eyebrow and turned toward Herbert. "The Tears of the Angel can be found only along the Cocytus, one of the rivers surrounding hell. Have you heard of Caina?"

Herbert turned on Hamelin. "Ca-Ca-Ca-Caina? The place where punishment is meted out to those who betray their own blood? Cain against Abel? Man against man? Elf against elf? That's your *Helldale*? Is this some sort of cruel joke? You people are out of your minds. Count me out," he said.

Nemie, who had been sitting unobtrusively in a corner, stirred to life. "You'll be fine," he said. "I do not think your sins here in Christmasville are so egregious as to condemn you to eternal suffering in the frozen lake, Caina."

"Like I'm interested in your presumptions," Herbert snapped. "I'm aware of your ties to the underworld." He turned to Santa. "What's to stop him from dealing on the devil's behalf? You and I shouldn't *both* be put in danger. Who will the village turn to if something happens to us? I should remain behind and hold down the fort."

Santa finished double-knotting the laces on his boots, stood up, and began adjusting his wide black belt. "Nemie will be fine, we'll be fine, and it might be a good time to remind you that you are no longer second in command around here."

"So I'm expendable, is that what you're saying? Well, thank you for that, *Mr. Claus.*"

Santa's head slowly tipped to the right and he regarded Herbert thoughtfully. "In times like this, Herbert, everyone must be ready to sacrifice. It's what we do for each other. The choice is yours, however. But remember, the only reason you are standing in Quonset Hut Alpha and not cottage three is that you are the sole elf licensed to drive the sleigh. How far along is my renewal, by the way?"

"It's in the works," Herbert said, fudging a little.

"Hmm. How unfortunate." Santa gave a final tug on his belt.

"Nevertheless, are you in or out, Herbert? We're not tarrying. If I must, I'll drive the sleigh myself. It will put Christmas at risk for the sweet children of the world, but that's my responsibility to bear."

Santa's stare forced Herbert to shift his eyes away. Hamelin and Nemie were also staring—judging in their own quiet way—but it was Santa's expression that gutted him. He'd never seen the Claus look so stern. Oh, bonbons, they had him! "For the children," he said quietly, nodding. "I'll meet you in the stable."

As he walked out, they didn't clap him on the back or even thank him. That made him feel even worse that he had initially balked. The question that Santa had flung at him earlier was spot on. *What the hell is wrong with you, Herbert?*

Nope, wrong question. Herbert walked out of Quonset Hut Alpha, into the midst of a throng of elves—a green sea of perhaps fifty shouting, sign-waving protesters chanting, "We strike! No bike! Under the Christmas tree! We strike! No bike! Under the Christmas tree." Melody was standing at the front of the pack with a neatly lettered sign that read, SAVE OUR JOBS. SEND JETSLA HOME.

"What are you doing? It was a *no* vote," he shouted at her over the din.

"Yeah, we're doing this, man. Rank and file pushed for a second vote, and it was *hell yes,* this time. Sick-outs on every line. No quotas will be met. And a big help you were. I don't know what's wrong with you Herbert, but you've changed. Just too busy to notice what's going on."

Herbert took her by the arm and escorted her through the crowd. "Look! This couldn't come at a worse time. You've got to back everybody off. Quonset Hut Alpha has, perhaps, the worst crisis in the history of Christmasville. Our very survival is at stake here. The old man and I are taking the sleigh out to try and fix—"

"No, you're not," she said, pulling her arm free. "Nothing flies in or out, including the sleigh, until we get what we want." She turned around and yelled back at the crowd, "Hey, you, Lumberyard Jody, take a group over to the barn and park 'em. We need to make sure the sleigh stays grounded."

"But . . ." Herbert began.

"Sorry, Herbert. All the managers are resigning their positions. As of . . ." She checked her watch. ". . . ten minutes ago. We're all rank and file now. What's it going to be with you? Resign and join us. There is no in-between; you're either with us or agin' us."

Herbert hesitated. Showing solidarity would be difficult. He had no position to resign, but revealing that he had been unceremoniously booted would put a big "L" for loser on his forehead.

"Traitor!" she snarled. She bumped past him and disappeared into the noisy throng.

He looked to the barn, where Jody was heading, and then back again at Melody's group. Dear lord, he was suddenly on the outs with everyone. Melody was right. To survive, he had to choose.

He bolted for Boston Charlie, made a quick left between it and Alpha, and headed for the locked side entrance that only he and Santa had a key for. He unlocked the unmarked metal door and raced down an unused corridor that ran straight to the command center.

"They're striking," he blurted out as he entered. "We'll have to push our way into the stable and, uh, trample a few elves in the process."

"Striking?" Santa rose from his tête-à-tête with the soul runners and swept out of the room, heading toward the front door of the Quonset hut, his heavy boots clomping through the uncharacteristically empty and, otherwise, eerily silent hut.

"Wait," Herbert said, pulling on his arm to slow him down. "Don't invite the attention, sir. I say we sneak out the side door and make a run for the stable. That's the only way we'll get out of here. Get Gustav on the horn and have him make everything ready, sir. Honestly, it's us against them. They won't listen. You must act boldly, or you'll be stuck here for hours in negotiations."

Santa halted midway through the vast front hall that served as a staging area in the months leading up to zero hour, Christmas Eve. The strikers' chants filled the space that used to echo with the happy sound of North Pole elf shanties. Today, the elves' mood was fiery, and their bobbing signs could be seen clearly through the windows of the Quonset doors. All that stood between the group and Santa were two gendarmes, who seemed polite and gentle enough to merely step aside if requested to. "Mow down fellow elves?" Santa said, slowly putting everything together.

"Well, hopefully, no. I would think they'd scatter when they see Rudolph bearing down on them."

Santa turned, and as he brushed past Herbert, he mumbled, "Let us hope so." He swept back into the command center.

"Go on ahead of us and make sure the Tears of the Angel plants are still where we think they are," Santa said, waving at the runners. "Wits about you, though. They're striking outside." He went directly to a computer console on the big desk, typed something in, and tapped Enter. "Herbert and I won't be far behind. I just gave Gustav a heads-up that we need him to clear take off immediately."

Neither runner moved. "He's willing to cross the picket line?" Hamelin asked.

"Guess we'll see when we get over there," Santa said. "He may be too busy to give it a second thought." Santa pulled the control room door open and stuck his head out. "Patterson, a minute, please. And you, Herbert," he said, turning around, "Grab that red sack on the chair over there. Fermier jerry-rigged a plant carrier for us."

Patterson entered, his wide eyes checking over his shoulder several times toward the ruckus outside. "S-sir?"

"I need someone I can rely on to man the center while we are away. You fit the bill, but I totally understand if you would feel more comfortable outside with your peers. Not to rush you, but we must be away immediately. Choose your place, and do it quickly. Inside or out, Mr. Patterson?"

"I, uh . . ." The young clerk frowned as his eyes darted back and forth between the strikers and the Claus. Then he said, "I'll keep it in good hands," and he sat down in the command chair at the computer console. He adjusted the height of the chair and began familiarizing himself with the equipment in front of him. "Godspeed," he whispered. "Let me know how it's going."

"Got it," Santa said. "But before you settle in, Patterson, please take the elevator up to the sky dome switches and flip 'er open. Give us about five minutes' lead time."

Santa walked back into his private sitting area and peered out the window a moment. Herbert joined him and was surprised to see that Jody the lumberman's group consisted of Jody and just two other elves. The other two were husky lads like Jody, but even so, the group was too few in number to stop the sleigh with a human blockade.

Santa sighed. "We can only hope, Herbert." He turned to find Hamelin and Nemie still in the control room. "Why are you still here?" he said. "Go, go, go! We'll be okay."

"Not like that, you won't," Nemie said, gesturing to Santa's suit. "At least cover up some of that look-at-me red." He pulled off his jacket and gave it to the Claus.

Herbert and Santa let themselves out the side door and fled. As they reached the stable, Jody slid in front of them, blocking their entrance. The violent emotion that Herbert had seen in Jody's eyes when that hulk of an elf pinned Walter to the wall was absent, but his sheer size was intimidating on its own. "Please respect the picket line, sir."

"Yes, yes," Santa said politely, walking peacefully around him. "Far be it from me to interfere. You go right along doing what you need to do, Jody. Shan't be but a minute in here. Gustav has new harnesses on the boys, and I want to personally make sure they're perfect before he makes some promotional videos."

Herbert looked to Gustav, and the stable manager gave him a thumbs-up. Behind him stood the reindeer team, hitched and ready, snorting and nervously dancing about as they yearned to cast off.

"Sorry, sir," Jody said. "You can't move the sleigh. The grooms shouldn't be forced to cross the line."

"Oh, certainly," Santa said, taking a quick right into one of the empty stalls. "No flying today. We're merely creating a documentary about reindeer for the little children. Come, Herbert," he said over his shoulder. "Take pictures in Cupid's stall. They'll love this." And with Herbert following dutifully behind with his cell phone, Santa began a dialogue about the feeding, housing, and maintenance of Christmasville's reindeer herd. For a while, Jody continued watching from a respectful distance, but the added stress of having to watch the main door at the same time eventually forced him to choose which front he would defend. He turned his back on Santa and resumed his watch at the stable door.

After a few minutes of letting the lumberman settle into a routine, the two elves suddenly made a mad dash for Santa's tricked-out ride and jumped in. With a low whistle from Santa and a crack of his whip, the Santa mobile took off with a jerk.

"Hey!" Jody yelled, rushing toward them, but it was too late. The reindeer team immediately found its stride, and the sleigh had runners in the air before Jody could interfere. The Santa mobile banked left and headed for the sky door which was slowly rolling back at the summit of the great biodome. The last Herbert heard from below was a string of naughty words, a roar from the crowd of protestors, and possibly a chunk of lobbed ice that surely left its mark on the bottom of the sleigh. Then the team shot through the opening in the dome and climbed into the clear blue sky.

"See? Piece of cake," Herbert said, sliding the driver's seat up until he felt comfortable. "No elves were harmed in the conduct of this mission."

"*Yet*," Santa said, fiddling with the buttons on the dashboard's elaborate GPS. "What is wrong with this thing?" he asked, still fumbling. "Give this a go, Herbert. We need to get it off autopilot." He reached over and took the reins from Herbert.

Herbert took the slip of paper Santa handed him. "I have no idea what this says. Who wrote this?" He tried to hand it back.

Santa kept both hands on the reins. "Nemie. And yes, it's strange looking, but he assured me that the code will get us where we need to be. Just punch it in." As he watched Herbert, he said, "You do realize that flying the sleigh doesn't absolve you of anything. You will still have to answer for what you have done."

"I know," Herbert said quietly. He spun the cylinder in the upper left corner of the GPS until he had the five correct numbers and symbols lined up. He hoped the payout would be healthy Tears of the Angel plants and a safe return trip with all souls accounted for. The sleigh made a course correction, banking ever so slowly to the right until it headed in the opposite direction. "West?" Has the sleigh ever gone west?"

"Not to our knowledge," Santa said, handing the reins back.

"Our? If you think I will be much help here, think again, sir. I've been on an official run precisely once. When your predecessor was, was . . ."

"Mortally injured," Santa finished. "No, your assistance with the GPS will be enough. They assured me that we will arrive where we need to be. When I said 'our,' I meant my predecessors and me. Apparently, not only did I inherit specific responsibilities and a certain look, but I also acquired the collective memories of the Sinterklaas who came before me. Picture a sort of software download. We have always flown from east to west. And now we must go west to east." He frowned a moment, seemingly intrigued by the thought. Then something must have clicked because his frown grew into a huge smile. He nodded once and settled back into his seat.

Herbert loosened up on the reins and gave the team permission to set their own pace. Rudolph tossed his head, and his teammates immediately lengthened their stride and picked up their speed.

"Yes," Santa said, "I knew how to drive the sleigh before I ever rode in it. Understood the naughty list, too. Everything, just everything."

Herbert scoffed. "You make it sound like such a burden. I can't imagine anything more glorious." His statement came out as slightly ambitious. He bit his lip and kept his eyes trained over the top of Rudolph's head as he felt Santa turn to stare at him.

"Oh, it is a burden, Herbert. You know the saying 'Before you judge an elf, walk a mile in his little pointed slippers?' No truer words were ever spoken. I have learned a lot in the past six months. Being Sinterklaas is something I never aspired to, and if given the chance—if it were not such a dishonor—I would gladly pass the position on to someone more apt. Frankly, I don't see how anyone would ever consider me worthy of such a lofty position."

Herbert bit down harder. He couldn't see it either.

"Those strikers won't understand why I had to leave or where we are headed. I just hope they aren't rioting in the lanes when we get back. All these problems, and now I've run out on another one."

"For Fudgesicles' sake, Claus, if they knew, they'd cringe in fear."

Santa shook his head and concentrated on the side view out of the sleigh.

They rode along in silence for some time, Herbert imagining what he would do if he were *king* of Christmasville, and Santa scribbling furiously in a small blue journal. Herbert didn't suppose the Claus was taking notes about their adventure. There was too much gazing off into blue sky. No, this was creative activity. Herbert vowed to peek the first time Santa left the notebook unattended. Not to be nosy, just to have a better understanding of what made the old man tick.

"Whoa! Is that normal?" Herbert said. The cylinder on the GPS was suddenly spinning uncontrollably. He watched the spinning stop with new numbers and symbols. The sleigh began descending, and the reindeer leaned into a slight course correction to the left.

Santa shook his head. "These symbols don't look familiar. Are they on Nemie's list?"

"Nope. I used them all up the first time." Herbert unbuttoned his suede jacket and dug the list out of an inside pocket. "You watched me the first time. Put these back in again."

Santa snatched the paper and twirled the cylinder back to where Herbert had initially set it. The sleigh team immediately began to ascend and the sleigh banked ever so gently right. "I'll just hang on to this if you don't mind," Santa said, waving the note at him.

Herbert nodded. "Hopefully—" and "Oh, dear Lord" came in quick succession. The cylinder started spinning again, stopping only when it had once more reset itself to the new code. The reindeer responded accordingly.

Santa's hand shot out, hovering over the dial.

"Do it!"

No sooner had Santa adjusted the tumblers than the GPS reset itself again to the new code, and Rudolph corrected course.

"One more course correction and I will vomit," Herbert said. "Wherever that's leading," he said, tipping his chin toward the GPS, "I think we're going there."

"Dear God, help us," Santa said, clutching the side of the sleigh. He peered into the cloud deck below them. "First the Tears, and now this. What will happen to Christmas without elves or a sleigh? Pray, Herbert, as you have never prayed, for I fear our days are numbered."

"No need to ask," Herbert said, cowering in his seat as the sleigh made another, sharper turn to the left. He gave up trying to steer. The sleigh dropped precipitously, and his stomach lurched.

## Chapter Thirty-Two
# Beware of Children Bearing Gifts

The sleigh landed with a gentle bounce and the sound of galloping hooves. Herbert popped his head up. They were alive, all reindeer accounted for, and this was the most beautiful landing field he had ever seen. To his left stretched a newly plowed field of rich brown soil; to his right a deep wood full of bird song, and bluets growing thickly in the play of light and shadow along its fringe. And somehow, the sleigh had managed to land in a long strip of meadow running between the two. "Where are we?" he asked.

"Tilldale" Santa said. He frowned, and then said, "Don't even ask me how . . ."

"Sinterklaas download?"

Santa shrugged. "Maybe he can tell us more," he said, pointing to an elderly man who had stepped away from a team of two white oxen yoked to a ramshackle farm wagon and was crossing toward them. Beyond the wagon stood an unremarkable house with two single windows in the front and a lean-to greenhouse on the side.

The man gave them a warm *ho* as he approached, and when near enough to read the expression on his face, Herbert decided they were in no danger of being shot as trespassers. The face was weathered but ageless, with intense, warm eyes, and a pointy chin that would have been comelier with a beard filling it out.

"Landed a sweet one, didn'tcha?" he said, sweeping the wide-brimmed straw hat from his head and bowing slightly. He walked past the sleigh and began caressing the reindeer, sharing a whisper in each one's ear that set them to snorting and pawing the ground.

"Santa's sleigh," he said to the elves once he had greeted the team and come back around the other side to Claus.

"The one and only," Herbert said. *Any fool could tell you that,* he added silently.

"Peace, brother, I mean no harm," the man said, smiling at him. "And who is it who drives such a magnificent contraption?"

Santa and Herbert both answered at once, pointing fingers at each other.

The man gave a chuckle that sounded so much like the Claus, Herbert had to look at Santa to make sure he wasn't laughing, too.

Santa wasn't, but he was smiling from ear to ear. He jumped out of the sleigh and offered his hand. "Santa, the Claus. You must be Minus."

"Indeed, I am. And you are?" he asked, turning to Herbert.

"Herbert, former first assistant to the Claus." Herbert shook the man's hand. The grip was firm, but if Minus worked the land for a living, his hands were much too smooth.

"No one else?" Minus asked, his eyes roving the sleigh.

"None," said Santa.

Minus walked to the rear of the sleigh and in one quick motion tugged out the green canvas tarp that was used during flight to keep Christmas presents from spilling out across the countryside over. "And you?"

Hoho's head popped up out of the cargo area. He offered a sheepish grin and a quiet, "Hoho, sir?"

200

"Asking or telling?" Minus said.

Hoho's face flushed pink. "Telling?"

"Quite harmless, I assure you," Santa said, a slight edge to his voice. "Hoho, I hope you have a good reason for inserting yourself where you don't belong."

"I was here first?" he offered. "Napping?" he added. "Gustav wanted a heavy box moved without emptying it, so Heath and I helped him, and then I took a nap. Six months until Christmas, and I didn't think anyone would be using the—"

"Oh, dear God, Heath's here, too?"

Hoho wagged his head. "No, sir."

Minus chuckled to himself. "Now that introductions have been made, the coat, if I might," he said, wiggling his fingers at Santa.

"Oh, this," Santa said, looking down at Nemie's coat. "Yes, of course." He peeled it off. "I'm only wearing it as a . . . Well, it's too long a story, and I'm sure you really don't care. It was a disguise. Let's leave it at that."

Minus stuck his hand inside Nemie's jacket pocket and pulled out a red plastic coin about the size of a quarter. "Crude but effective," he said, before stomping on it twice with the heel of his muddied work boot. He gave the coat back. "Now they can't follow you, and you are free to go."

"They?" Herbert ducked and his eyes roved the sky. Rusk had the money and the means to do most anything.

"Not Rusk," Minus said, speaking to Herbert's thoughts for a second time. "The owner of the coat has enemies, and they have been following the signal from the coin. Do not be afraid. No one can land without my permission."

"Yes, but we can't stay," Santa said, tossing the coat into the back of the sled. "We need to find—"

"And you will find it," Minus said.

The two men stood staring at each other. A moment of silent communication passed back and forth between the two, Santa nodding thoughtfully as Minus related something. The nodding was followed by a quick frown and a single nod, and finally an *okay*. Herbert felt insulted by his exclusion.

Minus disengaged from Santa. "Herbert, we have need of your masterly skills. Bring the sleigh around," he said, drawing his hand in a half-circle as he gestured at the expanse of meadow ahead of them, "and fly out in the opposite direction from whence you came. When you are aloft, the GPS will do the rest. And remember, redemption is always within reach. And you," he said, turning to Hoho. "Chin up. There may yet be a part for you to play in this. Now, go, while your pursuit is lost and confused."

Santa clambered back on board, and with a double click of his tongue, Herbert urged Rudolph and his crew into a wide sweep that set them in the right direction for flight. He looked Minus's way and got a half salute from him. "Away," he commanded, and the team sallied forth—first at a walk and then as they reached the end of the meadow, thundering on hoofs that suddenly leaped into the air and took them airborne. Minus, the house, and the well-tended land quickly disappeared.

Herbert watched the GPS spin, clicking as it set a course with Nemie's original code. The team banked slowly right, and the sleigh hurtled into a deep, starless night sky.

"Did I understand him correctly?" Herbert said, breaking the silence. "The demons are after us?"

"No longer," Santa said. "And it's not us they want, but our friend Nemie."

"But they wouldn't have known he wasn't in the sleigh until after they had waylaid us."

"True, but there will be no repeat of their Christmas attack. Minus said we will reach our destination."

"A little telepathic reassurance?"

"Something like that," Santa said.

At any rate, Santa seemed confident enough to stretch his legs out and close his eyes. Soon, he was snoring loudly, and it swept away a ton of anxiety from Herbert's overcrowded thoughts. Try as he might, though, he couldn't shake the feeling that everything wouldn't be well—no telepathy, just an instinct for self-preservation. So he stayed awake, one hand loosely holding the reins and both eyes searching the sky for an evil pursuit that he couldn't even begin to picture.

# Chapter Thirty-Three
# Helldale

Herbert awoke with a start, no longer gripping the reins and the reindeer at full gallop. His eyes went to the GPS. The code remained unchanged. To his right, Santa was leaning over the back of the seat playing rock-paper-scissors with Hoho.

"Relax, Herbert," Santa said. "Everything's fine and it's not far now."

"Bad dream," Herbert lied, feeling foolish and like a bit of a nervous Nellie. "Do you have that on good authority, or is it another unexplainable Sinterklaas download?"

"A little of both."

"What else did Minus say to you?"

"I can't beat you," Santa said to Hoho, and he turned back around in the seat. "That everything will be okay if we trust one another."

"You can trust me," Herbert said, a little too quickly. "Really. I've seen how fast things can jump the rails. I'm done playing the ends against the middle." He couldn't read Santa's unusual, stoic expression. "Don't you believe me?"

Santa nodded, but he never looked Herbert's way and he offered nothing more.

"That's it? Can't you at least tell me who Minus is?"

Santa leaned back and took a peek at Hoho, who had curled back up under the tarp in the sleigh's cargo bay. The big elf had said very little since their encounter with Minus, and by the sound of his heavy breathing, he had fallen into a deep, blissful slumber.

"He's a Keeper, Herbert."

"But . . . but I thought there weren't any more Keepers."

"So everyone thought," Santa said, the corners of his mouth turning up ever so slightly. "I'm sure they would have preferred it stay that way, but these are troubled times. And I don't think Minus is the only one we shall meet."

"But who *are* they?"

Santa shrugged. "Keepers."

Herbert thought about it a minute. "Who put the tracker in Nemie's coat?"

"No one from Christmasville, that's for sure. It would be the devil's own. It seems the affair that took the life of my predecessor is not yet over. Nemie's adoptive father still wants him back in hell. He has his minions looking for him and will do anything to drag him back there. Apparently, they thought—still do, probably—that Nemie is in the sleigh with us. Nemie screwed them over royally when he gave me his coat."

"You don't suppose he meant to take you out, too? Finish up what he started with the previous Claus?"

"Nemie? Oh, no, he's faultless. I'm sure he had no clue that he was being tracked. No, he dodged a bullet because of his kindness. At any rate, the pursuit is off now. Minus would not have let us proceed if he had thought otherwise."

Santa shifted his well-cushioned backside on the bench seat and propped his booted feet up on the edge of the sleigh. Herbert thought he heard a quiet sigh of contentment, too.

Santa was going incommunicado again. Attempting to keep the conversation going, Herbert said, "A lot of information passed between you and Minus. You know even more than you're saying, don't you? Please, Santa, you can tell me. Hoho won't hear, and who else could I possibly tell? You can share the burden, sir."

But Santa merely shook his head, tucked his chin into his chest and was soon loudly sawing logs again. Herbert checked over his shoulder as if he expected some unseen foe to sweep down on them. Forewarned would be forearmed, but if the Claus knew anything else, he wasn't yapping until Herbert needed to know.

Herbert tilted his head back against the top of the seat and settled in for a most uncomfortable nap. Immediately, he drifted into a deep slumber full of dark-suited figures who descended on him from the sky, their huge beating wings blotting out the light and filling the air with a cloud of rotting funk. One monster landed on the back of the reindeer nearest the sled and began slashing at the harness with a blade of glowing silver as another settled beside Santa and began spinning the cylinder on the GPS. The sleigh took a nosedive. Herbert let out a bloodcurdling shriek.

He awoke with his hand gripping the rail of the sleigh, one leg slung over the side, and the other one moving to join it. Santa had latched on to his shirt and was yanking him backward. He tumbled back into the sleigh, his head almost striking the dashboard, where the GPS was spinning madly.

"A final course correction," Santa said. "We'll be landing soon."

"Food?" Hoho asked, popping up to hang over the seat.

"No. Go back to sleep," Santa said to the bleary-eyed elf. "We'll call you."

"Oh," Hoho said. He disappeared back under the dark green canvas.

Unlike in Herbert's dream, the sleigh was flying level, but as the GPS locked onto a new code, Rudolph and his buddies began a gentle descent, drawing the sleigh out of a dark sky, through clouds of puffy white, and into a sky of brilliant azure. Ahead, Herbert saw a wisp of black cloud stretching along the far horizon, rapidly approaching like an angry thunderhead.

"Oh, dear," Santa said. "That doesn't look good."

Within seconds, they hurtled into the new darkness. There was no howling wind, no lashing rain. The gloom, which was no storm at all, sucked them into eerie silence. The sleigh dropped again, shot through the murk, and, with a few bounces, came to rest in a lush, verdant countryside bathed in bright sunshine. Behind them, the dark cloud wall floated like a miasmic fog over a sandy riverbank. Herbert could not, however, see any water. This was Caina on Cocytus? He cocked an eyebrow at the Claus.

"I suppose," Santa said. He climbed out of the sleigh. "Don't touch the water," he admonished.

Herbert shuddered as he rose up on tiptoes. "Fat chance," he muttered, still not seeing anything, but he could feel a cool draft wrapping around his ankles, and the whole business smacked of malevolence. He turned back to the bright, inviting, sunlit world.

Santa had already moved away from the sleigh and was heading for a thicket of young trees. "Keeper Number Two?" Herbert asked, following him.

"Someone." Santa suddenly veered right. Whatever scent or Clausian-cum-Keeper download he was following led him back toward the water. Only this time, Herbert saw that the ominous cloud bank had lifted. And they were not alone. Just as Minus had appeared to assist them, on the fringe of the grove sat a man in a wide-brimmed hat with a pair of garden shears and a wheelbarrow filled with yellow and red flowers. Beside him stood soul runners Hamelin and Nemie. He rose from his portable garden seat as they approached, but remained where he stood and let them come to him.

When they drew close, Santa said, "Minus said you would be here. I don't know what has been shared with you, but Christmasville needs Tears of the Angel plants."

The man said nothing but eyed Santa closely before turning those keen, wide-set eyes on Herbert. The gardener was young, very tall but not lanky, and well-tanned, and unlike Minus, he possessed a strong chin that fit nicely with the rest of his face. He was by all accounts strikingly handsome. "I am Plus," he said at last, turning back to Santa. "We have been waiting for you."

"What took you so long?" Hamelin asked.

Santa raised a calming hand. "All is well now, but it seems young Nemie's coat had a tracking device—red coin with a biblical citation."

"The boy in Nevis," Nemie said, shaking his head in disgust. "Can no one be trusted?"

"Apparently, just us," Hamelin said.

"Your *friends*," Santa continued, looking at Nemie, "followed us as far as, uh, well, until we met Keeper Minus. He kindly removed the tracker. We've had no trouble since, so I would assume that we have lost them. Perhaps, though, we should move this along. This place gives me an eerie feeling, and I will feel much better when we are once again back at the Pole."

"I am sorry," Nemie said, shaking his head. "I would never have given you the coat if I had known. I had no idea—"

"We'll deal with it later," Hamelin said. "We are in a tenuous position here at this notorious river. Plus, the plant, if you will . . ."

"I will give you two plants," Plus said, leading them along the fringe of the trees where the level land began rolling down to the water. "Reproduction, of course, is asexual. I'm giving you an heir and a spare, of sorts. Guard it with your life. I will be loath to give you any more."

If truth be told, Herbert was loath to follow them any closer to the water's edge. Visions of an icy lake with the heads and body parts of unfortunates damned to spend eternity frozen into blocks of ice made him want to cut and run to the comfort of Hoho's sleeping cubby in the rear of the sleigh. "I should hang back and keep a lookout," he said.

"You can come," Plus said. "The runners can handle that."

"Just like they handled the tracking device," Herbert said to himself.

He straggled after them, vowing not to look at anything except his shoes and the plants. That lasted seconds as the fear of tripping and falling into the water overrode the horrible pictures spinning around in his head. He squinted toward the water. It wasn't so bad! The water was calm—its surface smooth as polished glass, but it wasn't clear, nor was it milky white like snow. He couldn't see into its depths, but its reputation was all he needed to know. He quickened his step to catch up with Santa and Plus. The runners were already dropping back to keep watch for any horrors that might descend on them.

Plus had already worked his way into the middle of a tiny patch of Tears of the Angel—their blue heads rising defiantly near the treacherous waters of the Caina. Ignoring the soggy ground, he dropped to his knees and dug out two plants from the ten or so growing there and deposited them into separate clay pots. He set them low in the planters and packed soil around them until they stood firm in their new, temporary homes. "Never out of your care," he said to Santa, handing them over, "or they will meet the same fate as their predecessor."

"Oh, no," Santa said. He tucked them inside his thick red coat. "Close to my heart until we are back in Christmasville. Now, let's get out of here."

A sudden gale picked Santa up and blew him back several feet and onto his backside. Herbert tumbled forward, somersaulting a number of times before he came to a bruising stop against a tree trunk as a whirlpool of leaves, sticks, and debris lashed them with a ferocious roar. The turbulence howled and moaned, and the wind took on the quality of shouting voices and pained cries.

"Get up," Plus said, pulling on his arm.

Herbert forced his watering, stinging eyes to open a crack, and he could make out the red of Santa's coat. He staggered to his feet only to be ripped out of Plus's grasp by a dark figure that rushed at him with a blood-curdling banshee cry. He tumbled again, rolling, rolling, rolling across boggy, wet ground. Where was the water?

And just as suddenly as it had arrived, the storm calmed, and an eerie silence and stillness descended. Someone dragged Herbert to his feet a second time. His eyes opened to nightmare made flesh. Three hooded figures clothed in black stood before him, and the frozen, evil, waters of the Caina loomed directly behind him.

"Over there," said the boldest of the three, ordering Santa to take his place beside Herbert. Herbert's terror deepened as he spied first the muddied work boots, then the prostrate figure of Plus lying on the ground behind the tree. He wasn't moving. If one had the power to dispatch a Keeper . . .

Herbert's eyes darted. Where were the runners? He searched the ground for more bodies. None. Had Hamelin and Nemie forsaken them?

"Who are you and what do you want?" Santa asked in a clear, calm voice. "We have nothing of value. If we have trespassed, we apologize most humbly. We were just leaving. With your permission, we'll just take our friend there and be out of your way."

Herbert nodded vigorously.

The leader pulled back his hood to reveal a grotesque face: one eye stitched closed, no lips, and a nose that had collapsed into his face. "Call Nemesis back," he croaked, his voice struggling to rise above a whisper.

"We don't have any means to do that," Santa said. "We would be glad to pass along your request, however."

Herbert's stomach heaved. His gaze dropped from the disfigured face to the ground and the demon's feet. Why was he wearing two left shoes? His eyes shifted again, this time over the monster's shoulder. Just beyond, something moved in the sleigh. Were they desecrating it? Merciful heavens! It was Hoho! Surely, the imbecile wouldn't amble over to inquire about lunch again.

"You!"

Herbert quailed as his gaze darted back to the leader's chin. He shrugged, a fallback reflex that worked in most situations. *Don't turn around. Don't turn around,* he silently pleaded as Hoho lowered himself out of the sleigh. Herbert blinked several times and shook his head ever so slightly as if Hoho would ever be smart enough to know Morse Code or interpret subtle body language.

Santa must have seen it too for he suddenly took a step forward, saying, "As I've already told you, we can't help you. We arrived separately from the others, and we were also leaving separately. Now, I'm sorry, but I really must be on my way. I invoke my right to free passage as recognized by—"

Who knew that an elf built like a refrigerator could move like a freight train? Hoho rammed into the dark figures as if he were bowling for a 3-6-9 spare. The right thug sailed to the right, the left one ate dirt. Just like a middle linebacker, Hoho rammed into the leader with a ferocity that drove Hoho past Santa and Herbert, and into the icy waters of the Caina.

# Chapter Thirty-Four
## Fragility of Life

As the hell-sent dark runners descended on them, Hamelin had grabbed Nemie by the arm and dragged him—fighting and gibbering—into the nearest Weigh Station portal, where they had been whisked away quicker than the speed of light.

"We can't leave them," Nemie said, tugging to pull free.

"We already have. Can I safely let you go?" Hamelin asked, his hand still firmly clasped around Nemie's upper arm.

Nemie gave him an evil look and jerked his arm free. "I'm not stupid."

"I never said you were, but my orders from Elder Stephen were clear: keep you out of trouble at all costs."

"And that doesn't include Santa Claus? What's wrong with you, Hamelin? We should have stayed and bluffed them out. We can't just leave them there. I never pegged you for a chicken."

Hamelin began to see red, and it wasn't Santa's coat. He pulled in a long, slow breath and let it out the same way. Duking it out in the portal would solve nothing. He shook his head. "Too many. We might have handled the three, but the other twelve minions would have gotten the best of us. Far better to get a flyboy or two."

"I thought you wanted nothing to do with the angels."

"Typically, no. They really are idiots. But in this case, their presence is required. They're the only ones who can send these guys back to the sweltering cesspit they call home. Relax, they want you and not Santa. You'll enjoy watching Miguel whip their rear ends, particularly Martin Westwood Cobb's."

Nemie's eyes brightened. "The former runner?"

"Leading the posse." Hamelin snickered.

"And that's funny *why*, exactly?"

"Oh, the irony. HTBT, Nemie. Had to be there. He can no longer be recognized by face, but you'll always know him by his shoes: two lefts. Must be terribly painful. He always had nice designer shoes at the Weigh Station. No more, no more. If you've grown attached to anything, best get rid of it before you descend, because it'll come back to bite you in the foot."

Whatever else Nemie might say on the subject was put to rest when the portal jerked to a stop at the Weigh Station's White Corridor. "Which way?" he asked instead.

"Miguel," Hamelin responded, pointing across the hallway, where Miguel already stood waiting for them. The runners quickly followed the angel into an empty conference room. Miguel closed the door behind them, and within seconds, Hamelin described the situation.

Miguel immediately spun them around, and before they could reach the door, the flyboy had used his own angelic method of transportation to have them standing once more on the banks of Caina Lake.

*** 

The cool lake air suddenly changed direction, and goosebumps ran up Herbert's arms. *What evil*, he thought. He whirled around. The demons were gone, but Miguel, Hamelin, and Nemie rushed toward him. He gestured helplessly toward the water. "Hoho is out there somewhere. You've got to find him."

Santa didn't turn to acknowledge them, but kept his eyes glued to a spot directly in front of him on the frozen lake. He pointed. "He went in here," he said, pointing, "but he hasn't come up again. They fell through the ice, and then it healed itself over, sealing them in."

Miguel stood beside him, lifted his arms, and closed his eyes. His lips moved, but his speech was too low to hear. Why didn't the angel just dive in and pull the poor elf out?

The spot Santa had been watching suddenly liquified. The water there began to roil—bubbling and sending out ripples that washed the shore and forced everyone to back up. At the center of the turbulence, the water spun itself up into a column some ten feet tall and wide. As Miguel held his ground—arms still raised, and still praying—the others fled the water, clearing a path for the waterspout as it headed ashore. When the spout hit land, it spun itself out, collapsing in a deluge on the sandy shore, and depositing Hoho with it.

Herbert pulled him away from the lake, fell to his knees, and put his ear to Hoho's chest. Oh, what a beautiful strong beat he heard!

Hoho opened his eyes. "Hi!"

"Hi, you big doof," Herbert cried. "I, uh . . ." He patted Hoho awkwardly on his chest and scrambled back to his feet. "He's alive," he said, shouting unnecessarily at Santa, who was already hitting his knees beside Hoho.

Herbert looked at Miguel, Hoho's savior. He hadn't moved from his spot but had dropped his arms and was smiling broadly. And then sudden annoyance arose in Herbert as he saw the two runners still hanging back, watching with dispassionate expressions. "No transport today," he snarled at them.

He and Santa helped Hoho to his feet and hung on to him long enough to make sure he had his land legs. Then they walked him back to the sleigh, had him pull off his wet clothing, and wrapped him in the tarp. Herbert would have gladly given up his own clothes to redress him, but size was an issue, so the Claus peeled down to his skivvies and they had the big elf clothed and warm in a jiffy. They made him promise to remain in the sleigh and went to tend to Plus, who still lay prostrate on the ground. Hamelin was already kneeling beside him, holding his hand as Nemie and Miguel stood solemnly over them.

Nemie intercepted the elves before they could come too close. "You need to take the big elf and the plant and head back immediately. There is nothing like the mighty power of an angel to run the devil off, but as long as they think I am here, they will try again."

The solution to that was pretty clear to Herbert, but he kept his mouth shut because it was also clear that the Plus was not long for—or had already departed—this world. "How is this possible!"

"Life is fragile," Nemie said. "Even a Keeper's. Now, go, or everything he did for you will be for naught. Go!"

Santa nodded as a single teardrop journeyed down his cheek. "We wouldn't think of intruding. What about the rest of the plants? I fear for their safety. Should we take them with us?"

"You worry needlessly. We will not leave them unprotected. Miguel will want to talk to Hoho soon. Until then, watch him closely."

Santa nodded a second time. "Please extend our thanks and condolences to . . . to anyone touched by this tragedy." He gave Herbert a pointed look, and they hurried back to the sleigh.

"You still have the plants?" Herbert asked as he checked the buckles on the reindeer harnesses.

"Yes, safely tucked away," Santa said, showing him the plants nestled in his hat.

Herbert climbed in beside Santa and took up the reins. Hoho was styling it in Santa's flashy coat in the cargo bay, watching the ministrations of the runners and the angel. "You still okay?" Herbert asked.

"Yes."

"What happened back—"

Santa placed a hand on Herbert's arm. "Later," he whispered. "Unless he volunteers it."

Herbert nodded. Hoho wasn't his buoyant self, but surely Miguel would get to the bottom of it. "Up," he said, and the reindeer obeyed instantly. Within seconds, they were airborne, and their meeting at the Caina was hopefully a closed chapter and an ever-receding memory.

# Chapter Thirty-Five
# Neat and Safe

Miguel watched the sky window on the great Christmasville dome roll back and the sleigh descend through it. The craft made a graceful arc around the airfield and came to a gentle, perfect landing in the middle of the airstrip. He needed a chat with Hoho. The road to recovering from what had befallen him would not be easy, he thought, noting the sluggish way the big guy conducted himself across the tarmac. Even the huge crowd of chanting, sign-waving elves on strike didn't draw Hoho's attention. Thank heavens for a newly constructed barricade that kept the strikers from swarming him and the other returnees.

"Herbert," Miguel said, greeting them at the entrance to Quonset Hut Alpha, "where can I find you later? We should talk after the Claus, Hoho, and I are through."

Herbert arched an eyebrow, but he didn't offer up any sass at being summarily dismissed. "I'll be in Alpha."

Santa spent a moment watching the strikers, his forehead scrunched into worry lines that made him look older and more exhausted than usual.

Miguel put a hand on his shoulder. "I won't need you for long, Santa; then you can do what you feel you must. If you'll find a quiet space for us . . ."

Santa dragged his eyes away from the raucous crowd. "Yes, of course. You can use my private study. No one will bother you there."

Miguel followed him through the silent, empty, cavernous staging room, which only six months earlier would have resonated with the joyous carols of busy, happy elves. Miguel knew that it would do so once again, but convincing the Claus without revealing everything he knew would be a delicate matter.

Santa ushered them into the command center. "Here," he said, "or you're welcome to use my personal room." He opened the door to his bedroom.

"This will do," Miguel said. "Hoho, have a seat at the fireside? I'd like to have brief chat with you. Maybe put some things in perspective for you."

Hoho shot a wary look at Santa, who nodded and directed him to sit. "You're in good hands. I'll be back shortly." He started out the door, reconsidered, and then came back in. He put the Tears plants on his bookcase. "I don't feel comfortable toting these around. Keep them safe for me, Miguel." Then he left, closing the door behind him.

Miguel sat down in the chair beside Hoho. "Well, Hoho, as far as I know, you are the only one ever to fall into the Caina and live to talk about it."

Hoho nodded. "But why?"

"Would you like the long explanation, or the simple one?"

"Simple, please."

"Because you're good-hearted, that's why. The Caina could never claim the soul of someone as pure as you."

Hoho's eyes began to well, and his lip quivered. "B-but I couldn't get out. I was going to die in there."

Miguel chuckled. "No, actually, the lake was so puzzled by what it had swallowed that it couldn't decide how to spit you back out again. Even if I had not arrived when I did, the water would have cast you back onto the land. Trust me, amigo, it was not your time. Nor will it be for quite a while."

Hoho brightened "Really?"

"Yes, really. And you are a hero, too. If you had not intervened, it would have turned out badly for your friends."

"But I couldn't save *him*."

"The Keeper? Don't give Plus another thought. He has moved on to a much better place than this. His reward is great."

Hoho smiled. "Are we done, then? I have chores to do."

Miguel smiled, too. "Yes, but I'm afraid your calling will have to wait. I don't think you should alienate your coworkers by crossing their picket line. Maybe go have something to eat in the lunchroom, and then take a nice long nap after that. You can make other decisions later." Miguel cocked his head and considered Hoho. The simple goodness of the elf filled him with joy. Hoho's eyes were brighter now, and he would be okay.

"As for me, I have one more chore before I am off. Please send the Claus back in. I suspect he hasn't gone far."

***

Herbert didn't know whether he was included in Santa's invitation to speak with Miguel, but it felt like two birds with one stone, so he accompanied the Claus back into the command center. Miguel had kicked back at the main command console, calmly playing a game of solitaire with cards bearing the image of la Catrina and other bright Día de los Muertos designs on the reverse. Herbert didn't understand how anyone could be comfortable with such hideous pictures. These afterlife immortals were a little too cavalier about death.

Miguel swept his cards into a neat stack and stowed them away in a pocket. "There are just a few loose ends to attend to, and then I'll take my leave. First, Hoho will be just fine. He's a resilient type and a delightful soul. More people should strive to be like him."

Herbert kept his eyes glued to the floor. Even if the remark wasn't directed at him, it still stung a little. Nobody was that perfect.

Santa sat down at the table. "I feel as if I've mismanaged everything. Maybe they chose the wrong elf."

Herbert's head came up sharp. Aha, he thought. Now they were getting somewhere.

"Not you," Miguel said, looking at Herbert. "Definitely not you, amigo. You are definitely not part of the solution. More of the problem, I would say."

Herbert bristled. "I've already apologized for my mistake with the plant, and I've vowed to change my ways. What else do you want me to say? That I killed my friends with some bad 'shine? Because if that's what you want, I can't do that."

"Oh, I would never expect that, Herbert. Because that would be one more lie, wouldn't it?"

"Look! I don't remember much about that night, but I'm pretty sure I drank the same stuff they did. I have no idea why I'm still alive."

"I don't intend to interfere," Miguel said, "but I will set your feet on the right path to figuring it out on your own." He turned to Santa. "I would suppose you have a watchmaker, or someone who excels at crafting devices that pulse at regular intervals?"

Santa nodded. "That would be Waterbury, our horologist."

"Call him, and tell him to bring one of his pendulum clocks with him."

"He has many such things, but maybe it would be better to go to him. His workshop is full to overflowing with any number of—"

"Any number will do," Miguel said.

Miguel was first out the door and set a scorching pace that told Herbert that while the angel could stay a while longer, he didn't have all day.

Waterbury's workshop—an A-frame chalet heavily ornamented on the exterior with dark vertical and horizontal wooden beams—was deep in the village in a prime spot at the corner of Tinsel and Holly. The interior space was a one-up-one-down: the shop and workspace on the bottom floor and living quarters above. Timepieces covered every horizontal and vertical surface except the tiny three-foot square table that the old man worked on. Waterbury, a wizened old elf with a thin, snow-white beard, a few matching wisps over his ears, and a lively whistle that could wake the dearly departed, was alone at his workbench. He looked up as they entered, grumbled something, and returned quickly to his work.

"Good day," Santa said, sounding more chipper than usual. "We have need of your expertise."

"Between two and four," Waterbury said, pointing to the tiny handwritten sign by the register that said just that. "I'm closed now."

"Yes, as we can see," Miguel said. "And as we need it. Twenty minutes of your time, and then we shall leave you alone." He walked over and picked up a mantle clock shoved against the cash register, opened the glass covering the brass dial, tapped the dial once, and wound the key. As soon as he closed the glass, the timepiece began to chime.

Waterbury dropped the tool in his hand and dashed across the room. "How did you do that?" he asked, pulling the clock from

Miguel's grasp. "For months I've tried . . .Who *are* you?" he asked peering over the top of his half glasses. "All these clocks . . . I could use your help."

"Just a friend," Miguel said. "And now that your clock is fixed, will you help us? Mr. Tuddy needs some assistance in remembering things." He began moving around the room, admiring Waterbury's work with quiet *oohs* and *aahs* before stopping before an unusual grandfather clock with its face behind glass, but its pendulum swinging freely within an open case. He pulled a nearby shipping crate over and positioned it in front of the clock. "Come, Herbert, this will do nicely."

When he had Herbert positioned just so, Miguel said, "All I want you to do is listen to my voice and stare at that pendulum. Nothing else in your thoughts except the rhythmic swing of that lovely bob. Okay?"

Herbert nodded. Easiest job he ever had. And as he sat there listening to Miguel's quiet, mellifluous voice, he found himself growing sleepier by the second.

"Eyes open," Miguel whispered. "Now, tell me about the party, Herbert."

Herbert just couldn't. Seeing his friends laughing, and smiling once again would tear him up inside. He shouldn't. Once he started, he would have to shoulder even more awful memories. He wouldn't put himself through that. He started up from the chair.

Miguel placed a hand on his shoulder. "Peace, brother. We will walk with you."

Herbert began in a slow, halting voice. "We met at an unused storage room in Quonset Hut Dickens. Tocker brought chips and those little corn puffs that Tina from the Paper Division makes." Herbert broke out into a smile and chuckled. "Beltzer had the record.

Fifteen tosses in a row without missing a catch into his mouth. He was the best." His smile melted away.

"And what did you bring?"

Herbert's voice dropped to a whisper. "*Lacrima ambrotos.*"

"That was all? Did anyone else bring anything?"

"Beer, brandy, some excellent Guinness. Huban brought a big-ass bowl of ice. The color was a hoot. Bright blue. Never saw ice like that before."

Miguel turned to Waterbury. "I think he needs a drink of brandy. Top shelf, left-hand cabinet?"

The clockmaker's eyes flashed to the cabinet over his worktable. "Uh, yes. Someone might have left their cooking . . ."

Miguel merely smiled. "Neat or on the rocks, Herbert?"

"Uh, none, sir. I'm on the clock."

"Yes, and it's a beautiful clock. Santa won't mind. Answer the question."

"Neat, sir." Herbert's skin popped out in a sweat.

Miguel handed him the drink. "Never take it on the rocks?"

Herbert shook his head and took a sip.

"But your other buddies did, didn't they?"

Herbert thought a moment. He nodded.

Miguel patted him on the back. "Be at peace. Your 'shine, as you call it, had nothing to do with your friends' deaths." He looked at Santa. "It was tainted ice that killed the other elves. Contaminated, no doubt, by the Jetsla spill."

Santa's eyes grew wide. "*Blue* ice. Solomon mentioned festive party ice. Dear God, it positively was Jetsla! I've created a monster."

"An unfortunate accident," Miguel said. "But you can still prevent other needless deaths if you act quickly and authoritatively."

Herbert felt his head spinning. Not the ambrotos? He picked up the brandy and downed it in three gulps.

"Wake up!"

Herbert started, a drink in his hand, his gaze fixed on the grandfather clock, and Santa snapping his fingers in his ear. He looked around. "Where's Miguel?"

"Other things." Santa turned to Waterbury. "Thank you for your time and patience. Sorry to have interrupted you. How is the timing device for the new Zoom Eight-Ten remote-controlled car coming along? I hear it's expected to be a showstopper at the New York Toy Expo."

Waterbury shrugged as he walked back to his workbench. "Coming."

Santa's pocket began playing "Edelweiss." He pulled out his cell phone. "Yes?" His eyes drifted from Waterbury to Herbert before striding to the door and looking out. "No. Thanks for the heads-up." He clicked off and put his phone away. "It's been a very rough day, Herbert. Hoho's already been sent off to the cafeteria, but I'm sure that Mrs. Claus can set out a lovely spread for us on short notice."

Herbert would rather have hit the sack and slept for a month of Sundays, but he didn't get a chance to put in his two cents. Much as Miguel had done earlier, Santa was out the door in a flash.

"Where's the fire?" Herbert asked, scurrying to catch up.

"Everywhere, Herbert. Swear to goodness, everywhere. Just when I think I have things under control, he gets a bee in his bonnet and—"

"Who, sir?" Herbert said, huffing as he finally pulled abreast.

"Well, actually, I do have control," Santa said, continuing the conversation as if Herbert weren't there. "I just don't like confrontation. I do much better on the line, doodling with a nice piece of wood and a knife."

Herbert stopped in the middle of the sidewalk, directly outside Freda's Intimate Apparel Shop (pastel-hued bras and panties half price through the end of the week). He walked it forward a bit to a less embarrassing location: Speckly's Fun and Fitness Center. Creating Beach Bodies Since 1907. "*Who*, sir?" he said, much louder this time.

Santa toddled around in surprise. "No stopping now," he said, coming back to take Herbert by the arm. "Noël Rusk is on the warpath. Now that we have Tears of the Angel, we don't need him anymore. As soon as we meet, I'm going to give Jetsla the heave-ho, but I would like him to calm down before I do it."

Rusk was the last man on earth Herbert wanted to tangle with right now. He shook loose from Santa and hurried the fat man toward the cottages.

## Chapter Thirty-Six

# Take a Hike

A fabled meal from the reclusive Violet Claus would have been nice, but a desperate call from Patterson sent Herbert and Santa scurrying back to Quonset Hut Alpha, where an angry crowd of strikers was directing its frustration at Noël Rusk.

The billionaire stood trapped in the midst of the rowdy group, and for the first time, he looked as if he had lost his cool—giving what for to someone who had gotten into his personal space. Both participants were nose to nose, and Herbert suspected that they weren't too far from blows.

"I thought you settled them down," Herbert said.

"Not exactly," Santa said. "I promised to give them new information that would do that, but too many things on too many fronts."

Herbert slowed his pace as he took in the jostling and the vitriol. "Maybe we shouldn't wander into the middle of that. How about we go over there?" he said, tipping his head toward a service vehicle parked outside Boston Charlie. "At least, you can get above the fray."

They commandeered the set of wheels and drove it right up behind the fracas. Santa climbed up on the seat and shouted, "Here! Here! Good news!" He had to shout it twice to get a response. When he finally connected, the crowd pivoted toward the jeep.

"Effective today," Santa said, pausing a moment to consult his wristwatch, "five minutes from now, at exactly noon, the contractual relationship between Christmasville and Jetsla will be history. There follows—"

"What about our jobs?" someone yelled. The voice was female, Melody's maybe, but Herbert wouldn't stake his life on it.

"Safe! Secure!" Santa yelled. "We get an analysis of how we can modernize, but it's up to us how we choose to implement—"

Wild cheers drowned him out. Cardboard signs flew up into the air, and merry shouts and dancing broke out in the crowd, leaving Noël Rusk on the sidewalk by his lonesome. He immediately took refuge in Quonset Hut Alpha.

"Take the day off," Santa said, waving his arms over the crowd. The roar quieted a bit. "And there will be a kegger this evening to celebrate just how wonderful it is to be in Christmasville." He hopped down out of the jeep.

Herbert gave Santa a hard look and followed him into Alpha. Rusk was nowhere in sight. Herbert could picture him right now cowering in Santa's office. *"Kegger?"*

"That's right, Herbert," Santa said, stopping before his portrait in the Sinterklaas hall. "I won't have my fellow villagers dying because they had to sneak a little liquor. From now on, we will be up front, safe, and happy. We're lowering quarterly goals and reverting to the simple basics that have worked so well in the past."

"But what about the children? Some will go without, sir."

"Johnny doesn't need a turbo-powered fleet of toy cars, Herbert— pushing one across the floor works just as well with imaginative play. We don't need to waste production time with fancy gimmicks. Hula hoops, yo-yos, and bicycles with handlebar bells—that's what this world needs more of!" Santa ran his finger along the bridge of his nose in the picture, nodded once, and set off for the command center.

As they drew near, he slowed to a creep. Someone had left his door open. A quiet sigh escaped Santa's lips.

"Should I call for reinforcements?" Herbert whispered, trying to see who was inside.

Santa waved dismissively and made a beeline for his office. "Mr. Rusk, we need to talk."

Rusk was standing near the door to Santa's private room, his hand on the knob, ready to lock himself in there, if necessary. "I'll get to you in a minute," Rusk said, pointing a finger at Santa, his eyes homing in on Herbert. Herbert began backing up, but Rusk continued advancing until Herbert's back was against one of the bookcases.

"What did you say to my wife?"

Herbert's eyes widened. "Wife?"

"Yes," Rusk said. "The one who requested a divorce and left earlier today for God knows where on my private jet."

"N-nothing. I said nothing." Herbert stepped sideways and retreated to stand beside the door and Santa. "Where did you get the idea that I said something to her?"

"Because you met her in the stable. Isn't that where she gave you the Tears of the Angel?"

"Uh, no. I mean, sort of."

"Don't lie. P. J. Foos saw it."

"Ah, well, Foos," Herbert said, eyes rolling. "I can tell you that it's not so, because she gave the plant to . . ." Herbert clamped his mouth shut and shot Santa a pleading look.

"Mr. Rusk, let's not get sidetracked," Santa said. "Whatever family problems you are having at the moment don't concern us. The heart of the matter is that Jetsla's negligence resulted in a chemical spill that can now be directly linked to the deaths of Christmasville elves. Once the postmortem toxicology reports come back, we intend to keep your lawyers busy into the next millennium—not an unmanageable length of time for us, but I'm afraid it will plague your descendants for generations."

"Poppycock! My chemists have assured me—"

"You've shown us nothing," Santa said. "It's your word—"

"Foos's word," Herbert interjected.

"—on this, and your word on that. Trust me, trust me, trust me, trust me. Well, no longer, sir. I want your group to cease and desist immediately and vacate your business space by COB tomorrow. Now, if you'll excuse me, I have Christmas affairs to attend to."

Rusk didn't move. In fact, he appeared to have tuned Santa out, his interest suddenly piqued by the knickknacks from Herbert's collection of stolen trinkets. "Where did you get this?" he asked, picking up a round blue metal knob.

Santa turned to Herbert. "Where did you appropriate that from?"

Herbert's jaw dropped. "Me? Uh, that's not mine. I've never seen it before in my life."

The entrepreneur ran his index finger along the fitting. "This is a Jetsla valve knob. It even says *Jetsla*," he noted, pointing along the metal edge. "This is what the engineers determined was missing from the pipeline and what contributed to the spillage. I'll be damned. You sabotaged the project, didn't you? I just can't fathom why. If you weren't satisfied, why didn't you say something? Unless it's to settle some score with Mr. Foos."

Santa's hands went to his hips as he drew himself up to all of his five-feet (and a skosh more) height. "How dare you! We make toys,

Rusk, not construction equipment. It was probably brought in by Anatoli, the groundskeeper, because he didn't know what it was. There was no ill intent, I can assure you."

"No, not you. *Him*," Rusk said, looking at Herbert. "Your little wheeler-dealer here."

"I couldn't pick that doo-dad out of a line-up," Herbert said. "And whatever feelings I have about P. J. Foos are more than tempered by my unquestioning dedication to my job and allegiance to this community. Your accusation is without merit, and I am highly offended."

"Oh, come on. "You're never satisfied, are you Mr. Tuddy? I paid you handsomely for the Tears plant—"

Santa turned on Herbert. "*What?*"

"Oh, didn't he tell you the whole story, Nicholas? Why does that not surprise me? Your Mr. Tuddy here has no scruples. No matter what, he always wants more. If you're smart, you'll kick him to the curb and find someone you can trust, because if you can't trust one of your closest advisers, you'll fail, fail, and fail again."

"You're a great one to discuss scruples," Herbert shot back. "We have better things to do, Mr. Rusk, than to stand here and listen to the ravings of an egotistical bully billionaire who only came to the North Pole because no one else on Earth trusts him enough to strike a deal with him. Santa has asked you to leave. You should do it now before we have to call someone to throw you out."

"Have it your way," Rusk said, nodding. "Sort of. You can sue if you want, but your attorneys better be damn good—the best money can buy." He held up the wheel handle. "And you'd better be able to explain this." He stormed out, only to return seconds later. "Oh, and that plane ticket? Canceled!"

"Well?" Santa said as soon as the door slammed shut a second time. "Did you?"

Herbert shook his head. "I've done a lot of things I'm not proud of, Santa, but vandalizing property isn't one of them. Honest to God, I've never seen that before in my life. I have no idea where it came from."

"And the ticket?"

Herbert hung his head. "First class to St. Thomas. And there might have been a deed to a beachfront condo. I don't suppose he can cancel that one."

Santa dropped down into a chair. "Why, Herbert? Why are you so unhappy that you would give up what you were born to do, and destroy the one place that exists solely to make people happy? Why?"

Herbert's foot began tapping. *Don't go there*, he cautioned himself. *A word is dead when it is said*, he reminded himself. Emily Dickinson was never wrong. "Oh, for crap's sake," Herbert yelled. "Because I was born to be the Claus! That's why!"

"I, uh . . ." Claus closed his mouth and shook his head. "Herbert, no one is *born* to be Santa. It's unobtainable—a gift . . . and a burden," he quickly added. "If it's meant to be, it will be. If not ..."

Herbert heaved a heavy sigh. "I realize that now. The harder I try for the prize, the further away I seem to get. I will never be perfect enough to be the Claus."

"*Perfect?* You think you have to be *perfect* to be the Claus? Oh, Herbert, nothing could be further from the truth. I feel shamed by my imperfections, and I fight a constant battle to rationalize why someone so flawed would receive the title. It took Minus to straighten me out on that. He said to me, 'Have faith and patience. It is you no matter what.' And so, as inferior as I may be, I will power on, and someday, maybe, I will feel worthy of this office."

"And now that you know you're not the only Keeper left, how does it feel?"

Santa took his time before answering. When he did, his eyes welled with emotion. "Less lonely when I think of Minus, but more fragile when I think of Plus."

The last of Herbert's self-control vanished, and tears began to trickle down his face. "I'm so sorry for the trouble that I've caused. And if you'll let me," he said, placing his hand over his heart, "I will put my heart and soul into making your journey easier, Santa. With no thought to personal enrichment. I know it will take time for you to trust me again, but I'll work toward that every day."

"I guess we will both have to work on it, Herbert. Let's just move past it because we have a whole village to heal. If you'll draw up a list of what we'll need for the shindig, we can start right away. Just remember, everybody's drinking neat tonight. And send out a memo right away. From now on, it is forbidden to use any ice that hasn't come out of an ice machine. Explain that the prohibition begins forthwith and will continue until it's been determined that the Jetsla industrial accident is no longer contaminating ice outside the dome."

"What about Patterson? I don't want to step on his toes."

"Nonsense. I'd never let anyone but my first assistant allocate money for a kegger. Hop to, Mr. Tuddy!"

Herbert pointed in the direction of the vacant office next door.

"Well, who else would it belong to?"

"I'm back?"

"Yes. Now get out of here before I reconsider."

Herbert offered a crisp salute and scampered out. All this, and he didn't even ask for it. Tonight's party would be the best ever.

As much as he might wish Jetsla to disappear in the blink of an eye—

just as the separation wall between the two domes had—there would be one more day of putting up with the folks. That included Noël Rusk, who, Herbert noted, had made it as far as Boston Charlie and was now sitting in a service vehicle, yelling at Foos. If Herbert had been a bit closer, he might have caught every word. As it was, the few he caught were enough: *terminated, moving,* and *now* gave him the gist. The exchange was short, and when Rusk finished, the little vehicle took off at speed toward the Jetsla compound.

# Chapter Thirty-Seven
# Herbert Tuddy Action Hero

The best thing about being in charge was that Herbert could plan on a grand scale, then delegate the hard work to underlings. Today, he did it early and with relish. He spent the early afternoon overseeing the Jetsla bunch clear out their stuff with the clock ticking. They didn't like him hanging around—he had a few bumps and bruises from wayward flatbed trolleys to prove it—but the satisfaction in seeing the obnoxious entrepreneur's North Pole dreams crumble made the pain worth it.

They were an efficient bunch. Team leaders coordinated everything from who got on or off the elevator to who ran the cartloads of boxes out to the airfield. Rusk already had one sizable cargo plane—his initials elegantly scripted in blue on the tail fin—on the ground and at least one more due to touch down shortly before seven p.m. With the exception of some of Jetsla's chemical reserves, which would need a slightly longer time frame to remove, vacating the Pole on Santa's timetable was quite doable.

After several hours of gloating, Herbert concluded that half of Jetsla had to be on the plane by now, and the other half would soon follow. He headed back to Quonset Hut Alpha to let Santa know he was right on top of things, best man for the job, and to ensure he wasn't left out of any important discussions.

As his service jeep crept past the cargo plane, he noticed P. J. Foos in deep conversation with three individuals. The four were bundled up in heavy weather gear: bulky blue down parkas with fur-edged hoods, red-soled knee-high black rubber boots, and waterproof mittens. It wasn't exactly haute couture for the comfortable temperature of the tarmac or the plane ride home, and definitely overkill for a desk-bound, never-leave-the-dome administrative type like Foos. What a poser.

Fascinated, Herbert stopped and watched them jump into a nearby vehicle and disappear around the side of Jetsla's main building. Doubly odd, Herbert thought. There were no entrances on the backside of the building—just an expeditionary airlock that Rusk had insisted on for access to a storage facility containing chemicals that the Claus had forbidden him from bringing inside the dome.

Herbert swung the jeep around in a broad arc and followed them, but before he could round the building, their vehicle came roaring back toward him. Three occupants—where was Foos? Herbert parked on the side of the building and walked until he could peek around the back corner. Foos was gone, already through the lock and moving rapidly outside the biodome through the heavily falling snow. That direction would lead him to only one place: Jetsla's off-campus lab and storage unit. A final check before movers cleared it out? Herbert's gut screamed no; Foos was up to no-good.

Herbert secured the airlock from the inside so Foos couldn't get back in. If he was up to mischief and returned with some sort of incriminating evidence or flaky story, they'd have him red-handed. Then Herbert sped off for Quonset Hut Alpha. He wasn't dressed to follow Foos, and his cell phone was still on its charger in his office. "Where's the Snow Patrol?" he blurted as he burst into the control room. "I think Foos may be up to no good. We need Elliot."

Santa sprang out of his chair, if someone of his considerable girth could ever be said to *spring*. "Wh—"

"Foos! He just went out the Jetsla airlock, and he's headed for their lab and storage facility."

Santa raised two calming hands. "Now, Herbert, settle down. They're probably giving it one last check. Rusk may be hard to deal with, but he's also a perfectionist."

"It's Foos, not Rusk. And I guarantee you, a desk rat like him doesn't know peanuts from walnuts when it comes to Jetsla's technical stuff."

"Breathe, Herbert. Maybe they already have a crew out there. He could be checking on the checkers."

"Come on, Santa, you know he's never had our best interests at heart. If he did, he never would have deserted us for fame and riches. He's taking one last, vindictive shot at us. I feel it in my gut."

"That's yesterday's veggie burger you're feeling. Mr. Foos was nothing short of professional for the short time he was here. You've got to let your little vendetta go. It's most unbecoming. I thought we agreed that what's past is past."

"Oh, you think so, do you? Your terribly *professional* Mr. Foos facilitated the sale of the Tears plant. He and I cut the deal right next door in his office. With due respect, sir," Herbert said, and he pushed past the Claus to flick on the microphone at the main communications console.

"Come in, Snow Patrol. This is Alpha One. Elliot, are you there?"

Santa tried to pull the microphone from him. "Don't force me to add your name to the naughty list in permanent ink," he said.

Herbert held the phone just out of reach as static crackled on the line. It was Elliot, but the speech was garbled. "What's your ten-twenty, Elliot?"

"Twen . . . min . . . out. Wh . . . y . . . need?"

"Twenty minutes out?"

"Affirm . . ."

"We need you to go check the security—"

"Herbert! Now!" Santa screamed at him, holding out his hand for the phone.

Herbert shoved the microphone at him and headed for the door. "It's up to me. He's too far away."

"Hold on, Elliot," Santa said, bobbling the phone. "Herbert, what are you planning? Hold on, Elliot. Herbert!"

Herbert called back over his shoulder, "Tell Elliot to meet me at the plant and be prepared for trouble. No good is going on."

Herbert turned right at Claus's door and jogged down to the maintenance room near the elevator bay. Protective outerwear would be here and in the bunker's utility room. He plowed through several closets without success and then searched the piles of stuff dumped on a table in the back corner. Not so much as a neck scarf. The workers in the snowcat must be wearing it.

He hit the stairs to the bunker at a dead run, bouncing down them two at a time and jumping the last three. He landed with his ankle at an odd angle. As he crumpled to the floor, he also came down hard on his hands. *Come on, Herbert, it can't end like this. Foos might already be done with his dirty work.* He pulled himself up, put a hand against the wall, and hobbled to the utility room.

The door was locked. He rattled it several times and tried to put his shoulder against it, but the dad-blasted thing held firm. He reached up for the skeleton key on his neck chain. Where was the damn key? He fumbled through his jacket, shirt, and pants until he found it in a back pocket. He unlocked the door with a shaking hand.

The room was empty—not a piece of furniture or a storage box, and certainly not any protective gear. What the what? He exited from the space, mumbling profanity that would make his drinking pals spit liquor back into their glasses. What to do? He couldn't just let Foos win. He began opening doors, searching every room for some protection he could wear against the brutal elements outside the biodome.

And then there it was: a roller cart sitting outside the laundry room, and it was full of long johns, midlayers, down parkas, and hats and gloves. Paydirt—literally! They were filthy but dry. Herbert piled on the layers, limped back up the stairs, and, with the help of another cart, rolled himself to Alpha's front door. Within seconds, he had gunned his jeep halfway across the tarmac and was bearing down hard on the Jetsla airlock.

They say discretion is the better part of valor. At the moment, Herbert had none. It was do or die. He grabbed a wrench from the utility box in the back of the jeep and exited from the biodome. If Foos was breaking anything, the dirty, backstabbing traitor of an elf could fix it, or else.

# Chapter Thirty-Eight
# The Boom Boom Room

Herbert had been outside the big dome many times, but only once to the mini dome housing Jetsla's chemical compound. Still, he didn't need a map. Elliot and the security patrol prowled this area regularly—plowing and maintaining a flagged throughway. Minutes after passing through the airlock, he stood alone before the windowless slate-gray single-story building. To his right sprawled a much bigger structure, three times longer in length and two stories tall with windows set up high on the second floor. It was Jetsla's off-campus lab, and a concession to Santa, who wanted to keep as much of Jetsla's proprietary work away from Christmasville as possible. Who knew what they might be involved in?

Herbert hesitated. A small snowmobile was outside the dome, but there was no sign of a driver. Did he really need to be a hero? Suddenly, the whooping warning blasts of a security system burst forth from the smaller building and continued blasting every ten seconds or so. In between the whoops, Herbert heard thumps and glass breaking. He slid the wrench into his back pocket and entered the smaller building. The interior was all one room. He tipped the door closed.

Above the relentless blaring of the alarm, Foos's voice floated out from the middle of the room. Herbert worked his way around stacks of wooden moving crates until he saw the imbecile hovering over a section of pipe leading from one of the large circular tanks. The turncoat elf was alone and talking to himself. Did he intend to flood the place? Herbert stood a moment more, taking in the gauges hanging in tatters behind the elf—the broken glass, the bent copper tubing, and wiring that had been ripped from its housing and clipped. And just beyond that sprawled Felix, a member of Elliot's snow patrol. Foos had totally lost it.

Herbert stood up from his hiding place. "Stop!"

Foos bolted upright, his eyes roving. "Herbert," he said, finally locking eyes. "Good old Herbert. Did they throw you out of the dome, too? I'm amazed that despite every stupid thing you've done, you've somehow managed to keep yourself out of trouble for so long." He chuckled and picked up a long, adjustable wrench leaning against the holding vat. "Want to take a whack? It's very soul cleansing."

"What's in there?"

Foos lifted a shoulder.

"Hmm," Herbert said. He limped out of the shadows toward Foos. "They just don't understand us, do they, P. J.? Instead of recognizing and promoting the talented people, they always seem to go with the political expedient. You never being recognized for your organizational skills, and me coming in second-best in the Claus sweepstakes back in December—we both deserved better. Give me that," he said, reaching for the thirty-inch wrench. "I'd love to have a go at it."

Foos's eyes widened. "Really? They actually bounced you?"

"Yeah. Scoundrels." He slipped the tool out of Foos's grip and hefted it in his hand. "Ooh, nice and heavy." He stepped toward the pipe, and before Foos could respond, Herbert clocked him in the head—a good, hard swing. The blow was cushioned by Foos's thick parka hood and didn't draw blood, but it did send him staggering sideways and into a heap on the floor, where his head hit hard against the floorboards. Herbert jumped on him, grabbed his ears, and tried to bang his head a second time.

But Foos was too agile. He twisted, forcing the two elves to roll. Once on top, Foos put his hands around Herbert's neck and tightened his grip. "If they had only given me the assistant position, everything would have been fine."

Herbert clawed at Foos's hands, but he couldn't ease the relentless pressure or turn away from the ferocious, hating eyes glowering at him. Herbert raked his fingers across them. Foos shrieked, released his grip, and rolled away screaming. Herbert grabbed a crowbar from atop a stack of wooden packing crates and came at him as he writhed in pain.

"Uncle! Uncle! Uncle!" Foos yelled. He shielded his face with his arm.

"It wasn't Rusk's idea to destroy everything, was it?" Herbert said, raising the crowbar over his head.

"No," Foos whimpered.

"Didn't think so. For all his bad traits, he's not completely faithless. And you were the one who planted the Jetsla handle in my stuff."

"Maybe."

Herbert sighed in disgust. "You had everything, P. J., and you blew it. Position, power, probably a ridiculous amount of money. What's your problem?"

"Nobody should know the answer to that better than you," Foos scoffed. "You think it was my idea to come back to Christmasville? All my hard work to get away from this desolate place, and where does Rusk send me the first chance he gets? Yeah." Foos nodded wistfully. "Well, there wasn't any way that I was gonna get stuck pushing papers at the North Pole with a bunch of simpleton, off-key-singing toy peddlers. There's a big old world out there, Herbert."

"You thought Noël Rusk would cut and run once a little sabotage started bleeding the coffers?"

"Oh, without a doubt. The man is all about succeeding."

"No, not everyone is like you."

"Or you," Foos sneered. "Herbert the job-hopper, Herbert the next in line to be Santa. You'll never become the Claus. You have more flaws than good qualities—and you'll never be able to fix them all. Go ahead. Take that final whack. It will feel oh, so good, Herbert. Go ahead. I dare you."

"Liar!" Herbert snarled, and he brought the crowbar down hard. Foos screamed. The claw end of the tool lodged in the floorboards about six inches from Foos's head.

Herbert took the wrench from his pocket and shook it at him. "Get up again and I'll take your head off." He whirled around to the pipe Foos had been destroying. There was no damage, just a shorter piece of steel pipe duct-taped to it. Both ends were capped and it had a fuse running to a battery and a timer sitting on the floor beneath it. And the timer? It was ticking down with about five minutes remaining until one hell of an explosion.

Herbert never saw the blow that smashed into the back of his noggin. He stumbled forward, staggering into the broken meters and clutching at the copper tubing to stop his fall. Foos hit him hard again, this time in the middle of his back, with something small and heavy. He fell to his knees and braced for another blow.

It never came. As the alarm whooped and thoughts of Santa, Hoho, and the good things in his life raced through his head, he thought he heard pounding feet and a slamming door. Then again, it might have been the throbbing in, his head. He fell forward. Death would be mercifully quick.

"Dear God! Herbert! You've got to get up." Hands grabbed the back of his coat.

Herbert looked up to find two Santas hovering over him. He smiled weakly. "Run, Santa. I've got it covered."

Santa rolled him over and pulled him into a sitting position. "Can you get to your feet? Please, Herbert. Meet me halfway. You can rest outside."

"Sure," Herbert mumbled. But he couldn't seem to get his hands and feet to work together, and he couldn't figure out which Santa to grab hold of. "Can't," he said, trying to lie back down. "My head is exploding."

"*Everything* is going to explode if we don't get out of here." Santa yanked hard on Herbert's parka, which got him to his feet, then wrapped an arm around his middle and began dragging him across the room.

Fifty feet or so, and Santa dropped him like a sack of spuds. Herbert stayed where he fell, as dark shapes swirled around him, and his ears rang. A flash of light, and a thunderous explosion shook the ground beneath him, and he closed his eyes to the heat and the debris that began raining down on him.

Hands grabbed him again, this time not so roughly. For God's sake, why couldn't they let him die in peace? He opened his eyes to Elliot's blond hair and serious face.

"Are you okay?" Elliot asked.

"What?"

"Are you all right?"

"Yes!" he yelled back. Elliot and another member of the security patrol helped him stand up. He sagged against Elliot and looked around. Somehow, he had made it out of the building. With Santa? By himself? He had no idea. After he looked twice, he realized there was no building—just a smoldering, flaming pile of debris. Foos was lying a few feet away in the snow. "He's not dead . . ."

"Oh, no," Elliot said, looking horrified. "One good sucker punch laid him out. I would have preferred to look him in the eyes, but Santa was on the losing end of the fisticuffs, and we do what we must. Still, it was nice to get in a few good licks."

"He's being humble," the other security elf interjected. "He beat the snot out of him."

Herbert nodded. The effort made everything spin. "Where's Santa?" he asked, looking around his shaky surroundings.

"Everything's under control," Elliot said. "Let's get you in the cat, where we can check you out more thoroughly." He tried to guide him to a nearby gurney.

"No Santa? I could have sworn I saw him . . . *two* actually." Herbert stopped. There was something in Elliot's face. "Where's Santa, Elliot?"

"You're right," Elliot said, pushing harder to get him to lie down. "He's here. Just one of him. We're looking after him. Now, lie down so we can get you back inside the dome. Dr. Dash is waiting."

Herbert saw the boots first, then the big man himself, prostrate on the ground near Foos. His magnificent red Santa coat was in tatters.

"Santa?" Herbert said, and he began to sway.

"You've got to lie down, sir," Elliot said, catching him.

"Is he dead?"

And then everything went dark.

# Chapter Thirty-Nine
## A Better Place

Herbert opened his eyes to bright light and a pair of feathery red eyebrows.

"He's awake," Solomon yelled. "How do you feel?" he asked, hovering in Herbert's face.

"Better without you all up in my business," Herbert said, shooing him away. "Tone it down. You're echoing all over the place."

The room was white with dazzling overhead lighting and, once Solomon put a sock in it, as quiet as the landscape outside the biodome in a gently falling snow. Herbert sat up. Too white, too quiet, and the walls were lined with large stainless-steel drawers. "Am I, uh, in the morgue?"

"Of course," Solomon said. "Where else would they put you?"

Herbert flopped back down on the cold, hard gurney. Damn his misfortune and damn that Foos. What would he do now?

"Wait a minute," he said, sitting up again. "If I'm dead, how can you talk to me?"

Solomon's flight dropped precipitously before regaining altitude again. "We're both dead? How did Saturday come so fast?" His scarlet feathers faded to a muddy brown color. "Oh, my dear! How did that happen?"

Three or four gasps followed. Crying, Herbert supposed. And as the tiny fairy descended and buried his face into Herbert's chest, Herbert began crying too. "I wonder if they've selected a new Santa yet," he blubbered.

"I'm not going anywhere."

Herbert rose up on his elbows, which sent Solomon rolling off his chest and into his lap. Santa was stretched out on a nearby gurney, covered up to his chin in a red wool blanket. "Heaven! We're in heaven, Solomon. Santa would never end up in the naughty place." Tears began rolling down Herbert's cheeks. "Dear Santa, it's wonderful to see you again!"

"And you, too," Dr. Dash said, appearing at Herbert's side.

Herbert frowned. "What . . . how . . . I'm confused," he said. "Is everyone dead?"

Dr. Dash chuckled. "No one's dead, Mr. Tuddy. Not you or Solomon, nor Santa or Foos, or Felix. All are well and accounted for."

Solomon buzzed off Herbert's chest. "So what day is it really?" Solomon asked.

"Tuesday, as in your christening day," Santa said. "Why don't you go celebrate?"

"Excellent idea," Solomon said, and he was gone in a blink.

"Lying to the little fellow, are you?" Dash said after he was gone.

"Just a little white one. Telling him it's actually Saturday would just confuse him. By the time he figures out he should be dying today, we'll be back to Monday again. Let him go."

Dash chuckled and put a gentle hand on Herbert's chest to make him lie down. "Bumps on the head can put you out of sorts, and it was touch and go there for most of the week. In a few more days, you'll be seeing—and hearing—everything with a lot more clarity."

"Days? You're kidding me, right?"

"Santa?" Dash asked.

"I followed you out to the storage facility," Santa said. "The alarm was sounding, but I didn't see anyone outside, so I went in. I found both you and Felix, but neither hide nor hair of Foos. With the bomb ticking down, I hauled you as far as the door, and then went back for Felix. That's when Foos came out of nowhere and began whaling on me. In my thinner days, I might have taken him, but now . . ." He put his hands on his belly, rising like a mountain beneath the blanket. "Well, I was on the losing end. If it hadn't been for Elliot, I probably wouldn't be here to talk about it. None of us would. The security patrol cleared everyone out of the building before everything went kaboom." Santa looked at Dash. "Did I miss anything?"

"That seems to cover it," Dash said, nodding. "Heroes, the lot of you, and I'm just tickled that I won't have to put any of you in my walk-in freezer over there."

"Yeah," Herbert said. "Exactly why are we in the morgue?"

"Space and privacy," Dash said. "It was rather full in the infirmary when you were brought it, so I thought you both would prefer to be in here rather than the curtained-off beds in the sick bay. Felix is out there. And so was Foos, but as soon as we turned our backs, he gave us the slip. He was last sighted boarding Jetsla's final plane out."

"And good riddance," Santa said. "I'm sorry, Herbert, that I didn't heed your warnings about him. You had him pegged from the very beginning."

A week ago, Herbert might have gloated at such an admission. Today, after Foos's antics, it barely registered. "No offense taken, sir. I can truthfully say that even I didn't expect him to resort to attacking people and planting a bomb. We elves can get mad, and we can argue, but violence isn't in our nature. It had to be from his nonelvish side. Why on earth would he do such a thing?"

"You mean the bomb?" Santa scratched his beard. "I guess we'll never know, "but sometimes, if people can't get what they want, they'll destroy it to make sure nobody else gets anything. If Foos couldn't be happy, nobody would be happy. Santa shrugged. "But I'm no psychologist. It may be a cry for help. If so, I hope he gets it."

"Me, too," Herbert said. "I mean, uh, I intend to get help, too. None of this would have happened if I had been able to control my impulses. I admit it. I'm a five-fingered elf. I'm petty and jealous and can't let go of a grudge, and if I don't get a handle on those things, I will never be happy."

Herbert turned to Dash. "Can you help me, Doc?"

"Not personally, but I can refer you to a good specialist in New York who might help you explore those issues. You'll have to go there, but with Santa's permission—"

"Which he has," Santa said, smiling. "I think it will do you a world of good, Herbert, and will go a long way in atoning for your recent indiscretions."

Herbert bit his lip. "New York, huh? Well, I'm not so keen anymore on escaping Christmasville. I think Foos's behavior proved that the temptations of the outside world do corrupt. But I don't want to feel like this anymore, and I don't want people to mistrust and hate me, and I want to be the best first assistant this village has ever had. Let's do it! Right after we get operations up and running smoothly again."

"Sold!" Santa said. "But you'll have to do your own paperwork." With that, he sat up, pulled the blanket off, and swung his legs off the gurney. "Well, the rest has been pleasant," he said to Dash, handing him the blanket, "but I have a Christmas operation to run. Tuddy, as soon as you feel one hundred percent, I want you back in the office. But not before. Understood?"

Herbert nodded. He'd give Santa a couple of hours' head start and then he'd be back in the swing of things, too. It was great to be excited about life again.

# Chapter Forty

# Brotherhood

For the first in what seemed like ages, Santa was looking forward to work. Oh, pressing issues still remained, but somehow, they didn't seem quite as daunting as before. Jetsla's report on Christmasville process improvements was sitting on his desk, and it would help enormously, but it did lack some of the specificity he had hoped for. Rusk would get an immediate personal call. With all the chaos Foos had caused, the billionaire could at least provide a follow-up report with specific action items.

Santa entered the Sinterklaas hall and was surprised to see Hoho standing before the portraits, his hand to his chin and a frown on his face. "Fascinating, aren't they?" Santa said, drawing up beside him. "I do believe if we took them down and mixed them up, we'd never get them up in the right order again."

"Yes," Hoho said, his eyes not leaving the pictures. He held out a sealed envelope. "Communication, sir."

The letter was on Noël Rusk's personal monogrammed stationery. The billionaire wrote:

*Dear Mr. Claus,*

*I wanted to let you know that it seems I need to take my own advice about whom to include in one's inner circle. The matter of the blue Jetsla valve knob has been explained in full, and P. J. Foos's employment has been terminated with prejudice. He is a loose cannon that Jetsla can ill afford. I urge you to consider Mr. Tuddy in the same light.*

*I hope and pray that Christmasville bounces back from its tribulations. If you will allow us to return temporarily, I have a maintenance team at the ready to clean up the mess Mr. Foos created—a team big enough to be in and out in a couple of days, with little trouble to you. And, of course, as soon as my analysis staff complete their report on how to implement our earlier broad areas of concern about your operations, I will have my secretary, Sherri, forward it to you. If you have any questions, please do not hesitate to reach out to me personally. Jetsla always stands behind its work. I do regret, Nicholas, that we were unable to accomplish more. At this time more than ever, the world needs us, but I bear no ill feelings about our too-short collaboration and hope that someday you will feel the same.*

*Sincerely,*
*Noël Rusk*

"But where is yours?" Hoho asked, interrupting Santa's second reading.

"Haven't you ever been back here before? The portraits hang in chronological order. I'm down on the far end." Santa started over at the beginning of the note.

Hoho shuffled closer to the last picture. "No. Where's yours?"

With Hoho blabbing, Santa gave up trying to read. "Here," he said, walking to the end of the row. But that picture didn't look like him.

The face staring back was virtually identical to the other portraits, with all the right wrinkles and all the right twinkles. Well, maybe not the slight eye glimmer that Santa recognized as his own, but everything else screamed Sinterklaas Brotherhood.

"Lord Almighty, I've done it," he muttered. A certain spot in the middle of his chest began to glow and warm, and the heat gradually fanned throughout his body from the wispy tips of his snowy hair to the ends of his toes in his spit-polished black boots. By golly, he had been found worthy!

"Trust me, Hoho," he said quietly. "This is me. If we're doing it right, we just become one of the many."

He patted the kindly elf on the back and continued on his way. He could already hear laughter spilling out of Herbert's office. That was a first. When had Herbert ever cut loose and had a good time? It was Wednesday, and if he had heard correctly, Solomon was sporting a tuxedo and spouting something about getting hitched to some honey named Phoebe. This he had to see.

"A little to the left," Solomon was saying as Santa peeked inside the door.

"We just had it there," Herbert said, but he obliged, tapping a miniature desk half an inch to the left on the corner of his enormous executive desk. "That's as much space as I can give you. My in-box has to go somewhere." He added a matching chair and a bookcase to create a perfectly scaled office setting. "Okay now?"

"Acceptable," Solomon said as he adjusted the tails on his black full-dress tuxedo and made himself at home in the chair. "But where's my in-box?"

"I'll work on that," Herbert said. He noticed Santa and gave him a wink.

"Two workers in one office?" Santa said. "Excellent use of space, Mr. Tuddy. From now on, I'll expect twice as much work out of here. Solomon, make sure you have a work status report on my desk bright and early every Tuesday morning—right after your christening."

"Yes, sir," Solomon said, jumping to attention with a crisp salute.

"Excellent. You're looking very sharp today, I might add. Is what I'm hearing true?"

"Best man," Herbert said, jerking a thumb at himself.

Santa chuckled. "Yes, you certainly are, Herbert, and to celebrate the nuptials, I want you to shut everything down this afternoon. I'll ask Violet and some of the kitchen staff to whip up something grand for a buffet luncheon. Enough for two hundred or so, Solomon?"

The tips of Solomon's feathers vibrated in brilliant candy-apple red. "I would be honored," he said, and he bowed deeply. "But only two hundred?"

"You pick the number," Santa said, "and I'm sure it will be fine. After all, if you can't celebrate love and family, how can you possibly celebrate Christmas? Now, hop to! We've got less than a hundred and eighty days to make everyone else in the world happy."

"Yes, sir, Santa," Herbert and Solomon said in unison, and as Santa disappeared into his office, he thought he heard them bickering over the thermostat. Herbert would have his work cut out for him. Somehow, though, Santa suspected that his new and improved first assistant would be more than up to the task.

Thank you for reading *The Five-Fingered Elf*. I hope you enjoyed the story. If you have a moment, please consider leaving a quick review on the book's Amazon page.

Would you like to know when I release new books?
Here are three ways:

Join my mailing list at:
https://www.louisegordaybooks.com/contact

Like me on Facebook:
https://www.facebook.com/louisegordayauthor

Follow me on Twitter:
https://twitter.com/LouiseGorday

Made in the USA
Middletown, DE
03 August 2023

35642084R00156